**JORJ X. McKIE, saboteur extraordinaire**

A smile touched McKie's wide mouth. He turned, crossed to the room's only door, paused there, hand on knob.

"What have you done?" Watt exploded.

McKie continued to look at him.

Watt's scalp began itching madly. He put a hand there, felt a long tangle of . . . tendrils! They were lengthening under his fingers, growing out of his scalp, waving and writhing.

"A Jicuzzi stim," Watt breathed.

—The Tactful Saboteur

# The Worlds of Frank Herbert

## Frank Herbert

A BERKLEY MEDALLION BOOK
published by
BERKLEY PUBLISHING CORPORATION

# CONTENTS

# THE TACTFUL SABOTEUR

"Better men than you have tried!" snarled Clinton Watt.

"I quote paragraph four, section ninety-one of the Semantic Revision to the Constitution," said saboteur extraordinary Jorj X. McKie. "'The need for obstructive processes in government having been established as one of the chief safeguards for human rights, the question of immunities must be defined with extreme precision.'"

McKie sat across a glistening desk from the Intergalactic Government's Secretary of Sabotage, Clinton Watt. An air of tension filled the green-walled office, carrying over into the screenview behind Watt which showed an expanse of the System Government's compound and people scurrying about their morning business with a sense of urgency.

Watt, a small man who appeared to crackle with suppressed energy, passed a hand across his shaven head. "All right," he said in a suddenly tired voice. "This is the only Secretariat of government that's never immune from sabotage. You've satisfied the legalities by quoting the law. Now, do your damnedest!"

McKie, whose bulk and fat features usually gave him the appearance of a grandfatherly toad, glowered like a gnome-dragon. His mane of red hair appeared to dance with inner flame.

"Damnedest!" he snapped. "You think I came in here to try to unseat you? You think that?"

And McKie thought: *Let's hope he thinks that!*

"Stop the act, McKie!" Watt said. "We both know you're eligible for this chair." He patted the arm of his chair. "And we both know the only way you can eliminate me and qualify yourself for the appointment is to overcome me with a masterful sabotage. Well, McKie, I've sat here more than eighteen years. Another five months and it'll be a new record. Do your damnedest. I'm waiting."

"I came in here for only one reason," McKie said. "I want to report on the search for saboteur extraordinary Napoleon Bildoon."

McKie sat back wondering: *If Watt knew my real purpose here would he act just this way? Perhaps.* The man had been behaving oddly since the start of this interview, but it was difficult to determine real motive when dealing with a fellow member of the Bureau of Sabotage.

Cautious interest quickened Watt's bony face. He wet his lips with his tongue and it was obvious he was asking himself if this were more of an elaborate ruse. But McKie had been assigned the task of searching for the missing agent, Bildoon, and it was just possible . . .

"Have you found him?" Watt asked.

"I'm not sure," McKie said. He ran his fingers through his red hair. "Bildoon's a Pan-Spechi, you know."

"For disruption's sake!" Watt exploded. "I know who and what my own agents are! But we take care of our own. And when one of our best people just drops from sight . . . What's this about not being sure?"

"The Pan-Spechi are a curious race of creatures," McKie said. "Just because they've taken on humanoid shape we tend to forget their five-phase life cycle."

"Bildoon told me himself he'd hold his group's ego at least another ten years," Watt said. "I think he was being truthful, but . . ." Watt shrugged and some of the bursting energy seemed to leave him. "Well, the group ego's the only place where the Pan-Spechi show vanity so . . ." Again he shrugged.

"My questioning of the other Pan-Spechi in the Bureau has had to be circumspect, of course," McKie said. "But I did follow one lead clear to Achus."

"And?"

McKie brought a white vial from his copious jacket, scattered a metallic powder on the desktop.

Watt pushed himself back from the desk, eyeing the powder with suspicion. He took a cautious sniff, smelled chalf, the quick-scribe powder. Still . . .

"It's just chalf," McKie said. And he thought: *If he buys that, I may get away with this.*

"So scribe it," Watt said.

Concealing his elation, McKie held a chalf-memory stick over the dusted surface. A broken circle with arrows pointing to a right-hand flow appeared in the chalf. At each break in the circle stood a symbol—in one place the Pan-Spechi character for ego, then the delta for fifth gender and, finally, the three lines that signified the dormant creche-triplets.

McKie pointed to the fifth gender delta. "I've seen a Pan-Spechi in this position who looks a bit like Bildoon and *appears* to have some of his mannerisms. There's no identity response from the creature, of course. Well, you know how the quasi-feminine fifth gender reacts."

"Don't ever let that amorous attitude fool you,"

Watt warned. "In spite of your nasty disposition I wouldn't want to lose you into a Pan-Spechi creche."

"Bildoon wouldn't rob a fellow agent's identity," McKie said. He pulled at his lower lip, feeling an abrupt uncertainty. Here, of course, was the most touchy part of the whole scheme. "If it was Bildoon."

"Did you meet this group's ego holder?" Watt asked and his voice betrayed real interest.

"No," McKie said. "But I think the ego-single of this Pan-Spechi is involved with the Tax Watchers."

McKie waited, wondering if Watt would rise to the bait.

"I've never heard of an ego change being forced onto a Pan-Spechi," Watt said in a musing tone, "but that doesn't mean it's impossible. If those Tax Watcher do-gooders found Bildoon sabotaging their efforts and . . . Hmmm."

"Then Bildoon *was* after the Tax Watchers," McKie said.

Watt scowled. McKie's question was in extreme bad taste. Senior agents, unless joined on a project or where the information was volunteered, didn't snoop openly into the work of their fellows. Left hand and right hand remained mutually ignorant in the Bureau of Sabotage and for good reason. Unless . . . Watt stared speculatively at his saboteur extraordinary.

McKie shrugged as Watt remained silent. "I can't operate on inadequate information," he said. "I must, therefore, resign the assignment to search for Bildoon. Instead, I will now look into the Tax Watchers."

"You will not!" Watt snapped.

McKie forced himself not to look at the design he had drawn on the desktop. The next few moments were the critical ones.

"You'd better have a legal reason for that refusal," McKie said.

Watt swiveled sideways in his chair, glanced at the screenview, then addressed himself to the side wall. "The situation has become one of extreme delicacy, Jorj. It's well known that you're one of our finest saboteurs."

"Save your oil for someone who needs it," McKie growled.

"Then I'll put it this way," Watt said, returning his gaze to McKie. "The Tax Watchers in the last few days have posed a real threat to the Bureau. They've managed to convince a High Court magistrate they deserve the same immunity from our ministrations that a ... well, public water works or ... ah ... food processing plant might enjoy. The magistrate, Judge Edwin Dooley, invoked the Public Safety amendment. Our hands are tied. The slightest suspicion that we've disobeyed the injunction and ..."

Watt drew a finger across his throat.

"Then I quit," McKie said.

"You'll do nothing of the kind!"

"This TW outfit is trying to eliminate the Bureau, isn't it?" McKie asked. "I remember the oath I took just as well as you do."

"Jorj, you couldn't be that much of a simpleton," Watt said. "You quit, thinking that absolves the Bureau from responsibility for you! That trick's as old as time!"

"Then fire me!" McKie said.

"I've no legal reason to fire you, Jorj."

"Refusal to obey orders of a superior," McKie said.

"It wouldn't fool anybody, you dolt!"

McKie appeared to hesitate, said: "Well, the public

5

doesn't know the inner machinery of how we change the Bureau's command. Perhaps it's time we opened up."

"Jorj, before I could fire you there'd have to be a reason so convincing that ... Just forget it."

The fat pouches beneath McKie's eyes lifted until the eyes were mere slits. The crucial few moments had arrived. He had managed to smuggle a Jicuzzi stim into this office past all of Watt's detectors, concealing the thing's detectable radiation core within an imitation of the lapel badge that Bureau agents wore.

"In Lieu of Red Tape," McKie said and touched the badge with a finger, feeling the raised letters there— "ILRT." The touch focused the radiation core onto the metallic dust scattered over the desktop.

Watt gripped the arms of the chair, studying McKie with a new look of wary tension.

"We are under legal injunction to keep hands off the Tax Watchers," Watt said. "Anything that happens to those people or to their project for scuttling us—even legitimate accidents—will be laid at our door. We must be able to defend ourselves. No one who has ever been connected with us dares fall under the slightest suspicion of complicity."

"How about a floor waxed to dangerous slickness in the path of one of their messengers? How about a doorlock changed to delay—"

"Nothing."

McKie stared at his chief. Everything depended now on the man holding very still. He knew Watt wore detectors to warn him of concentrated beams of radiation. But this Jicuzzi stim had been rigged to diffuse its charge off the metallic dust on the desk and that required several seconds of relative quiet.

The men held themselves rigid in the staredown until

Watt began to wonder at the extreme stillness of McKie's body. The man was even holding his breath!

McKie took a deep breath, stood up.

"I warn you, Jorj," Watt said.

"Warn me?"

"I can restrain you by physical means if necessary."

"Clint, old enemy, save your breath. What's done is done."

A smile touched McKie's wide mouth. He turned, crossed to the room's only door, paused there, hand on knob.

"What have you done?" Watt exploded.

McKie continued to look at him.

Watt's scalp began itching madly. He put a hand there, felt a long tangle of...tendrils! They were lengthening under his fingers, growing out of scalp, waving and writhing.

"A Jicuzzi stim," Watt breathed.

McKie let himself out, closed the door.

Watt leaped out of his chair, raced to the door.

Locked!

He knew McKie and didn't try unlocking it. Frantically, Watt slapped a molecular dispersion wad against the door, dived through as the wad blasted. He landed in the outer hall, stared first in one direction, then the other.

The hall was empty.

Watt sighed. The tendrils had stopped growing, but they were long enough now that he could see them writhing past his eyes—a rainbow mass of wrigglers, part of himself. And McKie with the original stim was the only one who could reverse the process—unless Watt were willing to spend an interminable time with the Jicuzzi themselves. No. That was out of the question.

7

Watt began assessing his position.

The stim tendrils couldn't be removed surgically, couldn't be tied down or contained in any kind of disguise without endangering the person afflicted with them. Their presence would hamper him, too, during this critical time of trouble with the Tax Watchers. How could he appear in conferences and interviews with these things writhing in their Medusa dance on his head? It would be laughable! He'd be an object of comedy.

And if McKie could stay out of the way until a Case of Exchangement was brought before the full Cabinet...But, no! Watt shook his head. This wasn't the kind of sabotage that required a change of command in the Bureau. This was a gross thing. No subtlety to it. This was like a practical joke. Clownish.

But McKie was noted for his clownish attitude, his irreverence for all the blundering self-importance of government.

*Have I been self-important?* Watt wondered.

In all honesty, he had to admit it.

*I'll have to submit my resignation today,* he thought. *Right after I fire McKie. One look at me and there'll be no doubt of why I did it. This is about as convincing a reason as you could find.*

Watt turned to his right, headed for the lab to see if they could help him bring this wriggling mass under control.

*The President will want me to stay at the helm until McKie makes his next move,* Watt thought. *I have to be able to function somehow.*

McKie waited in the living room of the Achusian mansion will ill-concealed unease. Achus was the administrative planet for the Vulpecula region, an area of great wealth, and this room high on a mountaintop commanded a natural view to the southwest across lesser peaks and foothills misted in purple by a westering G3 sun.

But McKie ignored the view, trying to watch all corners of the room at once. He had seen a fifth gender Pan-Spechi here in company with the fourth-gender ego-holder. That could only mean the creche with its three dormants was nearby. By all accounts, this was a dangerous place for someone not protected by bonds of friendship and community of interest.

The value of the Pan-Spechi to the universal human society in which they participated was beyond question. What other species had such refined finesse in deciding when to hinder and when to help? Who else could send a key member of its group into circumstances of extreme peril without fear that the endangered one's knowledge would be lost?

There was always a dormant to take up where the lost one had left off.

Still, the Pan-Spechi did have their idiosyncrasies. And their hungers were at times bizarre.

"Ahhh, McKie."

The voice, deep and masculine, came from his left. McKie whirled to study the figure that came through a door carved from a single artificial emerald of glittering creme de menthe colors.

The speaker was humanoid but with Pan-Spechi multifaceted eyes. He appeared to be a terranic man (except for the blue-green eyes) of an indeterminate, well-preserved middle age. The body suggested a certain daintiness in its yellow tights and singlet. The head was squared in outline with close-cropped blond hair, a fleshy chunk of nose and thick splash of mouth.

"Panthor Bolin here," the Pan-Spechi said. "You are welcome in my home, Jorj McKie."

McKie relaxed slightly. Pan-Spechi were noted for honoring hospitality once it was extended ... provided the guest didn't violate their mores.

"I'm honored that you've agreed to see me," McKie said.

"The honor is mine," Bolin said. "We've long recognized you as a person whose understanding of the Pan-Spechi is most subtle and penetrating. I've longed for the chance to have uninhibited conversation with you. And here you are." He indicated a chairdog against the wall to his right, snapped his fingers. The semi-sentient artifact glided to a position behind McKie. "Please be seated."

McKie, his caution realerted by Bolin's reference to "uninhibited conversation," sank into the chairdog, patting it until it assumed the contours he wanted.

Bolin took a chairdog facing him, leaving only about a meter separating their knees.

"Have our egos shared nearness before?" McKie asked. "You appeared to recognize me."

"Recognition goes deeper than ego," Bolin said. "Do you wish to join identities and explore this question?"

McKie wet his lips with his tongue. This was delicate ground with the Pan-Spechi, whose one ego moved somehow from member to member of the unit group as they traversed their *circle of being*.

"I ... ah ... not at this time," McKie said.

"Well spoken," Bolin said. "Should you ever change your mind, my ego-group would consider it a most signal honor. Yours is a strong identity, one we respect."

"I'm ... most honored," McKie said. He rubbed

10

nervously at his jaw, recognizing the dangers in this conversation. Each Pan-Spechi group maintained a supremely jealous attitude of and about its wandering ego. The ego imbued the holder of it with a touchy sense of honor. Inquiries about it could be carried out only through such formula questions as McKie already had asked.

Still, if this were a member of the pent-archal life circle containing the missing saboteur extraordinary Napoleon Bildoon...if it were, much would be explained.

"You're wondering if we really can communicate," Bolin said. McKie nodded.

"The concept of *humanity*," Bolin said, "—our term for it would translate approximately as *comsentiency*—has been extended to encompass many differing shapes, life systems and methods of mentation. And yet we have never been sure about this question. It's one of the major reasons many of us have adopted your life-shape and much of your metabolism. We wished to experience your strengths and your weaknesses. This helps...but is not an absolute solution."

"Weaknesses?" McKie asked, suddenly wary.

"Ahhh-hummm," Bolin said. "I see. To allay your suspicions I will have translated for you soon one of our major works. Its title would be, approximately, *The Developmental Influence of Weaknesses*. One of the strongest sympathetic bonds we have with your species, for example, is the fact that we both originated as extremely vulnerable surface-bound creatures, whose most sophisticated defense came to be the social structure."

"I'll be most interested to see the translation," McKie said.

11

"Do you wish more amenities or do you care to state your business now?" Bolin asked.

"I was ... ah ... assigned to seek out a missing agent of our Bureau," McKie said, "to be certain no harm has befallen this ... ah ... agent."

"Your avoidance of gender is most refined," Bolin said. "I appreciate the delicacy of your position and your good taste. I will say this for now: the Pan-Spechi you seek is not at this time in need of your assistance. Your concern, however, is appreciated. It will be communicated to those upon whom it will have the most influence."

"That's a great relief to me," McKie said. And he wondered: *What did he really mean by that?* This thought elicited another, and McKie said: "Whenever I run into this problem of communication between species I'm reminded of an old culture/teaching story."

"Oh?" Bolin registered polite curiosity.

"Two practioners of the art of mental healing, so the story goes, passed each other every morning on their way to their respective offices. They knew each other, but weren't on intimate terms. One morning as they approached each other, one of them turned to the other and said, 'Good morning.' The one greeted failed to respond, but continued toward his office. Presently, though, he stopped, turned and stared at the retreating back of the man who'd spoken, musing to himself: 'Now what did he really mean by that?'"

Bolin began to chuckle, then laugh. His laughter grew louder and louder until he was holding his sides.

*It wasn't that funny,* McKie thought.

Bolin's laughter subsided. "A very educational story," he said. "I'm deeply indebted to you. This story shows your awareness of how important it is in

12

communication that we be aware of the other's identity."

*Does it?* McKie wondered. *How's that?*

And McKie found himself caught up by his knowledge of how the Pan-Spechi could pass a single ego-identity from individual to individual within the life circle group of five distinct protoplasmic units. He wondered how it felt when the ego-holder gave up the identity to become the fifth gender, passing the ego spark to a newly matured unit from the creche. Did the fifth gender willingly become the creche nurse and give itself up as a mysterious identity-food for the three dormants in the creche? he wondered.

"I heard about what you did to Secretary of Sabotage Clinton Watt," Bolin said. "The story of your dismissal from the service preceded you here."

"Yes," McKie said. "That's why I'm here, too."

"You've penetrated to the fact that our Pan-Spechi community here on Achus is the heart of the Tax Watchers' organization," Bolin said. "It was very brave of you to walk right into our hands. I understand how much more courage it takes for your kind to face unit extinction than it does for our kind. Admirable! You are indeed a prize."

McKie fought down a sensation of panic, reminding himself that the records he had left in his private locker at Bureau headquarters could be deciphered in time even if he did not return.

"Yes," Bolin said, "you wish to satisfy yourself that the ascension of a Pan-Spechi to the head of your Bureau will pose no threat to other human species. This is understandable."

McKie shook his head to clear it. "Do you read minds?" he demanded.

13

"Telepathy is not one of our accomplishments," Bolin said, his voice heavy with menace. "I do hope that was a generalized question and in no way directed at the intimacies of my ego-group."

"I felt that you were reading my mind," McKie said, tensing himself for defense.

"That was how I interpreted the question," Bolin said. "Forgive my question. I should not have doubted your delicacy or your tact."

"You do hope to place a member in the job of Bureau Secretary, though?" McKie said.

"Remarkable that you should've suspected it," Bolin said. "How can you be sure our intention is not merely to destroy the Bureau?"

"I'm not," McKie glanced around the room, regretting that he had been forced to act alone.

"Where did we give ourselves away?" Bolin mused.

"Let me remind you," McKie said, "that I have accepted the hospitality you offered and that I've not offended your mores."

"Most remarkable," Bolin said. "In spite of all the temptations I offered, you have not offended our mores. This is true. You are an embarrassment, indeed you are. But perhaps you have a weapon. Yes?"

McKie lifted a wavering *shape* from an inner pocket.

"Ahhh, the Jicuzzi stim," Bolin said. "Now, let me see, is that a weapon?"

McKie held the *shape* on his palm. It appeared flat at first, like a palm-sized sheet of pink paper. Gradually, the flatness grew a superimposed image of a tube laid on its surface, then another image of an S-curved spring that coiled and wound around the tube.

"Our species can control its shape to some extent," Bolin said. "There's some question on whether I can

14

consider this a weapon."

McKie curled his fingers around the *shape*, squeezed. There came a pop, and fumeroles of purple light emerged between his fingers accompanied by an odor of burnt sugar.

"Exit stim," McKie said. "Now I'm completely defenseless, entirely dependent upon your hospitality."

"Ah, you are a tricky one," Bolin said. "But have you no regard for Ser Clinton Watt? To him, the change you forced upon him is an affliction. You've destroyed the instrument that might have reversed the process."

"He can apply to the Jicuzzi," McKie said, wondering why Bolin should concern himself over Watt.

"Ah, but they will ask your permission to intervene," Bolin said. "They are so formal. Drafting their request should take at least three standard years. They will not take the slightest chance of offending you. And you, of course, cannot volunteer your permission without offending them. You know, they may even build a nerve-image of you upon which to test their petition. You are not a callous person, McKie, in spite of your clownish poses. I'd not realized how important this confrontation was to you."

"Since I'm completely at your mercy," McKie said, "would you try to stop me from leaving here?"

"An interesting question," Bolin said. "You have information I don't want revealed at this time. You're aware of this, naturally?"

"Naturally."

"I find the Constitution a most wonderful document," Bolin said. "The profound awareness of the individual's identity and its relationship to society as a whole. Of particular interest is the portion dealing with

15

the Bureau of Sabotage, those amendments recognizing that the Bureau itself might at times need...a-h...adjustment."

*Now what's he driving at?* McKie wondered. And he noted how Bolin squinted his eyes in thought, leaving only a thin line of faceted glitter.

"I shall speak now as chief officer of the Tax Watchers," Bolin said, "reminding you that we are legally immune from sabotage."

*I've found out what I wanted to know*, McKie thought. Now if I can only get out of here with *it!*

"Let us consider the training of saboteurs extraordinary," Bolin said. "What do the trainees learn about the make-work and featherbedding elements in Bureau activity?"

*He's not going to trap me in a lie*, McKie thought. "We come right out and tell our trainees that one of our chief functions is to create jobs for the politicians to fill," he said. "The more hands in the pie, the slower the mixing."

"You've heard that telling a falsehood to your host is a great breach of Pan-Spechi mores, I see," Bolin said. "You understand, of course, that refusal to answer certain questions is interpreted as a falsehood?"

"So I've been told," McKie said.

"Wonderful! And what are your trainees told about the foot dragging and the monkeywrenches you throw into the path of legislation?"

"I quote from the pertinent training brochure," McKie said. "'A major function of the Bureau is to slow passage of legislation.'"

"Magnificent! And what about the disputes and outright battles Bureau agents have been known to incite?"

"Strictly routine," McKie said. "We're duty bound

to encourage the growth of anger in government wherever we can. It exposes the temperamental types, the ones who can't control themselves, who can't think on their feet."

"Ah," Bolin said. "How entertaining."

"We keep entertainment value in mind," McKie admitted. "We use drama and flamboyance wherever possible to keep our activities fascinating to the public."

"Flamboyant obstructionism," Bolin mused.

"Obstruction is a factor in strength," McKie said. "Only the strongest surmount the obstructions to succeed in government. The strongest . . . or the most devious, which is more or less the same thing when it comes to government."

"How illuminating," Bolin said. He rubbed the backs of his hands, a Pan-Spechi mannerism denoting satisfaction. "Do you have special instructions regarding political parties?"

"We stir up dissent between them," McKie said. "Opposition tends to expose reality, that's one of our axioms."

"Would you characterize Bureau agents as troublemakers?"

"Of course! My parents were happy as the devil when I showed troublemaking tendencies at an early age. They knew there'd be a lucrative outlet for this when I grew up. They saw to it that I was channeled in the right directions all through school—special classes in Applied Destruction, Advanced Irritation, Anger I and II . . . only the best teachers."

"You're suggesting the Bureau's an outlet for society's regular crop of troublemakers?"

"Isn't that obvious? And troublemakers naturally call for the services of troubleshooters. That's an outlet for do-gooders. You've a check and balance system serving society."

McKie waited, watching the Pan-Spechi, wondering if his answers had gone far enough.

"I speak as a Tax Watcher, you understand?" Bolin asked.

"I understand."

"The public pays for this Bureau. In essence, the public is paying people to cause trouble."

"Isn't that what we do when we hire police, tax investigators and the like?" McKie asked.

A look of gloating satisfaction came over Bolin's face. "But these agencies operate for the greater good of humanity!" he said.

"Before he begins training," McKie said, and his voice took on a solemn, lecturing tone, "the potential saboteur is shown the entire sordid record of history. The do-gooders succeeded once...long ago. They eliminated virtually all red tape from government. This great machine with its power over human lives slipped into high speed. It moved faster and faster." McKie's voice grew louder. "Laws were conceived and passed in the same hour! Appropriations came and were gone in a fortnight. New bureaus flashed into existence for the most insubstantial reasons."

McKie took a deep breath, realizing he'd put sincere emotional weight behind his words.

"Fascinating," Bolin said. "Efficient government, eh?"

"Efficient?" McKie's voice was filled with outrage. "It was like a great wheel thrown suddenly out of balance! The whole structure of government was in imminent danger of fragmenting before a handful of people, wise with hindsight, used measures of desperation and started what was called the Sabotage Corps."

18

"Ahhh, yes, I've heard about the Corps' violence."

*He's needling me,* McKie thought, but found that honest anger helped now. "All right, there was bloodshed and terrible destruction at the beginning," he said. "But the big wheels were slowed. Government developed a controllable speed."

"Sabotage," Bolin sneered. "In lieu of red tape."

*I needed that reminder,* McKie thought.

"No task too small for Sabotage, no task too large," McKie said. "We keep the wheel turning slowly and smoothly. Some anonymous Corpsman put it into words a long time ago: 'When in doubt, delay the big ones and speed the little ones.'"

"Would you say the Tax Watchers were a 'big one' or a 'little one'?" Bolin asked, his voice mild.

"Big one," McKie said and waited for Bolin to pounce.

But the Pan-Spechi appeared amused. "An unhappy answer."

"As it says in the Constitution," McKie said, "'The pursuit of unhappiness is an inalienable right of all humans.'"

"Trouble is as trouble does," Bolin said and clapped his hands.

Two Pan-Spechi in the uniforms of system police came through the creme de menthe emerald door.

"You heard?" Bolin asked.

"We heard," one of the police said.

"Was he defending his bureau?" Bolin asked.

"He was," the policeman said.

"You've seen the court order," Bolin said. "It pains me because Ser McKie accepted the hospitality of my house, but he must be held incommunicado until he's needed in court. He's to be treated kindly, you understand?"

19

*Is he really bent on destroying the Bureau?* McKie asked himself in sudden consternation. *Do I have it figured wrong?*

"You contend my words were sabotage?" McKie asked.

"Clearly an attempt to sway the chief officer of the Tax Watchers from his avowed duties," Bolin said. He stood, bowed.

McKie lifted himself out of the chairdog, assumed an air of confidence he did not feel. He clasped his thick-fingered hands together and bowed low, a grandfather toad rising from the deep to give his benediction. "In the words of the ancient proverb," he said, "'The righteous man lives deep within a cavern and the sky appears to him as nothing but a small round hole.'"

Wrapping himself in dignity, McKie allowed the police to escort him from the room.

Behind him, Bolin gave voice to puzzlement: "Now, what did he mean by that?"

"Hear ye! Hear ye! System High Court, First Bench, Central Sector, is now in session!"

The robo-clerk darted back and forth across the cleared lift dais of the courtarena, its metal curves glittering in the morning light that poured down through the domed weather cover. Its voice, designed to fit precisely into the great circular room, penetrated to the farthest walls: "All persons having petitions before this court draw near!"

The silvery half globe carrying First Magistrate Edwin Dooley glided through an aperture behind the lift dais and was raised to an appropriate height. His white sword of justice lay diagonally across the bench in front of him. Dooley himself sat in dignified silence while the robo-clerk finished its stentorian announcement and rolled to a stop just beyond the lift field.

Judge Dooley was a tall, black browed man who affected the ancient look with ebon robes over white linen. He was noted for decisions of classic penetration.

He sat now with his face held in rigid immobility to conceal his anger and disquiet. Why had they put him in this hot spot? Because he'd granted the Tax Watchers' injunction? No matter how he ruled now, the result likely would be uproar. Even President Hindley was watching this one through one of the hotline projectors.

The President had called shortly before this session. It had been Phil and Ed all through the conversation, but the intent remained clear. The Administration was concerned about this case. Vital legislation pended; votes were needed. Neither the budget nor the Bureau of Sabotage had entered their conversation, but the President had made his point—*don't compromise the Bureau but save that Tax Watcher support for the Administration!*

"Clerk, the roster," Judge Dooley said.

And he thought: *They'll get judgment according to strict interpretation of the law! Let them argue with that!*

The robo-clerk's reelslate buzzed. Words appeared on the repeater in front of the judge as the clerk's voice announced: "The People versus Clifton Watt, Jorj X. McKie and the Bureau of Sabotage."

Dooley looked down into the courtarena, noting the group seated at the black oblong table in the Defense ring on his left: a sour-faced Watt with his rainbow horror of Medusa head, McKie's fat features composed in a look of someone trying not to snicker at a sly joke—the two defendants flanking their attorney,

21

Pander Oulson, the Bureau of Sabotage's chief counsel. Oulson was a great thug of a figure in defense white with glistening eyes under beetle brows and a face fashioned mostly of scars.

At the Prosecution table on the right sat Prosecutor Holjance Vohnbrook, a tall scarecrow of a man dressed in conviction red. Gray hair topped a stern face as grim and forbidding as a later day Cotton Mather. Beside him sat a frightened appearing young aide and Panthor Bolin, the Pan-Spechi complaintant, his multi-faceted eyes hidden beneath veined lids.

"Are we joined for trial?" Dooley asked.

Both Oulson and Vohnbrook arose, nodded.

"If the court pleases," Vohnbrook rumbled, "I would like to remind the Bureau of Sabotage personnel present that this court is exempt from their ministrations."

"If the prosecutor trips over his own feet," Oulson said, "I assure him it will be his own clumsiness and no act of mine nor of my colleagues."

Vohnbrook's face darkened with a rush of blood. "It's well known how you . . ."

A great drumming boomed through the courtarena as Dooley touched the handle of his sword of office. The sound drowned the prosecutor's words. When silence was restored, Dooley said: "This court will tolerate no displays of personality. I wish that understood at the outset."

Oulson smiled, a look like a grimace in his scarred face. "I apologize, Your Honor," he said.

Dooley sank back into his chair, noting the gleam in Oulson's eyes. It occurred to Dooley then that the defense attorney, sabotage-trained, could have brought on the prosecutor's attack to gain the court's sympathy.

"The charge is outlaw sabotage in violation of this court's injunction," Dooley said. "I understand that opening statements have been waived by both sides, the public having been admitted to causae in this matter by appropriate postings?"

"So recorded," intoned the robo-clerk.

Oulson leaned forward against the defense table, said: "Your Honor, defendant Jorj X. McKie has not accepted me as counsel and wishes to argue for separate trial. I am here now representing only the Bureau and Clinton Watt."

"Who is appearing for defendant McKie?" the judge asked.

McKie, feeling like a man leaping over a precipice, got to his feet, said: "I wish to represent myself, Your Honor."

"You should be cautioned against this course," Dooley said.

"Ser Oulson has advised me I have a fool for a client," McKie said. "But in common with most Bureau agents, I have legal training. I've been admitted to the System Bar and have practiced under such codes as the Gowachin where the double-negative innocence requirement must be satisfied before bringing criminal accusation against the prosecutor and proceeding backward the premise that..."

"This is not Gowachin," Judge Dooley said.

"May I remind the Court," Vohnbrook said, "that defendant McKie is a saboteur extraordinary. This goes beyond questions of champerty. Every utterance this man..."

"The law's the same for official saboteurs as it is for others in respect to the issue at hand," Oulson said.

"Gentlemen!" the judge said. "If you please? I will decide the law in this court." He waited through a long moment of silence. "The behavior of all parties in this matter is receiving my most careful attention."

McKie forced himself to radiate calm good humor.

Watt, whose profound knowledge of the saboteur extraordinary made this pose a danger signal, tugged violently at the sleeve of defense attorney Oulson. Oulson waved him away. Watt glowered at McKie.

"If the court permits," McKie said, "a joint defense on the present charge would appear to violate..."

"The court is well aware that this case was bound over on the basis of deposa summation through a ruling by a robo-legum," Dooley said. "I warn both defense and prosecution, however, that I make my own decisions in such matters. Law and robo-legum are both human constructions and require human interpretation. And I will add that, as far as I'm concerned, in all conflicts between human agencies and machine agencies the human agencies are paramount."

"Is this a hearing or a trial?" McKie asked.

"We will proceed as in trial, subject to the evidence as presented."

McKie rested his palms on the edge of the defense table, studying the judge. The saboteur felt a surge of misgiving. Dooley was a no-nonsense customer. He had left himself a wide avenue within the indictment. And this was a case that went far beyond immediate danger to the Bureau of Sabotage. Far-reaching precedents could be set here this day—or disaster could strike. Ignoring instincts of self-preservation, McKie wondered if he dared try sabotage within the confines of the court.

"The robo-legum indictment requires joint defense," McKie said. "I admit sabotage against Ser Clinton Watt, but remind the court of Paragraph Four, section

24

ninety-one, of the Semantic Revision to the Constitution, wherein the Secretary of Sabotage is exempted from all immunities. I move to quash the indictment as it regards myself. I was at the time a legal officer of the Bureau required by my duties to test the abilities of my superior."

Vohnbrook scowled at McKie.

"Mmmm," Dooley said. He saw that the prosecutor had detected where McKie's logic must lead. If McKie were legally dismissed from the Bureau at the time of his conversation with the Pan-Spechi, the prosecution's case might fall through.

"Does the prosecutor wish to seek a conspiracy indictment?" Dooley asked.

For the first time since entering the courtarena, defense attorney Oulson appeared agitated. He bent his scarred features close to Watt's gorgon head, conferred in whispers with the defendant. Oulson's face grew darker and darker as he whispered. Watt's gorgon tendrils writhed in agitation.

"We don't seek a conspiracy indictment at this time," Vohnbrook said. "However, we would be willing to separate..."

"Your Honor!" Oulson said, surging to his feet. "Defense must protest separation of indictments at this time. It's our contention that..."

"Court cautions both counsel in this matter that this is not a Gowachin jurisdiction," Dooley said in an angry voice. "We don't have to convict the defender and exonerate the prosecutor before trying a case! However, if either of you would wish a change of venue..."

Vohnbrook, a smug expression on his lean face, bowed to the judge. "Your Honor," he said, "we wish at this time to request removal of defendant McKie from the indictment and ask that he be held as a prosecution witness."

"Objection!" Oulson shouted.

"Prosecution well knows it cannot hold a key witness under trumped up..."

"Overruled," Dooley said.

"Exception!"

"Noted."

Dooley waited as Oulson sank into his chair. *This is a day to remember,* the judge thought. *Sabotage itself outfoxed!* Then he noted the glint of sly humor in the eyes of saboteur extraordinary McKie, realizing with an abrupt sense of caution that McKie, too, had maneuvered for this position.

"Prosecution may call its first witness," the judge said, and he punched a code signal that sent a robo-aide to escort McKie away from the defense table and into a holding box.

A look of almost-pleasure came over prosecutor Vohnbrook's cadaverous face. He rubbed one of his downdrooping eyelids, said: "Call Panthor Bolin."

The Achusian capitalist got to his feet, strode to the witness ring. The robo-clerk's screen flashed for the record: "Panthor Bolin of Achus IV, certified witness in case $A011\text{-}5BD_4gGY74R_6$ of System High Court $ZRZ^1$."

"The oath of sincerity having been administered, Panthor Bolin is prepared for testifying," the robo-clerk recited.

"Panthor Bolin, are you chief officer of the civil organization known as the Tax Watchers?" Vohnbrook asked.

"I...ah...y-yes," Bolin faltered. He passed a large

blue handkerchief across his forehead, staring sharply at McKie.

*He just now realizes what it is I must do,* McKie thought.

"I show you this recording from the robo-legum indictment proceedings," Vohnbrook said. "It is certified by System police as being a conversation between yourself and Jorj X. McKie in which..."

"Your Honor!" Oulson objected. "Both witnesses to this alleged conversation are present in this courtarena. There are more direct ways to bring out any pertinent information from this matter. Further, since the clear threat of a conspiracy charge remains in this case, I object to introducing this recording as forcing a man to testify against himself."

"Ser McKie is no longer on trial here and Ser Oulson is not McKie's attorney of record," Vohnbrook gloated.

"The objection does, however, have some merit," Dooley said. He looked at McKie seated in the holding box.

"There's nothing shameful about that conversation with Ser Bolin," McKie said. "I've no objection to introducing this record of the conversation."

Bolin rose up on his toes, made as though to speak, sank back.

*Now he is certain,* McKie thought.

"Then I will admit this record subject to judicial deletions," Dooley said.

Clinton Watt, seated at the defense table, buried his gorgon head in his arms.

Vohnbrook, a death's-head grin on his long face, said: "Ser Bolin, I show you this recording. Now, in this conversation, was Sabotage Agent McKie subjected to any form of coercion?"

"Objection!" Oulson roared, surging to his feet. His scarred face was a scowling mask. "At the time of this alleged recording, Ser McKie was not an agent of the Bureau!" He looked at Vohnbrook. "Defense objects to the prosecutor's obvious effort to link Ser McKie with..."

"*Alleged* conversation!" Vohnbrook snarled. "Ser McKie himself admits the exchange!"

In a weary voice, Dooley said: "Objection sustained. Unless tangible evidence of conspiracy is introduced here, references to Ser McKie as an agent of Sabotage will not be admitted here."

"But Your Honor," Vohnbrook protested, "Ser McKie's own actions preclude any other interpretation!"

"I've ruled on this point," Dooley said. "Proceed."

McKie got to his feet in the holding box, said: "Would Your Honor permit me to act as a friend of the Court here?"

Dooley leaned back, hand on chin, turning the question over in his mind. A general feeling of uneasiness about the case was increasing in him and he couldn't pinpoint it. McKie's every action appeared suspect. Dooley reminded himself that the saboteur extraordinary was notorious for sly plots, for devious and convoluted schemes of the wildest and most improbable inversions—like onion layers in a five dimensional klein-shape. The man's success in practicing under the Gowachin legal code could be understood.

"You may explain what you have in mind," Dooley said, "but I'm not yet ready to admit your statements into the record."

"The Bureau of Sabotage's own Code would clarify matters," McKie said, realizing that these words burned his bridges behind him. "My action in successfully sabotaging *acting* Secretary Watt is a matter of record."

McKie pointed to the gorgon mass visible as Watt lifted his head and glared across the room.

"*Acting* Secretary?" the judge asked.

"So it must be presumed," McKie said. "Under the Bureau's Code, once the Secretary is sabotaged he . . ."

"Your Honor!" Oulson shouted. "We are in danger of breach of security here! I understand these proceedings are being broadcast!"

"As Director-in-Limbo of the Bureau of Sabotage, I will decide what is a breach of security and what isn't!" McKie snapped.

Watt returned his head to his arms, groaned.

Oulson sputtered.

Dooley stared at McKie in shock.

Vohnbrook broke the spell. The prosecutor said: "Your Honor, this man has not been sworn to sincerity. I suggest we excuse Ser Bolin for the time being and have Ser McKie continue his *explanation* under oath."

Dooley took a deep breath, said: "Does defense have any questions of Ser Bolin at this time?"

"Not at this time," Oulson muttered. "I presume he's subject to recall?"

"He is," Dooley said, turning to McKie. "Take the witness ring, Ser McKie."

Bolin, moving like a sleepwalker, stepped out of the ring, returned to the prosecution table. The Pan-Spechi's multi-faceted eyes reflected an odd glitter, moving with a trapped sense of evasiveness.

McKie entered the ring, took the oath and faced

Vohnbrook, composing his features in a look of purposeful decisiveness that he knew his actions must reflect.

"You called yourself Director-in-Limbo of the Bureau of Sabotage," Vohnbrook said. "Would you explain that, please?"

Before McKie could answer, Watt lifted his head from his arms, growled: "You traitor, McKie!"

Dooley grabbed the pommel of his sword of justice to indicate an absolute position and barked: "I will tolerate no outbursts in my court!"

Oulson put a hand on Watt's shoulder. Both of them glared at McKie. The Medusa tendrils of Watt's head writhed as they ranged through the rainbow spectrum.

"I caution the witness," Dooley said, "that his remarks would appear to admit a conspiracy. Anything he says now may be used against him."

"No conspiracy, Your Honor," McKie said. He faced Vohnbrook, but appeared to be addressing Watt. "Over the centuries, the function of Sabotage in the government has grown more and more open, but certain aspects of changing the guard, so to speak, have been ˙ eld as a highly placed secret. The rule is that if a man can protect himself from sabotage he's fit to boss Sabotage. Once sabotaged, however, the Bureau's Secretary must resign and submit his position to the President and the full Cabinet."

"He's out?" Dooley asked.

"Not necessarily," McKie said. "If the act of sabotage against the Secretary is profound enough, subtle enough, carries enough far reaching effects, the Secretary is replaced by the successful saboteur. He is, indeed, out."

"Then it's now up to the President and the Cabinet

to decide between Ser Watt and yourself, is that what you're saying?" Dooley asked.

"Me?" McKie asked. "No, I'm Director-in-Limbo because I accomplished a successful *act* of sabotage against Ser Watt and because I happen to be senior saboteur extraordinary on duty."

"But it's alleged that you were fired," Vohnbrook objected.

"A formality," McKie said. "It's customary to fire the saboteur who's successful in such an effort. This makes him eligible for appointment as Secretary if he so aspires. However, I have no such ambition at this time."

Watt jerked upright, staring at McKie.

McKie ran a finger around his collar, realizing the physical peril he was about to face. A glance at the Pan-Spechi confirmed the feeling. Panthor Bolin was holding himself in check by a visible effort.

"This is all very interesting," Vohnbrook sneered, "but how can it possibly have any bearing on the present action? The charge here is outlaw sabotage against the Tax Watchers represented by the person of Ser Panthor Bolin. If Ser McKie..."

"If the distinguished Prosecutor will permit me," McKie said, "I believe I can set his fears at rest. It should be obvious to—"

"There's conspiracy here!" Vohnbrook shouted. "What about the..."

A loud pounding interrupted him as Judge Dooley lifted his sword, its theremin effect filling the room. When silence had been restored, the judge lowered his sword, replaced it firmly on the ledge in front of him.

Dooley took a moment to calm himself. He sensed now the delicate political edge he walked and thanked

31

his stars that he had left the door open to rule that the present session was a hearing.

"We will now proceed in an orderly fashion," Dooley said. "That's one of the things courts are for, you know." He took a deep breath. "Now, there are several people present whose dedication to the maintenance of law and order should be beyond question. I'd think that among those we should number Ser Prosecutor Vohnbrook; the distinguished defense counsel, Ser Oulson; Ser Bolin, whose race is noted for its reasonableness and humanity; and the distinguished representatives of the Bureau of Sabotage, whose actions may at times annoy and anger us, but who are, we know, consecrated to the principle of strengthening us and exposing our inner resources."

*This judge missed his calling,* McKie thought. *With speeches like that, he could get into the Legislative branch.*

Abashed, Vohnbrook sank back into his chair.

"Now," the judge said, "unless I'm mistaken, Ser McKie has referred to two acts of sabotage." Dooley glanced down at McKie. "Ser McKie?"

"So it would appear, Your Honor," McKie said, hoping he read the judge's present attitude correctly. "However, this court may be in a unique position to rule on that very question. You see, Your Honor, the alleged act of sabotage to which I refer was initiated by a Pan-Spechi agent of the Bureau. Now, though, the secondary benefits of that action appear to be sought after by a creche mate of that agent, whose . . ."

"You dare suggest that I'm not the holder of my cell's ego?" Bolin demanded.

Without knowing quite where it was or what it was, McKie was aware that a weapon had been trained on him by the Pan-Spechi. References in their culture to

32

the weapon for defense of the ego were clear enough.

"I make no such suggestion," McKie said, speaking hastily and with as much sincerity as he could put into his voice. "But surely you cannot have misinterpreted the terranic-human culture so much that you do not know what will happen now."

Warned by some instinct, the judge and other spectators to this interchange remained silent.

Bolin appeared to be trembling in every cell of his body. "I am distressed," he muttered.

"If there were a way to achieve the necessary rapport and avoid that distress I would have taken it," McKie said. "Can you see another way?"

Still trembling, Bolin said: "I must do what I must do."

In a low voice, Dooley said: "Ser McKie, just what is going on here?"

"Two cultures are, at last, attempting to understand each other," McKie said. "We've lived together in apparent understanding for centuries, but appearances can be deceptive."

Oulson started to rise, was pulled back by Watt.

And McKie noted that his former Bureau chief had assessed the peril here. It was a point in Watt's favor.

"You understand, Ser Bolin," McKie said, watching the Pan-Spechi carefully, "that these things must be brought into the open and discussed carefully before a decision can be reached in this court. It's a rule of law to which you've submitted. I'm inclined to favor your bid for the Secretariat, but my own decision awaits the outcome of this hearing."

"What things must be discussed?" Dooley demanded. "And what gives you the right, Ser McKie, to call this a hearing?"

"A figure of speech," McKie said, but he kept his

attention on the Pan-Spechi, wondering what the terrible weapon was that the race used in defense of its egos. "What do you say, Ser Bolin?"

"You protect the sanctity of your home life," Bolin said. "Dc you deny me the same right?"

"Sanctity, not secrecy," McKie said

Dooley looked from McKie to Bolin, noted the compressed-spring look of the Pan-Spechi, the way he kept a hand hidden in a jacket pocket. It occurred to the judge then that the Pan-Spechi might have a weapon ready to use against others in this court. Bolin had that look about him. Dooley hesitated on the point of calling guards, reviewed what he knew of the Pan-Spechi. He decided not to cause a crisis. The Pan-Spechi were admitted to the concourse of humanity, good friends but terrible enemies, and there were always those allusions to their hidden powers, to their ego jealousies, to the fierceness with which they defended the secrecy of their creches.

Slowly, Bolin overcame the trembling. "Say what you feel you must," he growled.

McKie said a silent prayer of hope that the Pan-Spechi could control his reflexes, addressed himself to the nexus of pickups on the far wall that was recording this courtarena scene for broadcast to the entire universe.

"A Pan-Spechi who took the name of Napoleon Bildoon was one of the leading agents in the Bureau of Sabotage," McKie said. "Agent Bildoon dropped from sight at the time Panthor Bolin took over as chief of the Tax Watchers. It's highly probable that the Tax Watcher organization is an elaborate and subtle sabotage of the Bureau of Sabotage itself, a move originated by Bildoon."

"There is no such person as Bildoon!" Bolin cried.

"Ser McKie," Judge Dooley said, "would you care to continue this interchange in the privacy of my chambers?" The judge stared down at the saboteur, trying to appear kindly but firm.

"Your Honor," McKie said, "may we, out of respect for a fellow human, leave that decision to Ser Bolin?"

Bolin turned his multi-faceted eyes toward the bench, spoke in a low voice: "If the court please, it were best this were done openly." He jerked his hand from his pocket. It came out empty. He leaned across the table, gripped the far edge. "Continue, if you please, Ser."

McKie swallowed, momentarily overcome with admiration for the Pan-Spechi. "It will be a distinct pleasure to serve under you, Ser Bolin," McKie said.

"Do what you must!" Bolin rasped.

McKie looked from the wonderment in the faces of Watt and the attorneys up to the questioning eyes of Judge Dooley. "In Pan-Spechi parlance, there is no person called Bildoon. But there was such a person, a group mate of Ser Bolin. I hope you notice the similarity in the names they chose for themselves?"

"Ah . . . yes," Dooley said.

"I'm afraid I've been somewhat of a nosy Parker, a peeping Tom and several other categories of snoop where the Pan-Spechi are concerned," McKie said. "But it was because I suspected the act of sabotage to which I've referred here. The Tax Watchers revealed too much inside knowledge of the Bureau of Sabotage."

"I . . . ah . . . am not quite sure I understand you," Dooley said.

"The best kept secret in the universe, the Pan-Spechi cyclic change of gender and identity, is no longer a secret where I'm concerned," McKie said. He swallowed as he saw Bolin's fingers go white where they tightly gripped the prosecution table.

"It relates to the issue at hand?" Dooley asked.

"Most definitely, Your Honor," McKie said. "You see, the Pan-Spechi have a unique gland that controls mentation, dominance, the relationship between reason and instinct. The five group mates are, in reality, one person. I wish to make that clear for reasons of legal necessity."

"Legal necessity?" Dooley asked. He glanced down at the obviously distressed Bolin, back to McKie.

"The gland, when it's functioning, confers ego dominance on the Pan-Spechi in whom it functions. But it functions for a time that's definitely limited— twenty-five to thirty years." McKie looked at Bolin. Again, the Pan-Spechi was trembling. "Please understand, Ser Bolin," he said, "that I do this out of necessity and that this is not an act of sabotage."

Bolin lifted his face toward McKie. The Pan-Spechi's features appeared contorted in grief. "Get it over with, man!" he rasped.

"Yes," McKie said, turning back to the judge's puzzled face. "Ego transfer in the Pan-Spechi, Your Honor, involves a transfer of what may be termed basic-experience-learning. It's accomplished through physical contractor when the ego holder dies, no matter how far he may be separated from the creche, this seems to fire up the eldest of the creche triplets. The ego-single also bequeaths a verbal legacy to his mate whenever possible—and that's most of the time. Specifically, it's this time."

Dooley leaned back. He was beginning to see the legal question McKie's account had posed.

"The act of sabotage which might make a Pan-Spechi eligible for appointment as Secretary of the

Bureau of Sabotage was initiated by a...ah...cell mate of the Ser Bolin in court today, is that it?" Dooley asked.

McKie wiped his brow "Correct, Your Honor."

"But that cell mate is no longer the ego dominant, eh?"

"Quite right, Your Honor."

"The...ah...former ego holder, this...ah...Bildoon, is no longer eligible?"

"Bildoon, or what was once Bildoon, is a creature operating solely on instinct now, Your Honor," McKie said. "Capable of acting as creche nurse for a time and, eventually, fulfilling another destiny I'd rather not explain."

"I see." Dooley looked at the weather cover of the courtarena. He was beginning to see what McKie had risked here. "And you favor this, ah, Ser Bolin's bid for the Secretariat?" Dooley asked.

"If President Hindley and the Cabinet follow the recommendation of the Bureau's senior agents, the procedure always followed in the past, Ser Bolin will be the new Secretary," McKie said. "I favor this."

"Why?" Dooley asked.

"Because of this unique roving ego, the Pan-Spechi have a more communal attitude toward fellow sentients than do most other species admitted to the concourse of humanity," McKie said. "This translates as a sense of responsibility toward all life. They're not necessarily maudlin about it. They oppose where it's necessary to build strength. Their creche life demonstrates several clear examples of this which I'd prefer not to describe."

"I see," Dooley said, but he had to admit to himself that he did not. McKie's allusions to unspeakable practices were beginning to annoy him. "And you feel that this Bildoon-Bolin act of sabotage qualifies him, provided this court rules they are one and the same person?"

"We are not the same person!" Bolin cried. "You don't dare say I'm that . . . that shambling, clinging . . ."

"Easy," McKie said. "Ser Bolin, I'm sure you see the need for this legal fiction."

"Legal fiction," Bolin said as though clinging to the words. The multi-faceted eyes glared across the courtarena at McKie. "Thank you for the verbal nicety, McKie."

"You've not answered my question, Ser McKie," Dooley said, ignoring the exchange with Bolin.

"Sabotaging Ser Watt through an attack on the entire Bureau contains subtlety and finesse never before achieved in such an effort," McKie said. "The entire Bureau will be strengthened by it."

McKie glanced at Watt. The acting Secretary's Medusa tangle had ceased its writhing. He was staring at Bolin with a speculative look in his eyes. Sensing the quiet in the courtarena, he glanced up at McKie.

"Don't you agree, Ser Watt?" McKie asked.

"Oh, yes. Quite," Watt said.

The note of sincerity in Watt's voice startled the judge. For the first time, he wondered at the dedication which these men brought to their jobs.

Sabotage is a very sensitive Bureau," Dooley said. "I've some serious reservations—"

"If Your Honor please," McKie said, "forbearance is one of the chief attributes a saboteur can bring to his duties. Now, I wish you to understand what our Pan-Spechi friend has done here this day. Let us suppose that I had spied upon the most intimate moments between you, Judge, and your wife, and that I reported them in detail here in open court with half the universe looking on. Let us suppose further that you had the strictest moral code against such discussions with outsiders. Let us suppose that I made these disclosures in the basest terms with every four-letter word at my command. Let us suppose that you were armed, traditionally, with a deadly weapon to strike at such blasphemers, such—"

"Filth!" Bolin grated.

"Yes," McKie said. "Filth. Do you suppose, Your Honor, that you could have stood by without killing me?"

"Good heavens!" Dooley said.

"Ser Bolin," McKie said, "I offer you and all your race my most humble apologies."

"I'd hoped once to undergo the ordeal in the privacy of a judge's chambers with as few outsiders as possible," Bolin said. "But once you were started in open court..."

"It had to be this way," McKie said. "If we'd done it in private, people would've come to be suspicious about a Pan-Spechi in control of..."

"People?" Bolin asked.

"Non Pan-Spechi," McKie said. "It'd have been a barrier between our species.

"And we've been strengthened by all this," McKie said. "Those provisions of the Constitution that provide the people with a slowly moving government have been demonstrated anew. We've admitted the public to the inner workings of Sabotage, shown them the valuable character of the man who'll be the new Secretary."

"I've not yet ruled on the critical issue here," Dooley said.

"But Your Honor!" McKie said.

"With all due respect to you as a saboteur extraordinary, Ser McKie," Dooley said, "I'll make my decision on evidence gathered under my direction." He looked at Bolin. "Ser Bolin, would you permit an agent of this court to gather such evidence as will allow me to render verdict without fear of harming my own species?"

"We're humans together," Bolin growled.

"But terranic humans hold the balance of power," Dooley said. "I owe allegiance to law, yes, but my terranic fellows depend on me, too. I have a . . ."

"You wish your own agents to determine if Ser McKie has told the truth about us?"

"Ah . . . yes," Dooley said.

Bolin looked at McKie. "Ser McKie, it is I who apologize to you. I had not realized how deeply xenophobia penetrated your fellows."

"Because," McKie said, "outside of your natural modesty, you have no such fear. I suspect you know the phenomenon only through reading of us."

"But all strangers are potential sharers of identity," Bolin said. "Ah, well."

"If you're through with your little chat," Dooley said, "would you care to answer my question, Ser Bolin? This is still, I hope, a court of law."

"Tell me, Your Honor," Bolin said, "would you permit me to witness the tenderest intimacies between you and your wife?"

Dooley's face darkened, but he saw suddenly in all of its stark detail the extent of McKie's analogy and it was to the judge's credit that he rose to the occasion. "If it were necessary to promote understanding," he rasped, "yes!"

"I believe you would," Bolin murmured. He took a deep breath. "After what I've been through here today, one more sacrifice can be borne, I guess. I grant your investigators the privilege requested, but advise that they be discreet."

"It will strengthen you for the trials ahead as Secretary of the Bureau," McKie said. "The Secretary, you must bear in mind, has no immunities from sabotage whatsoever."

"But," Bolin said, "the Secretary's legal orders carrying out his Constitutional functions must be obeyed by all agents."

McKie nodded, seeing in the glitter of Bolin's eyes a vista of peeping Tom assignments with endless detailed reports to the Secretary of Sabotage—at least until the fellow's curiosity had been satisfied and his need for revenge satiated.

But the others in the courtarena, not having McKie's insight, merely wondered at the question: *What did he really mean by that?*

# BY THE BOOK

*You will take your work seriously. Infinite numbers of yet-unborn humankind depend upon you who keep open the communications lines through negative space. Let the angle-transmission networks fail and Man will fail.*

"You and the Haigh Company"
(Employees Handbook)

He was too old for this kind of work even if his name was Ivar Norris Gump, admittedly the best troubleshooter in the company's nine-hundred-year history. If it'd been anyone but his old friend Poss Washington calling for help, there'd have been a polite refusal signed "Ing." Semi-retirement gave a troubleshooter the right to turn down dangerous assignments.

Now, after three hours on duty in a full vac suit within a Skoarnoff tube's blank darkness, Ing ached with tiredness. It impaired his mental clarity and his ability to survive and he knew it.

*You will take your work seriously at all times,* he thought. *Axiom: A troubleshooter shall not get into trouble.*

Ing shook his head at the handbook's educated ignorance, took a deep breath and tried to relax. Right

42

now he should be back home on Mars, his only concerns the routine maintenance of the Phobos Relay and an occasional lecture to new 'shooters.

*Damn that Poss,* he thought.

The big trouble was in here, though—in the tube, and six good men had died trying to find it. They were six men he had helped train—and that was another reason he had come. They were all caught up in the same dream.

Around Ing stretched an airless tubular cave twelve kilometers long, two kilometers diameter. It was a lightless hole carved through lava rock beneath the moon's Mare Nectaris. Here was the home of the "Beam"—the beautiful, deadly, vitally *serious* beam, a tamed violence which suddenly had become balky.

Ing thought of all the history which had gone into this tube. Some nine hundred years ago the Seedling Compact had been signed. In addition to its Solar System Communications duties, the Haigh Company had taken over then the sending out of small containers, their size severely limited by the mass an angtrans pulse could push. Each container held twenty female rabbits. In the rabbit uteri, dormant, their metabolism almost at a standstill, lay two hundred human embryos nestled with embryos of cattle, all the domestic stock needed to start a new human economy. With the rabbits went plant seeds, insect eggs and design tapes for tools.

The containers were rigged to fold out on a planet's surface to provide a shielded living area. There the embryos would be machine-transferred into inflatable gestation vats, brought to full term, cared for and educated by mechanicals until the human *seed* could fend for itself.

Each container had been pushed to trans-light speed

43

by angtrans pulses—"Like pumping a common garden swing," said the popular literature. The life mechanism was controlled by signals transmitted through the "Beam" whose tiny impulses went "around the corner" to bridge in milliseconds distances which took matter centuries to traverse.

Ing glanced up at the miniature beam sealed behind its quartz window in his suit. There was the hope and the frustration. If they could only put a little beam such as that in each container, the big beam could home on it. But under that harsh bombardment, beam anodes lasted no longer than a month. They made-do with reflection plates on the containers, then, with beam-bounce and programmed approximations. And somewhere the programmed approximations were breaking down.

Now, with the first Seedling Compact vessel about to land on Theta Apus IV, with mankind's interest raised to fever pitch—beam contact had turned unreliable. The farther out the container, the worse the contact.

Ing could feel himself being drawn toward that frail cargo out there. His instincts were in communion with those containers which would drift into limbo unless the beam was brought under control. The embryos would surely die eventually and the dream would die with them.

Much of humanity feared the containers had fallen into the hands of alien life, that the human embryos were being taken over by something *out there*. Panic ruled in some quarters and there were shouts that the SC containers betrayed enough human secrets to make the entire race vulnerable.

To Ing and the six before him, the locus of the problem seemed obvious. It lay in here and in the anomaly math newly derived to explain how the beam might be deflected from the containers. What to do about that appeared equally obvious. But six men had died following that obvious course. They had died here in this utter blackness.

Sometimes it helped to quote the book.

Often you didn't know what you hunted here—a bit of stray radiation perhaps, a few cosmic rays that had penetrated a weak spot in the force-baffle shielding, a dust leak caused by a moonquake, or a touch of heat, a hot spot coming up from the depths. The big beam wouldn't tolerate much interference. Put a pinhead flake of dust in its path at the wrong moment, let a tiny flicker of light intersect it, and it went whiplash wild. It writhed like a giant snake, tore whole sections off the tube walls. Beam auroras danced in the sky above the moon then and the human attendants scurried.

A troubleshooter at the wrong spot in the tube died.

Ing pulled his hands into his suit's barrel top, adjusted his own tiny beam scope, the unit that linked him through a short reach of angspace to beam control. He checked his instruments, read his position from the modulated contact ripple through the soles of his shielded suit.

He wondered what his daughter, Lisa, was doing about now. Probably getting the boys, his grandsons, ready for the slotride to school. It made Ing feel suddenly old to think that one of his grandsons already was in Mars Polytechnic aiming for a Haigh Company career in the footsteps of his famous grandfather.

The vac suit was hot and smelly around Ing after a three-hour tour. He noted from a dial that his canned-cold temperature balance system still had an hour and ten minutes before red-line.

*It's the cleaners,* Ing told himself. *It has to be the*

*vacuum cleaners. It's the old familiar cussedness of inanimate objects.*

What did the handbook say? *"Frequently it pays to look first for the characteristics of devices in use which may be such that an essential pragmatic approach offers the best chance for success. It often is possible to solve an accident or malfunction problem with straightforward and uncomplicated approaches, deliberately ignoring their more subtle aspects.*

He slipped his hands back into his suit's arms, shielded his particle counter with an armored hand, cracked open the cover, peered in at the luminous dial. Immediately, an angry voice crackled in the speakers:

"Douse that light! We're beaming!"

Ing snapped the lid closed by reflex, said: "I'm in the backboard shadow. Can't see the beam." Then: "Why wasn't I told you're beaming?"

Another voice rumbled from the speakers: "It's Poss here, Ing. I'm monitoring your position by sono, told them to go ahead without disturbing you."

"What's the supetrans doing monitoring a troubleshooter?" Ing asked.

"All right, Ing."

Ing chuckled, then: "What're you doing, testing?"

"Yes. We've an inner-space transport to beam down on Titan, thought we'd run it from here."

"Did I foul the beam?"

"We're still tracking clean."

*Inner-space transmission open and reliable,* Ing thought, *but the long reach out to the stars was muddied.* Maybe the scare mongers were right. Maybe it was outside interference, an alien intelligence.

"We've lost two cleaners on this transmission," Washington said. "Any sign of them?"

"Negative."

46

They'd lost two cleaners on the transmission, Ing thought. That was getting to be routine. The flitting vacuum cleaners—supported by the beam's field, patrolling its length for the slightest trace of interference, had to be replaced at the rate of about a hundred a year normally, but the rate had been going up. As the beam grew bigger, unleashed more power for the long reach, the cleaners proved less and less effective at dodging the angtrans throw, the controlled whiplash. No part of a cleaner survived contact with the beam. They were energy-charged in phase with the beam, keyed for instant dissolution to add their energy to the transmission.

"It's the damned cleaners," Ing said.

"That's what you all keep saying," Washington said.

Ing began prowling to his right. Somewhere off there the glassite floor curved gradually upward and became a wall—and then a ceiling. But the opposite side was always two kilometers away, and the moon's gravity, light as that was, imposed limits on how far he could walk up the wall. It wasn't like the little Phobos beam where they could use a low-power magnafield outside and walk right around the tube.

He wondered then if he was going to insist on riding one of the cleaners . . . the way the six others had done.

Ing's shuffling, cautious footsteps brought him out of the anode backboard's shadow. He turned, saw a pencil line of glowing purple stretching away from him to the cathode twelve kilometers distant. He knew there actually was no purple glow, that what he saw was a visual simulation created on the one-way surface of his faceplate, a reaction to the beam's presence displayed there for his benefit alone.

Washington's voice in his speaker said: "Sono has you in Zone Yellow. Take it easy, Ing."

Ing altered course to the right, studied the beam.

Intermittent breaks in the purple line betrayed the presence between himself and that lambent energy of the robot vacuum cleaners policing the perimeter, hanging on the sine lines of the beam field like porpoises gamboling on a bow wave.

"Transport's down," Washington said. "We're phasing into a long-throw test. Ten-minute program."

Ing nodded to himself, imagined Washington sitting there in the armored bubble of the control room, a giant, with a brooding face, eyes alert and glittering. Old Poss didn't want to believe it was the cleaners, that was sure. If it was the cleaners, someone was going to have to ride the wild goose. There'd be more deaths ... more rides ... until they tested out the new theory. It certainly was a helluva time for someone to come up with an anomaly *hole* in the angtrans math. But that's what someone back at one of the trans-time computers on Earth had done ... and if he was right— then the problem had to be the cleaners.

Ing studied the shadow breaks in the beam—robotic torpedoes, sensor-trained to collect the tiniest debris. One of the shadows suddenly reached away from him in both directions until the entire beam was hidden. A cleaner was approaching him. Ing waited for it to identify the Authorized Intruder markings which it could *see* the same way he saw the beam.

The beam reappeared.

"Cleaner just looked you over," Washington said. "You're getting in pretty close."

Ing heard the worry in his friend's voice, said: "I'm all right long's I stay up here close to the board."

He tried to picture in his mind then the cleaner lifting over him and returning to its station along the beam.

"I'm plotting you against the beam," Washington

said. "Your shadow width says you're approaching Zone Red. Don't crowd it, Ing. I'd rather not have to clean a fried troubleshooter out of there."

"Hate to put you to all that extra work," Ing said.

"Give yourself plenty of 'lash room."

"I'm miking the beam thickness against my helmet cross-hairs, Poss. Relax."

Ing advanced another two steps, sent his gaze traversing the beam's length, seeking the beginnings of the controlled whiplash which would *throw* the test message into angspace. The chained energy of the purple rope began to bend near its center far down the tube. It was an action visible only as a gentle flickering outward against the cross-hairs of his faceplate.

He backed off four steps. The throw was a chancy thing when you were this close—and if interfering radiation ever touched that beam...

Ing crouched, sighted along the beam, waited for the throw. An experienced troubleshooter could tell more from the way the beam whipped than banks of instruments could reveal. Did it push out a double bow? Look for faulty field focus. Did it waver up and down? Possible misalignment of vertical hold. Did it split or spread into two loops? Synchronization problem.

But you had to be in here close and alert to that fractional margin between good seeing and *good night!* forever.

Cleaners began paying more attention to him in this close, but he planted himself with his AI markings visible to them, allowing them to fix his position and go on about their business.

To Ing's trained eye, the cleaner action appeared more intense, faster than normal. That agreed with all the previous reports—unless a perimeter gap had admitted stray foreign particles, or perhaps tiny shades dislodged from the tube's walls by the pulse of the moon's own life.

Ing wondered then if there could be an overlooked hole in the fanatic quadruple-lock controls giving access to the tube. But they'd been sniffing along that line since the first sign of trouble. Not likely a hole would've escaped the inspectors. No—it was in here. And cleaner action *was* increased, a definite lift in tempo.

"Program condition?" Ing asked.

"Transmission's still Whorf positive, but we haven't found an angspace opening yet."

"Time?"

"Eight minutes to program termination."

"Cleaner action's way up," Ing said. "What's the dirt count?"

A pause, then: "Normal."

Ing shook his head. The monitor that kept constant count of the quantity of debris picked up by the cleaners shouldn't show normal in the face of this much activity.

"What's the word from Mare Nubium transmitter?" Ing asked.

"Still shut down and full of inspection equipment. Nothing to show for it at last report."

"Imbrium?"

"Inspection teams are out and they expect to be back into test phase by 0900. You're not thinking of ordering *us* to shut down for a complete clean-out?"

"Not yet."

"We've got a budget to consider, too, Ing. Remember that."

*Huh!* Ing thought. *Not like Poss to worry about*

*budget in this kind of an emergency. He trying to tell me something?*

What did the handbook say? *"The good trouble-shooter is cost conscious, aware that down time and equipment replacement are factors of serious concern to the Haigh Company."*

Ing wondered then if he should order the tube opened for thorough inspection. But the Imbrium and Nubium tubes had revealed nothing and the decontamination time *was* costly. They were the older tubes, though—Nubium the first to be built. They were smaller than Nectaris, simpler locks. But their beams weren't getting through any better than the Nectaris tube with its behemoth size, greater safeguards.

"Stand by," Washington said. "We're beginning to get whipcount on the program."

In the abrupt silence, Ing saw the beam curl. The whiplash came down the twelve kilometers of tube curling like a purple wave, traveling the entire length in about two thousandths of a second. It was a thing so fast that the visual effect was of seeing it *after* it had happened.

Ing stood up, began analyzing what he had seen. The beam had appeared clean, pure—a perfect throw...except for one little flare near the far end and another about midway. Little flares. The afterimage was needle shaped, rigid...pointed.

"How'd it look?" Washington asked.

"Clean," Ing said. "Did we get through?"

"We're checking," Washington said, then: "Limited contact. Very muddy. About thirty per cent...just about enough to tell us the container's still there and its contents seem to be alive."

"Is it in orbit?"

51

"Seems to be. Can't be sure."

"Give me the cleaner count," Ing said.

A pause, then: "Damnation! We're down another two."

"Exactly two?"

"Yes. Why?"

"Dunno yet. Do your instruments show beam deflections from hitting two cleaners? What's the energy sum?"

"Everyone thinks the cleaners are causing this," Washington muttered. "I tell you they couldn't. They're fully phased *with* the beam, just add energy to it if they hit. They're *not* debris!"

"But does the beam really eat them?" Ing asked. "You saw the anomaly report."

"Oh, Ing, let's not go into that again." Washington's voice sounded tired, irritated.

The stubborness of Washington's response confused Ing. This wasn't like the man at all. "Sure," Ing said, "but what if they're going somewhere we can't see?"

"Come off that, Ing! You're as bad as all the others. If there's one place we know they're *not* going, that's into angspace. There isn't enough energy in the universe to put cleaner mass around the corner."

"Unless that hole in our theories really exists," Ing said. And he thought: *Poss is trying to tell me something. What? Why can't he come right out and say it?* He waited, wondering at an idea that nibbled at the edge of his mind—a concept ... What was it? Some half-forgotten association ...

"Here's the beam report," Washington said. "Deflection shows only one being taken, but the energy sum's doubled all right. One balanced out the other. That happens."

Ing studied the purple line, nodding to himself. The

beam was almost the color of a scarf his wife had worn on their honeymoon. She'd been a good wife, Jennie—raising Lisa in Mars camps and blister pods, sticking with her man until the canned air and hard life had taken her.

The beam lay quiescent now with only the faintest auroral bleed off. Cleaner tempo was down. The test program still had a few minutes to go, but Ing doubted it'd produce another throw into angspace. You acquired an instinct for the transmission pulse after a while. You could sense when the beam was going to open its tiny signal window across the light-years.

"I saw both of those cleaners go," Ing said. "They didn't seem to be torn apart or anything—just flared out."

"Energy consumed," Washington said.

"Maybe."

Ing thought for a moment. A hunch was beginning to grow in him. He knew a way to test it. The question was: Would Poss go along with it? Hard to tell in his present mood. Ing wondered about his friend. Darkness, the isolation of this position within the tube gave voices from outside a disembodied quality.

"Poss, do me a favor," Ing said. "Give me a straight 'lash-gram. No fancy stuff, just a demonstration throw. I want a clean ripple the length of the beam. Don't try for angspace, just 'lash it."

"Have you popped your skull? Any 'lash can hit angspace. And you get one fleck of dust in that beam path . . ."

"We'd rip the sides off the tube; I know. But this is a clean beam, Poss. I can see it. I just want a little ripple."

"Why?"

*Can I tell him?* Ing wondered.

Ing decided to tell only part of the truth, said: "I

53

want to check the cleaner tempo during the program. Give me a debris monitor and a crossing count for each observation post. Have them focus on the cleaners, not on the beam."

"Why?"

"You can see for yourself cleaner activity doesn't agree with the beam condition," Ing said. "Something's wrong there—accumulated programming error or . . . I dunno. But I want some actual facts to go on—a physical count during a 'lash."

"You're not going to get new data running a test that could be repeated in the laboratory."

"This isn't a laboratory."

Washington absorbed this, then: "Where would you be during the 'lash?"

*He's going to do it,* Ing thought. He said: "I'll be close to the anode end here. 'Lash can't swing too wide here."

"And if we damage the tube?"

Ing hesitated remembering that it was a friend out there, a friend with responsibilities. No telling who might be monitoring the conversation, though . . . and this test was vital to the idea nibbling at Ing's awareness.

"Humor me, Poss," Ing said.

"Humor him," Washington muttered. "All right, but this'd better not be humorous."

"Wait till I'm in position," Ing said. "A straight 'lash."

He began working up the tube slope out of Zone Yellow into the Gray and then the White. Here, he turned, studied the beam. It was a thin purple ribbon stretching off left and right—shorter on the left toward the anode. The long reach of it going off toward the cathode some twelve kilometers to his right was a thin

54

wisp of color broken by the flickering passage of cleaners.

"Any time," Ing said.

He adjusted the suit rests against the tube's curve, pulled his arms into the barrel top, started the viewplate counter recording movement of the cleaners. Now came the hard part—waiting and watching. He had a sudden feeling of isolation then, wondering if he'd done the right thing. There was an element of burning bridges in this action.

What did the handbook say? *"There is no point in planning sophisticated research on a specific factor's role unless that factor is known to be present."*

*If it isn't there, you can't study it,* Ing thought.

"You will take your work seriously," he muttered. Ing smiled then, thinking of the tragicomic faces, the jowly board chairmen he visualized behind the handbook's pronouncements. Nothing was left to chance—no task, no item of personal tidiness, no physical exercise. Ing considered himself an expert on handbooks. He owned one of the finest collections of them dating from ancient times down to the present. In moments of boredom he amused himself with choice quotes.

"Program going in," Washington said. "I wish I knew what you hope to find by this."

"I quote," Ing said. "The objective worker makes as large a collection of data as possible and analyzes these in their entirety in relation to selected factors whose relationship to a questioned phenomenon is to be investigated."

"What the devil's that supposed to mean?" Washington demanded.

"Damned if I know," Ing said, "but it's right out of the Haigh Handbook." He cleared his throat. "What's the cleaner tempo from your stations?"

"Up a bit."

"Give me a countdown on the 'lash."

"No sign yet. There's ... wait a minute! Here's some action—twenty-five ... twenty seconds."

Ing began counting under his breath.

Zero.

A progression of tiny flares began far off to his right, flickered past him with increasing brightness. They were a blur that left a glimmering afterimage. Sensors in his suit soles began reporting the fall of debris.

"Holy O'Golden!" Washington muttered.

"How many'd we lose?" Ing asked. He knew it was going to be bad—worse than he'd expected.

There was a long wait, then Washington's shocked voice: "A hundred and eighteen cleaners down. It isn't possible!"

"Yeah," Ing said. "They're all over the floor. Shut off the beam before that dust drifts up into it."

The beam disappeared from Ing's faceplate responders.

"Is that what you thought would happen, Ing?"

"Kind of."

"Why didn't you warn me?"

"You wouldn't have given me that 'lash."

"Well how the devil're we going to explain a hundred and eighteen cleaners? Accounting'll be down on my neck like a ..."

"Forget Accounting," Ing said. "You're a beam engineer; open your eyes. Those cleaners weren't absorbed by the beam. They were cut down and scattered over the floor."

"But the ..."

"Cleaners are designed to respond to the beam's needs," Ing said. "As the beam moves they move. As the debris count goes up, the cleaners work harder. If one works a little too hard and doesn't get out of the way fast enough, it's supposed to be absorbed—its energy converted by the beam. Now, a false 'lash catches a hundred and eighteen of them off balance. Those cleaners weren't eaten; they were scattered over the floor."

There was silence while Washington absorbed this.

"Did that 'lash touch angspace?" Ing asked.

"I'm checking," Washington said. Then: "No...wait a minute: there's a whole ripple of angspace...contacts, very low energy—a series lasting about an eighty-millionth of a second. I had the responders set to the last decimal or we'd have never caught it."

"To all intents and purposes we didn't touch," Ing said.

"Practically not." Then: "Could somebody in cleaner programming have flubbed the dub?"

"On a hundred and eighteen units?"

"Yeah. I see what you mean. Well, what're we going to say when they come around for an explanation?"

"We quote the book. 'Each problem should be approached in two stages: (1) locate those areas which contribute most to the malfunction, and (2) take remedial action designed to reduce hazards which have been positively identified.' We tell 'em, Poss, that we were positively identifying hazards."

Ing stepped over the lock sill into the executive salon, saw that Washington already was seated at the corner table which convention reserved for the senior beam engineer on duty, the Supervisor of Transmission.

It was too late for day lunch and too early for the second shift coffee break. The salon was almost empty.

Three junior executives at a table across the room to the right were sharing a private joke, but keeping it low in Washington's presence. A security officer sat nursing a teabulb beside the passage to the kitchen tram on the left. His shoulders bore a touch of dampness from a perspiration reclaimer to show that he had recently come down from the surface. Security had a lot of officers on the station, Ing noted ... and there always seemed to be one around Washington.

The vidwall at the back was tuned to an Earthside news broadcast: There were hints of political upsets because of the beam failure, demands for explanations of the money spent. Washington was quoted as saying a solution would be forthcoming.

Ing began making his way toward the corner, moving around the empty tables.

Washington had a coffeebulb in front of him, steam drifting upward. Ing studied the man—Possible Washington (Impossible, according to his junior engineers) was a six-foot eight-inch powerhouse of a man with wide shoulders, sensitive hands, a sharply Moorish-Semitic face of café au lait skin and startingly blue eyes under a dark crewcut. (The company's senior medic referred to him as "a most amazing throw of the genetic dice.") Washington's size said a great deal about his abilities. It took a considerable expenditure to lift his extra kilos moonside. He had to be worth just that much more.

Ing sat down across from Washington, gestured to the waiter-eye on the table surface, ordered Marslichen tea.

"You just come from Assembly?" Washington asked.

"They said you were up here," Ing said. "You look

tired. Earthside give you any trouble about your report?"

"Until I used your trick and quoted the book: 'Every test under field conditions shall approximate as closely as possible the conditions set down by laboratory precedent.'"

"Hey, that's a good one," Ing said. "Why didn't you tell them you were following a hunch—you had a hunch I had a hunch."

Washington smiled.

Ing took a deep breath. It felt good to sit down. He realized he'd worked straight through two shifts without a break.

"You look tired yourself," Washington said.

Ing nodded. Yes, he was tired. He was too old to push this hard. Ing had few illusions about himself. He'd always been a runt, a little on the weak side— skinny and with an almost weaselish face that was saved from ugliness by widely set green eyes and a thick crewcut mop of golden hair. The hair was turning gray now, but the brain behind the wide brow still functioned smoothly.

The teabulb came up through the table slot. Ing pulled the bulb to him, cupped his hands around its warmth. He had counted on Washington to keep the worst of the official pressure off him, but now that it had been done, Ing felt guilty.

"No matter how much I quote the book," Washington said, "they don't like that explanation."

"Heads will roll and all that?"

"To put it mildly."

"Well we have a position chart on where every cleaner went down," Ing said. "Every piece of wreckage has been reassembled as well as possible. The undamaged cleaners have been gone over with the proverbial comb of fine teeth."

"How long until we have a clean tube?" Washington asked.

"About eight hours."

Ing moved his shoulders against the chair. His thigh muscles still ached from the long session in the Skoarnoff tube and there was a pain across his shoulders.

"Then it's time for some turkey talk," Washington said.

Ing had been dreading this moment. He knew the stand Washington was going to take.

The Security officer across the room looked up, met Ing's eyes, looked away. *Is he listening to us?* Ing wondered.

"You're thinking what the others thought," Washington said. "That those cleaners were kicked around the corner into angspace."

"One way to find out," Ing said.

There was a definite lift to the Security officer's chin at that remark. He *was* listening.

"You're not taking that suicide ride," Washington said.

"Are the other beams getting through to the Seed Ships?" Ing asked.

"You know they aren't!"

Across the room, the junior executives stopped their own conversation, peered toward the corner table. The Security officer hitched his chair around to watch both the executives and the corner table.

Ing took a sip of his tea, said: "Damn' tea here's always too bitter. They don't know how to serve it anywhere except on Mars." He pushed the bulb away from him. "Join the Haigh Company and save the Universe for Man."

"All right, Ing," Washington said. "We've known each other a long time and can speak straight out. What're you hiding from me?"

Ing sighed.

"I guess I owe it to you," he said. "Well, I guess it begins with the fact that every transmitter's a unique individual, which you know as well as I do. We map what it does and operate by prediction statistics. We play it by ear, as they say. Now, let's consider something out of the book. A tube is, after all, just a big cave in the rock, a controlled environment for the beam to do its work. The book says: *'By anglespace transmission, any place in the universe is just around the corner from any other place.'* This is a damned loose way to describe something we don't really understand. It makes it sound as though we know what we're talking about."

"And you say we're putting matter around that corner," Washington said, "but you haven't told me what you're—"

"I know," Ing said. "We place a modulation of energy where it can be *seen* by the Seed Ship's instruments. But that's a transfer of energy, Poss. And energy's interchangeable with matter."

"You're twisting definitions. We put a highly unstable, highly transitory reflection phenomenon in such a position that time/space limitations are changed. That's by the book, too. But you're still not telling me . . ."

"Poss, I have a crew rigging a cleaner for me to ride. We've analyzed the destruction pattern—which is what I wanted from that test 'lash—and I think we can kick

61

me into angspace aboard one of these wild geese."

"You fool! I'm still Supetrans here and I say you're not going in there on..."

"Now, take it easy, Poss. You haven't even..."

"Granting you get kicked around that stupid corner, how do you expect to get back? And what's the purpose, anyway? What can you do if you..."

"I can go there and look, Poss. And the cleaner we're rigging will be more in the nature of a lifeboat. I can get down on TA-IV, maybe take the container with me, give our *seeds* a better chance. And if we learn how to kick me around there, we can do it again with..."

"This is stupidity!"

"Look," Ing said. "What're we risking? One old man long past his prime."

Ing faced the angry glare in Washington's eyes and realized an odd thing about himself. He wanted to get through there, wanted to give that container of embryos its chance. He was drunk with the same dream that had spawned the Seeding Compact. And he saw now that the other troubleshooters, the six who'd gone before him, must have been caught in the same web. They'd all seen where the trouble had to be. One of them would get through. There were tools in the container; another beam could be rigged on the other side. There was a chance of getting back...afterward...

"I let them talk me into sending for you," Washington growled. "The understanding was you'd examine the set up, confirm or deny what the others saw—but I didn't have to send you into that..."

"I want to go, Poss," Ing said. He saw what was eating on his friend now. The man had sent six troubleshooters in there to die—or disappear into an untraceable void, which was worse. Guilt had him.

62

"And I'm refusing permission," Washington said.

The Security officer arose from his table, crossed to stand over Washington. "Mr. Washington," he said, "I've been listening and it seems to me if Mr. Gump wants to go you can't..."

Washington got to his feet, all six feet eight inches of him, caught the Security man by the jacket. "So they told you to interfere if I tried to stop him!" He shook the man with an odd gentleness. "If you are on my station after the next shuttle leaves, I will see to it personally that you have an unexplained accident." He released his grip.

The Security agent paled, but stood his ground. "One call from me and this no longer will be *your* station."

"Poss," Ing said, "you can't fight city hall. And if you try they'll take you out of here. Then I'll have to make do with second best at this end. I need you as beam jockey here when I ride that wild goose."

Washington glared at him. "Ing, it won't work!"

Ing studied his friend, seeing the pressures which had been brought to bear, understanding how Earthside had maneuvered to get that request sent from a friend to Ivar Norris Gump. It all said something about Earthside's desperation. The patterns of secrecy, the Security watch, the hints in the newscasts—Ing felt something of the same urgency himself which these things betrayed. And he knew if Washington could overcome this guilt block the man would share mankind's need to help those drifting containers.

"No matter how many people get hurt—or killed," Ing said, "we have to give the embryos in those containers their chance. You know, I'm right—this is the main chance. And we need you, Poss. I want everything going for me I can get. And no matter what happens, we'll know you did your best for me..."

Washington took two short breaths. His shoulders slumped. "And nothing I say..."

"Nothing you say."

"You're going?"

"I'm going where the wild goose goes."

"And who faces the family afterward?"

"A friend, Poss. A friend faces the family and makes the blow as soft as possible."

"If you'll excuse me," the Security officer said.

They ignored him as the man returned to his table.

Washington allowed himself a deep, sighing breath. Some of the fire returned to his eyes. "All right," he growled. "But I'm going to be on this end every step of the way. And I'm telling you now you get no Go signal until everything's rigged to my satisfaction."

"Of course, Poss. That's why I can't afford to have you get into a fracas and be booted out of here."

Ing's left ankle itched.

It was maddening. His hand could reach only to the calf inside the webbing of his shieldsuit. The ankle and its itch could not be lifted from the area of the sole contact controls.

The suit itself lay suspended in an oil bath within a shocktank. Around the shocktank was something that resembled a standard cleaner in shape but not in size. It was at least twice the length of a cleaner and it was fatter. The fatness allowed for phased shells—Washington's idea. It had grown out of analysis of the debris left by the test 'lash.

The faint hissing of his oxygen regenerators came to Ing through his suit sensors. His viewplate had been replaced by a set of screens linked to exterior pickups. The largest screen, at top center, reported the view from a scanner on the belly. It showed a rope of fluorescing purple surrounded by blackness.

The beam.

It was a full five centimeters across, larger than Ing had ever before seen it. The nearness of that potential violence filled him with a conditioned dread. He'd milked too many beams in too many tubes, wary of the slightest growth in size to keep him at a safe distance.

This was a monster beam. All his training and experience cried out against its size.

Ing reminded himself of the analysis which had produced the false cleaner around him now.

Eighty-nine of the cleaners recovered from the tube floor had taken their primary damage at the pickup orifice. They'd been oriented to the beam itself, disregarding the local particle count. But the most important discovery was that the cleaners had fallen through the beam without being sliced in two. They had passed completely through the blade of that purple knife without being severed. There'd been no break in the beam. The explanation had to rest in that topological anomaly—angspace. Part of the beam and/or the cleaners had gone into angspace.

He was gambling his life now that the angspace bounce coincided with the energy phasing which kept the cleaners from deflecting the beam. The outside carrier, Ing's false cleaner, was phased with the beam. It would be demolished. The next inner shell was one hundred and eighty degrees out of phase. The next shell was back in phase. And so on for ten shells.

In the center lay Ing his hands and feet on the controls of a suit that was in effect a miniature lifeboat.

As the moment of final commitment approached, Ing began to feel a prickly sensation in his stomach. And the ankle continued to itch. But there was no way he could turn back and still live with himself. He was a troubleshooter, the best in the Haigh Company. There was no doubt that the company—and those lonely drifting human embryos had never needed him more desperately.

"Report your condition, Ing."

The voice coming from the speaker beside Ing's facemask was Washington's with an unmistakable edge of fear in it.

"All systems clear," Ing said.

"Program entering its second section," Washington said. "Can you see any of the other cleaners?"

"Forty contacts so far," Ing said. "All normal." He gasped as his cleaner dodged a transient 'lash.

"You all right?"

"All right," Ing said.

The ride continued to be a rough one, though. Each time the beam 'lashed, his cleaner dodged. There was no way to anticipate the direction. Ing could only trust his suit webbing and the oil-bath shocktank to keep him from being smashed against a side of the compartment.

"We're getting an abnormal number of transients," Washington said.

That called for no comment and Ing remained silent. He looked up at his receiver above the speaker. A quartz window gave him a view of the tiny beam which kept him in contact with Washington. The tiny beam, less than a centimeter long, glowed sharply purple through its inspection window. It, too, was crackling and jumping. The little beam could stand more interference than a big one, but it clearly was disturbed.

Ing turned his attention to the big beam in the viewscreen, glanced back at the little beam. The difference was a matter of degree. It often seemed to Ing that the beams should illuminate the area around them, and he had to remind himself that the parallel quanta couldn't deviate that much.

"Getting 'lash count," Washington said. "Ing! Condition critical! Stand by."

Ing concentrated on the big beam now. His stomach was a hard knot. He wondered how the other troubleshooters had felt in this moment. The same, no doubt. But they'd been flying without the protection Ing had. They'd paved the way, died to give information.

The view of the beam was so close and restricted that Ing knew he'd get no warning of the whip—just a sudden shift in size or position.

His heart leaped as the beam flared in the screen. The cleaner rolled sideways as it dodged, letting the beam pass to one side, but there was an ominous bump. Momentarily, the screen went blank, but the purple rope flickered back into view as his cleaner's sensors lined up and brought him back into position.

Ing checked his instruments. That bump—what had that been?

"Ing!" Washington's voice came sharply urgent from the speaker.

"What's the word?"

"We have one of the other cleaners on grav-track," Washington said. "It's in your shadow. Hold on."

There came a murmur of voices, hushed words, indistinguishable, then: "The beam touched you, Ing. You've got a phase arc between two of your shells on the side opposite the beam. One of the other cleaners has locked onto that arc with one of its sensors. Its other sensors are still on the beam and it's riding parallel with you, in your shadow. We're getting you out of there."

67

Ing tried to swallow in a dry throat. He knew the danger without having it explained. There was an arc, light in the tube. His cleaner was between the arc and the beam, but the other cleaner was up there behind him, too. If they had to dodge a 'lash, the other cleaner would be confused because its sensor contacts were now split. It'd be momentarily delayed. The two cleaners would collide and release light in the tube. The big beam would go wild. The protective shells would be struck from all sides.

Washington was working to get him out, but that would take time. You couldn't just yank a primary program out. That created its own 'lash conditions. And if you damped the beam, the other cleaners would home on the arc. There'd be carnage in the tube.

"Starting phase out," Washington said. "Estimating three minutes to control the second phase. We'll just..."

"'Lash!"

The word rang in Ing's ears even as he felt his cleaner lift at the beginning of a dodge maneuver. He had time to think that the warning must've come from one of the engineers on the monitor board, then a giant gong rang out.

A startled: "What the hell!" blasted from his speaker to be replaced by a strident hissing, the ravening of a billion snakes.

Ing felt his cleaner still lifting, pressing him down against the webbing, his face hard against the protective mask. There was no view of the big beam in his screen and the small beam revealed a wavering, crackling worm of red-little window which should've showed the line of his own beam revealed a wavering, crackling worm of red-purple.

68

Abruptly, Ing's world twisted inside out.

It was like being squeezed flat into a one-molecule puddle and stretched out to infinity. He *saw* around the outside of an inner-viewed universe with light extended to hard rods of brilliance that poked through from one end to the other. He realized he wasn't seeing with his eyes, but was absorbing a sensation compounded from every sense organ he possessed. Beyond this inner view everything was chaos, undefined madness.

*The beam got me,* he thought. *I'm dying.*

One of the light rods resolved itself into a finite row of spinning objects—over, under, around... over, under, around.... The movement was hypnotic. With a feeling of wonder, Ing recognized that the object was his own suit and a few shattered pieces of the protective shells. The tiny beam of his own transmitter had been opened and was spitting shards of purple.

With the recognition came a sensation of being compressed. Ing felt himself being pushed down into the blackness that jerked at him, twisting, pounding. It was like going over a series of rapids. He felt the web harness bite into his skin.

Abruptly, the faceplate viewscreens showed jewel brilliance against velvet black—spots of light: sharp blue, red, green, gold. A glaring white light spun into view surrounded by whipping purple ribbons. The ribbons looked like beam auroras.

Ing's body ached. His mind felt as though immersed in fog, every thought laboring against deadly slowness.

Jewel brilliance—spots of light.

Again, glaring white.

Purple ribbons.

The speaker above him crackled with static. Through its window, he saw his tiny beam spattering and jumping. It seemed important to do something about that. Ing slipped a hand into one of his suit arms, encountered a shattered piece of protective shell drifting close.

The idea of drifting seemed vital, but he couldn't decide why.

Gently, he nudged the piece of shell up until it formed a rough shield over his receiver beam.

Immediately, a tinny little voice came from his speaker: "Ing! Come in, Ing! Can you hear me, Ing?" Then, more distant: "You there! To hell with the locks! Suit up and get in there. He must be down..."

"Poss?" Ing said.

"Ing! Is that you, Ing?"

"Yeah, Poss. I'm...I seem to be all in one piece."

"Are you down on the floor some place? We're coming in after you. Hold on."

"I dunno where I am. I can see beam auroras."

"Don't try to move. The tube's all smashed to hell. I'm patched through the Imbrium tube to talk to you. Just stay put. We'll be right with you."

"Poss, I don't think I'm in the tube."

From some place that Ing felt existed on a very tenuous basis, he felt his thoughts stirring, recognition patterns forming.

Some of the jewel brilliance he saw was stars. He saw that now. Some of it was...debris, bits and pieces of cleaners, odd chunks of matter. There was light somewhere toward his feet, but the sensors there appeared to've been destroyed or something was covering them.

Debris.

Beam auroras.

The glaring white spun once more into view. Ing

adjusted his spin with a short burst from a finger jet. He saw the thing clearly now, recognized it: the ball and sensor tubes of a Seeding Compact container.

He grew conscious that the makeshift shield for his little beam had slipped. Static filled his speakers. Ing replaced the bit of shell.

". . . Do you mean you're not in the tube?" Washington's voice asked. "Ing, come in. What's wrong?"

"There's an SC container about a hundred meters or so directly in front of me," Ing said. "It's surrounded by cleaner debris. And there're auroras, angspace ribbons, all over the sky here. I . . . think I've come through."

"You couldn't have. I'm receiving you too strong. What's this about auroras?"

"That's why you're receiving me," Ing said. "You're stitching a few pieces of beam through here. Light all over the place; there's a sun down beneath my feet somewhere. You're getting through to me, but the container's almost surrounded by junk. The reflection and beam spatter in there must be enormous. I'm going in now and clean a path for the beam contact."

"Are you sure you're . . ." *Hiss, crackle.*

The little piece of shell had slipped again.

Ing eased it back into position as he maneuvered with his belt jets.

"I'm all right, Poss."

The turn brought the primary into view—a great golden ball that went dim immediately as his scanner filters adjusted. To his right beyond the sun lay a great ball of blue with chunks of cottony clouds drifting over it. Ing stared, transfixed by the beauty of it.

A virgin planet.

A check of the lifeboat instruments installed in his suit showed what the SC container had revealed before

71

contact had gone intermittent—Theta Apus IV, almost Earth normal except for larger oceans, smaller land masses.

Ing took a deep breath, smelled the canned air of his suit.

*To work*, he thought.

His suit jets brought him in close to the debris and he began nudging it aside, moving in closer and closer to the container. He lost his beam shield, ignored it, cut down receiver volume to reduce the static.

Presently, he drifted beside the container.

With an armored hand, he shielded his beam.

"Poss? Come in, Poss."

"Are you really there, Ing?"

"Try a beam contact with the container, Poss."

"We'll have to break contact with you."

"Do it."

Ing waited.

Auroral activity increased—great looping ribbons over the sky all around him.

*So that's what it looks like at the receiving end,* Ing thought. He looked up at the window revealing his own beam—clean and sharp under the shadow of his upraised hand. The armored fingers were black outlines against the blue world beyond. He began calculating then how long his own beam would last without replacement of anode and cathode. Hard bombardment, sharp tiny beam—its useful life would only be a fraction of what a big beam could expect.

*Have to find a way to rig a beam once we get down,* he thought.

"Ing? Come in, Ing?"

Ing heard the excitement in Washington's voice.

"You got through, eh, Poss, old hoss?"

"Loud and clear. Now, look—if you can weld yourself fast to the tail curve of that container we can get you down with it. It's over-engineered to handle twice your mass on landing sequence."

Ing nodded to himself. Riding the soft, safe balloon, which the container would presently become, offered a much more attractive prospect than maneuvering his suit down, burning it out above a watery world where a landing on solid ground would take some doing.

"We're maneuvering to give re-entry for contact with a major land mass," Washington said. "Tell us when you're fast to the container."

Ing maneuvered in close, put an armored hand on the container's surface, feeling an odd sensation of communion with the metal and life that had spent nine hundred years in the void.

*Old papa Ing's going to look after you,* he thought.

As he worked, welding himself solidly to the tail curve of the container, Ing recalled the chaos he had glimpsed in his spewing, jerking ride through angspace. He shuddered.

"Ing, when you feel up to it, we want a detailed report," Washington said. "We're planning now to put people through for every one of the containers that's giving trouble."

"You figured out how to get us back?" Ing asked.

"Earthside says it has the answer if you can assemble enough mass at your end to anchor a full-sized beam."

Again, Ing thought of that ride through chaos. He wasn't sure he wanted another such trip. Time to solve that problem when it arose, though. There'd be something in the book about it.

Ing smiled at himself then, sensing an instinctive reason for all the handbooks of history. Against chaos, man had to raise a precise and orderly alignment of actions, a system within which he could sense his own existence.

*A watery world down there,* he thought. *Have to find some way to make paper for these kids before they come out of their vats. Plenty of things to teach them.*

*Watery world.*

He recalled then a sentence of swimming instructions from the "Blue Jackets Manual," one of the ancient handbooks in his collection: "Breathing may be accomplished by swimming with the head out of water."

*Have to remember that one,* he thought. *The kids'll need a secure and orderly world.*

# COMMITTEE OF THE WHOLE

With an increasing sense of unease, Alan Wallace studied his client as they neared the public hearing room on the second floor of the Old Senate Office Building. The guy was too relaxed.

"Bill, I'm worried about this," Wallace said. "You could damn well lose your grazing rights here in this room today."

They were almost into the gantlet of guards, reporters and TV cameramen before Wallace got his answer.

"Who the hell cares?" Custer asked.

Wallace, who prided himself on being the Washington-type lawyer—above contamination by complaints and briefs, immune to all shock—found himself tongue-tied with surprise.

They were into the ruck then and Wallace had to pull on his bold face, smiling at the press, trying to soften the sharpness of that necessary phrase:

"No comment. Sorry."

"See us after the hearing if you have any questions, gentlemen," Custer said.

The man's voice was level and confident.

*He has himself over-controlled,* Wallace thought. *Maybe he was just joking . . . a graveyard joke.*

The marble-walled hearing room blazed with lights. Camera platforms had been raised above the seats at the rear. Some of the smaller UHF stations had their cameramen standing on the window ledges.

The subdued hubbub of the place eased slightly, Wallace noted, then picked up tempo as William R. Custer—"The Baron of Oregon" they called him—entered with his attorney, passed the press tables and crossed to the seats reserved for them in the witness section.

Ahead and to their right, that one empty chair at the long table stood waiting with its aura of complete exposure.

*"Who the hell cares?"*

That wasn't a Custer-type joke, Wallace reminded himself. For all his cattle-baron pose, Custer held a doctorate in philosophy, math and electronics. His western neighbors called him "The Brain."

It was no accident that the cattlemen had chosen him to represent them here.

Wallace glanced covertly at the man, studying him. The cowboy boots and string tie added to a neat dark business suit would have been affectation on most men. They merely accented Custer's good looks—the sunburned, windblown outdoorsman. He was a little darker of hair and skin than his father had been, still light enough to be called blond, but not as ruddy and without the late father's drink-tumescent veins.

But then young Custer wasn't quite thirty.

Custer turned, met the attorney's eyes. He smiled.

"Those were good patent attorneys you recommended, Al," Custer said. He lifted his briefcase to his lap, patted it. "No mincing around or mealy-mouthed excuses. Already got this thing on the way." Again he tapped the briefcase.

76

*He brought that damn' light gadget here with him?* Wallace wondered. *Why?* He glanced at the briefcase. *Didn't know it was that small ... but maybe he's just talking about the plans for it.*

"Let's keep our minds on this hearing," Wallace whispered. "This is the only thing that's important."

Into a sudden lull in the room's high noise level, the voice of someone in the press section carried across them: "greatest political show on earth."

"I brought this as an exhibit," Custer said. Again, he tapped the briefcase. It *did* bulge oddly.

*Exhibit?* Wallace asked himself.

It was the second time in ten minutes that Custer had shocked him. This was to be a hearing of a subcommittee of the Senate Interior and Insular Affairs Committee. The issue was Taylor grazing lands. What the devil could that ... *gadget* have to do with the battle of words and laws to be fought here?

"You're supposed to talk over all strategy with your attorney," Wallace whispered. "What the devil do you ..."

He broke off as the room fell suddenly silent.

Wallace looked up to see the subcommittee chairman, Senator Haycourt Tiborough, stride through the wide double doors followed by his coterie of investigators and attorneys. The senator was a tall man who had once been fat. He had dieted with such savage abruptness that his skin had never recovered. His jowls and the flesh on the back of his hands sagged. The top of his head was shiny bald and ringed by a three-quarter tonsure that purposely been allowed to grow long and straggly so that it fanned back over his ears.

The senator was followed in close lock step by syndicated columnist Anthony Poxman who was speaking fiercely into Tiborough's left ear. TV cameras tracked the pair.

*If Poxman's covering this one himself instead of sending a flunky, it's going to be bad,* Wallace told himself.

Tiborough took his chair at the center of the committee table facing them, glanced left and right to assure himself the other members were present.

Senator Spealance was absent, Wallace noted, but he had party organization difficulties at home, and the Senior Senator from Oregon was, significantly, not present. Illness, it was reported.

A sudden attack of caution, that common Washington malady, no doubt. He knew where his campaign money came from . . . but he also knew where the votes were.

They had a quorum, though.

Tiborough cleared his throat, said: "The committee will please come to order."

The senator's voice and manner gave Wallace a cold chill. *We were nuts trying to fight this one in the open,* he thought. *Why'd I let Custer and his friends talk me into this? You can't butt heads with a United States senator who's out to get you. The only way's to fight him on the inside.*

*And now Custer suddenly turning screwball.*

*Exhibit!*

"Gentlemen," said Tiborough, "I think we can . . . that is, today we can dispense with preliminaries . . . unless my colleagues . . . if any of them have objections."

Again, he glanced at the other senators—five of them. Wallace swept his gaze down the line behind that table—Plowers of Nebraska (a horse trader), Johnstone of Ohio (a parliamentarian—devious), Lane of

South Carolina (a Republican in Democrat disguise), Emery of Minnesota (new and eager—dangerous because he lacked the old inhibitions) and Meltzer of New York (poker player, fine old family with traditions).

None of them had objections.

*They've had a private meeting—both sides of the aisle—and talked over a smooth steamroller procedure,* Wallace thought.

It was another ominous sign.

"This is a subcommittee of the United States Senate Committee on Interior and Insular Affairs," Tiborough said, his tone formal. "We are charged with obtaining expert opinion on proposed amendments to the Taylor Grazing Act of 1934. Today's hearing will begin with testimony and ... ah, questioning of a man whose family has been in the business of raising beef cattle in Oregon for three generations."

Tiborough smiled at the TV cameras.

*The son-of-a-bitch is playing to the galleries,* Wallace thought. He glanced at Custer. The cattleman sat relaxed against the back of his chair, eyes half lidded, staring at the senator.

"We call as our first witness today Mr. William R. Custer of Bend, Oregon," Tiborough said. "Will the clerk please swear in Mr. Custer."

Custer moved forward to the "hot seat," placed his briefcase on the table. Wallace pulled a chair up beside his client, noted how the cameras turned as the clerk stepped forward, put the Bible on the table and administered the oath.

Tiborough ruffled through some papers in front of him, waited for full attention to return to him, said: "This sub-committee ... we have before us a bill, this is a United States Senate Bill entitled SB-1024 of the current session, an act amending the Taylor Grazing Act of 1934 and, the intent is, as many have noted, that we would broaden the base of the advisory committees to the Act and include a wider public representation."

Custer was fiddling with the clasp of his briefcase.

*How the hell could that light gadget be an exhibit here?* Wallace asked himself. He glanced at the set of Custer's jaw, noted the nervous working of a muscle. It was the first sign of unease he'd seen in Custer. The sight failed to settle Wallace's own nerves.

"Ah, Mr. Custer," Tiborough said. "Do you—did you bring a preliminary statement? Your counsel..."

"I have a statement," Custer said. His big voice rumbled through the room, requiring instant attention and the shift of cameras that had been holding tardily on Tiborough, expecting an addition to the question.

Tiborough smiled, waited, then: "Your attorney—is your statement the one your counsel supplied to the committee?"

"With some slight additions of my own," Custer said.

Wallace felt a sudden qualm. They were too willing to accept Custer's statement. He leaned close to his client's ear, whispered: "They know what your stand is. Skip the preliminaries."

Custer ignored him, said: "I intend to speak plainly and simply. I oppose the ammendment. Broaden the base and wider public representation are phases of political double talk. The intent is to pack the committees, to put control of them into the hands of people who don't know the first thing about the cattle business and whose private intent is to destroy the Taylor Grazing Act itself."

"Plain, simple talk," Tiborough said. "This committee...we welcome such directness. Strong words. A majority of this committee...we have taken the position that the public range lands have been too long subjected to the tender mercies of the stockmen advisors, that the lands...stockmen have exploited them to their own advantage."

*The gloves are off*, Wallace thought. *I hope Custer knows what he's doing. He's sure as hell not accepting advice.*

Custer pulled a sheaf of papers from his briefcase and Wallace glimpsed shiny metal in the case before the flap was closed.

*Christ! That looked like a gun or something!*

Then Wallace recognized the papers—the brief he and his staff had labored over—and the preliminary statement. He noted with alarm the penciled markings and marginal notations. How could Custer have done that much to it in just twenty-four hours?

Again, Wallace whispered in Custer's ear: "Take it easy, Bill. The bastard's out for blood."

Custer nodded to show he had heard, glanced at the papers, looked up directly at Tiborough.

A hush settled on the room, broken only by the scraping of a chair somewhere in the rear, and the whirr of cameras.

"First, the nature of these lands we're talking about," Custer said. "In my state..." He cleared his throat, a mannerism that would have indicated anger in the old man, his father. There was no break in Custer's expression, though, and his voice remained level. "... in my state, these were mostly Indian lands. This nation took them by brute force, right of conquest. That's about the oldest right in the world, I guess. I don't want to argue with it at this point."

"Mr. Custer."

It was Nebraska's Senator Plowers, his amiable

81

farmer's face set in a tight grin. "Mr. Custer, I hope . . ."

"Is this a point of order?" Tiborough asked.

"Mr. Chairman," Plowers said, "I merely wished to make sure we weren't going to bring up that old suggestion about giving these lands back to the Indians."

Laughter shot across the hearing room. Tiborough chuckled as he pounded his gavel for order.

"You may continue, Mr. Custer," Tiborough said.

Custer looked at Plowers said: "No, Senator, I don't want to give these lands back to the Indians. When they had these lands, they only got about three hundred pounds of meat a year off eighty acres. We get five hundred pounds of the highest grade proteins— premium beef—from only ten acres."

"No one doubts the efficiency of your factory-like methods," Tiborough said. "You can . . . we know your methods wring the largest amount of meat from a minimum acreage."

*Ugh!* Wallace thought. *That was a low blow— implying Bill's overgrazing and destroying the land value.*

"My neighbors, the Warm Springs Indians, use the same methods I do," Custer said. "They are happy to adopt our methods because we use the land while maintaining it and increasing its value. We don't permit the land to fall prey to natural disasters such as fire and erosion. We don't . . ."

"No doubt your methods are meticulously correct," Tiborough said. "But I fail to see where . . ."

"Has Mr. Custer finished his preliminary statement yet?" Senator Plowers cut in.

Wallace shot a startled look at the Nebraskan. That was help from an unexpected quarter.

"Thank you, Senator," Custer said. "I'm quite willing to adapt to the Chairman's methods and explain the meticulous correctness of my operation. Our lowliest cowhands are college men, highly paid. We travel ten times as many jeep miles as we do horse miles. Every outlying division of the ranch—every holding pen and grazing supervisor's cabin is linked to the central ranch by radio. We use the..."

"I concede that your methods must be the most modern in the world," Tiborough said. "It's not your methods as much as the results of those methods that are at issue here. We..."

He broke off at a disturbance by the door. An Army colonel was talking to the guard there. He wore Special Services fouragere—Pentagon.

Wallace noted with an odd feeling of disquiet that the man was armed—a .45 at the hip. The weapon was out of place on him, as though he had added it suddenly on an overpowering need... emergency.

More guards were coming up outside the door now—Marine and Army. They carried rifles.

The colonel said something sharp to the guard, turned away from him and entered the committee room. All the cameras were tracking him now. He ignored them, crossed swiftly to Tiborough, and spoke to him.

The senator shot a startled glance at Custer, accepted a sheaf of papers the colonel thrust at him. He forced his attention off Custer, studied the papers, leafing through them. Presently, he looked up, stared at Custer.

A hush fell over the room.

"I find myself at a loss, Mr. Custer," Tiborough said. "I have here a copy of a report... it's from the Special

Services branch of the Army... through the Pentagon, you understand. It was just handed to me by, ah... the colonel here."

He looked up at the colonel who was standing, one hand resting lightly on the holstered .45. Tiborough looked back at Custer and it was obvious the senator was trying to marshal his thoughts.

"It is," Tiborough said, "that is... this report supposedly... and I have every confidence it is what it is represented to be... here in my hands... they say that... uh, within the last, uh, few days they have, uh, investigated a certain device... weapon they call it, that you are attempting to patent. They report..." He glanced at the papers, back to Custer, who was staring at him steadily. "... this, uh, weapon, is a thing that... it is extremely dangerous."

"It is," Custer said.

"I... ah, see." Tiborough cleared his throat, glanced up at the colonel who was staring fixedly at Custer. The senator brought his attention back to Custer.

"Do you in fact have such a weapon with you, Mr. Custer?" Tiborough asked.

"I have brought it as an exhibit, sir."

"Exhibit?"

"Yes, sir."

Wallace rubbed his lips, found them dry. He wet them with his tongue, wished for the water glass, but it was beyond Custer. *Christ! That stupid cowpuncher!* He wondered if he dared whisper to Custer. Would the senators and that Pentagon lackey interpret such an action as meaning he was part of Custer's crazy antics?

"Are you threatening this committee with your weapon, Mr. Custer?" Tiborough asked. "If you are, I may say special precautions have been taken... extra guards in this room and we... that is, we will not allow ourselves to worry too much about any action you may take, but ordinary precautions are in force."

Wallace could no longer sit quietly. He tugged Custer's sleeve, got an abrupt shake of the head. He leaned close, whispered: "We could ask for a recess, Bill. Maybe we..."

"Don't interrupt me," Custer said. He looked at Tiborough. "Senator, I would not threaten you or any other man. Threats in the way you mean them are a thing we no longer can indulge in."

"You...I believe said this device is an exhibit," Tiborough said. He cast a worried frown at the report in his hands. "I fail...it does not appear germane."

Senator Plowers cleared his throat. "Mr. Chairman," he said.

"The chair recognizes the senator from Nebraska," Tiborough said, and the relief in his voice was obvious. He wanted time to think.

"Mr. Custer," Plowers said, "I have not seen the report, the report my distinguished colleague alludes to; however, if I may...is it your wish to use this committee as some kind of publicity device?"

"By no means, Senator," Custer said. "I don't wish to profit by my presence here...not at all."

Tiborough had apparently come to a decision. He leaned back, whispered to the colonel, who nodded and returned to the outer hall.

"You strike me as an eminently reasonable man, Mr. Custer," Tiborough said. "If I may..."

"May I," Senator Plowers said. "May I, just permit me to conclude this one point. May we have the Special Services report in the record?"

"Certainly," Tiborough said. "But what I was about to suggest..."

"May I," Plowers said. "May I, would you permit

me, please, Mr. Chairman, to make this point clear for the record?"

Tiborough scowled, but the heavy dignity of the Senate overcame his irritation. "Please continue, Senator. I had thought you were finished."

"I respect...there is no doubt in my mind of Mr. Custer's truthfulness," Plowers said. His face eased into a grin that made him look grandfatherly, a kindly elder statesman. "I would like, therefore, to have him explain how this...ah, weapon, can be an exhibit in the matter before our committee."

Wallace glanced at Custer, saw the hard set to the man's jaw, realized the cattleman had gotten to Plowers somehow. This was a set piece.

Tiborough was glancing at the other senators, weighing the advisability of high-handed dismissal...perhaps a star chamber session. No...they were all too curious about Custer's device, his purpose here.

The thoughts were plain on the senator's face.

"Very well," Tiborough said. He nodded to Custer. "You may proceed, Mr. Custer."

"During last winter's slack season," Custer said, "two of my men and I worked on a project we've had in the works for three years—to develop a sustained-emission laser device."

Custer opened his briefcase, slid out a fat aluminum tube mounted on a pistol grip with a conventional appearing trigger.

"This is quite harmless," he said. "I didn't bring the power pack."

"That is...this is your weapon?" Tiborough asked.

"Calling this a weapon is misleading," Custer said. "The term limits and oversimplifies. This is also a brush-cutter, a substitute for a logger's saw and axe, a diamond cutter, a milling machine . . . and a weapon. It is also a turning point in history."

"Come now, isn't that a bit pretentious?" Tiborough asked.

"We tend to think of history as something old and slow," Custer said. "But history is, as a matter of fact, extremely rapid and immediate. A President is assassinated, a bomb explodes over a city, a dam breaks, a revolutionary device is announced."

"Lasers have been known for quite a few years," Tiborough said. He looked at the papers the colonel had given him. "The principle dates from 1956 or thereabouts."

"I don't wish it to appear that I'm taking credit for inventing this device," Custer said. "Nor am I claiming sole credit for developing the sustained-emission laser. I was merely one of a team. But I do hold the device here in my hand, gentlemen."

"Exhibit, Mr. Custer," Plowers reminded him. "How is this an exhibit?"

"May I explain first how it works?" Custer asked. "That will make the rest of my statement much easier."

Tiborough looked at Plowers, back to Custer. "If you will tie this all together, Mr. Custer," Tiborough said. "I want to . . . the bearing of this device on our— we are hearing a particular bill in this room."

"Certainly, Senator," Custer said. He looked at his device. "A ninety-volt radio battery drives this particular model. We have some that require less voltage, some that use more. We aimed for a construction with simple parts. Our crystals are common quartz. We shattered them by bringing them to a boil in water and then plunging them into ice water . . . repeatedly. We chose twenty pieces of very close to the same size—about one gram, slightly more than fifteen grains each."

Custer unscrewed the back of the tube, slid out a round length of plastic trailing lengths of red, green, brown, blue and yellow wire.

Wallace noted how the cameras of the TV men centered on the object in Custer's hands. Even the senators were leaning forward, staring.

*We're gadget crazy people,* Wallace thought.

"The crystals were dipped in thinned household cement and then into iron filings," Custer said. "We made a little jig out of a fly-tying device and opened a passage in the filings at opposite ends of the crystals. We then made some common celluloid— nitrocellulose, acetic acid, gelatin and alcohol—all very common products, and formed it into a length of garden hose just long enough to take the crystals end to end. The crystals were inserted in the hose, the celluloid poured over them and the whole thing was seated in a magnetic waveguide, while the celluloid was cooling. This centered and aligned the crystals. The waveguide was constructed from wire salvaged from an old TV set and built following the directions in the Radio Amateur's Handbook."

Custer reinserted the length of plastic into the tube, adjusted the wires. There was an unearthly silence in the room with only the cameras whirring. It was as though everyone were holding his breath.

"A laser requires a resonant cavity, but that's complicated," Custer said. "Instead, we wound two layers of fine copper wire around our tube, immersed it in the celluloid solution to coat it and then filed one end flat. This end took a piece of mirror cut to fit. We then pressed a number eight embroidery needle at right angles into the mirror end of the tube until it touched the side of the number one crystal."

Custer cleared his throat.

Two of the senators leaned back. Plowers coughed. Tiborough glanced at the banks of TV cameras and there was a questioning look in his eyes.

We then determined the master frequency of our crystal series," Custer said. "We used a test signal and oscilloscope, but any radio amateur could do it without the oscilloscope. We constructed an oscillator of that master frequency, attached it at the needle and a bare spot scraped in the opposite end of the waveguide."

"And this...ah...worked?" Tiborough asked.

"No." Custer shook his head. "When we fed power through a voltage multiplier into the system we produced an estimated four hundred joules emission and melted half the tube. So we started all over again."

"You are going to tie this in?" Tiborough asked. He frowned at the papers in his hands, glanced toward the door where the colonel had gone.

"I am, sir, believe me," Custer said.

"Very well, then," Tiborough said.

"So we started all over," Custer said. "But for the second celluloid dip we added bismuth—a saturate solution, actually. It stayed gummy and we had to paint over it with a sealing coat of the straight celluloid. We then coupled this bismuth layer through a pulse circuit so that it was bathed in a counter wave—180 degrees out of phase with the master frequency. We had, in effect, immersed the unit in a thermoelectric cooler that exactly countered the heat production. A thin beam issued from the unmirrored end when we powered it. We have yet to find something that thin beam cannot cut."

"Diamonds?" Tiborough asked.

"Powered by less than two hundred volts, this device

could cut our planet in half like a ripe tomato," Custer said. "One man could destroy an aerial armada with it, knock down ICBMs before they touched atmosphere, sink a fleet, pulverize a city. I'm afraid, sir, that I haven't mentally catalogued all the violent implications of this device. The mind tends to boggle at the enormous power focused in . . ."

"Shut down those TV cameras!"

It was Tiborough shouting, leaping to his feet and making a sweeping gesture to include the banks of cameras. The abrupt violence of his voice and gesture fell on the room like an explosion. "Guards!" he called. "You there at the door. Cordon off that door and don't let anyone out who heard this fool!" He whirled back to face Custer. "You irresponsible idiot!"

"I'm afraid, Senator," Custer said, "that you're locking the barn door many weeks too late."

For a long minute of silence Tiborough glared at Custer. Then: "You did this deliberately, eh?"

"Senator, if I'd waited any longer, there might have been no hope for us at all."

Tiborough sat back into his chair, still keeping his attention fastened on Custer. Plowers and Johnstone on his right had their heads close together whispering fiercely. The other senators were dividing their attention between Custer and Tiborough, their eyes wide and with no attempt to conceal their astonishment.

Wallace, growing conscious of the implications in what Custer had said, tried to wet his lips with his tongue. *Christ!* he thought. *This stupid cowpoke has sold us all down the river!*

Tiborough signaled an aide, spoke briefly with him, beckoned the colonel from the door. There was a buzzing of excited conversation in the room. Several of

90

the press and TV crew were huddled near the windows on Custer's left, arguing. One of their number—a florid-faced man with gray hair and horn-rimmed glasses, started across the room toward Tiborough, was stopped by a committee aide. They began a low-voiced argument with violent gestures.

A loud curse sounded from the door. Poxman, the syndicated columnist, was trying to push past the guards there.

"Poxman!" Tiborough called. The columnist turned. "My orders are that no one leaves," Tiborough said. "You are not an exception." He turned back to face Custer.

The room had fallen into a semblance of quiet, although there still were pockets of muttering and there was the sound of running feet and a hurrying about in the hall outside.

"Two channels went out of here live," Tiborough said. "Nothing much we can do about them, although we will trace down as many of their viewers as we can. Every bit of film in this room and every sound tape will be confiscated, however." His voice rose as protests sounded from the press section. "Our national security is at stake. The President has been notified. Such measures as are necessary will be taken."

The colonel came hurrying into the room, crossed to Tiborough, quietly said something.

"You should've warned me!" Tiborough snapped. "I had no idea that . . ."

The colonel interrupted with a whispered comment.

"These papers . . . your damned report is *not* clear!" Tiborough said. He looked around at Custer. "I see you're smiling, Mr. Custer. I don't think you'll find much to smile about before long."

"Senator, this is not a happy smile," Custer said.

"But I told myself several days ago you'd fail to see the implications of this thing." He tapped the pistol-shaped device he had rested on the table. "I told myself you'd fall back into the old, useless pattern."

"Is that what you told yourself, really?" Tiborough said.

Wallace, hearing the venom in the senator's voice, moved his chair a few inches farther away from Custer.

Tiborough looked at the laser projector. "Is that thing really disarmed?"

"Yes, sir."

"If I order one of my men to take it from you, you will not resist?"

"Which of your men will you trust with it, Senator?" Custer asked.

In the long silence that followed, someone in the press section emitted a nervous guffaw.

"Virtually every man on my ranch has one of these things," Custer said. "We fell trees with them, cut firewood, make fence posts. Every letter written to me as a result of my patent application has been answered candidly. More than a thousand sets of schematics and instructions on how to build this device have been sent out to varied places in the world."

"You vicious traitor!" Tiborough rasped.

"You're certainly entitled to your opinion, Senator," Custer said. "But I warn you I've had time for considerably more concentrated and considerably more painful thought than you've applied to this problem. In my estimation, I had no choice. Every week I waited to make this thing public, every day, every minute, merely raised the odds that humanity would be destroyed by..."

"You said this thing applied to the hearings on the grazing act," Plowers protested, and there was a plaintive note of complaint in his voice.

"Senator, I told you the truth," Custer said. "There's no real reason to change the act, now. We intend to go on operating under it—with the agreement of our neighbors and others concerned. People are still going to need food."

Tiborough glared at him. "You're saying we can't force you to..." He broke off at a disturbance in the doorway. A rope barrier had been stretched there and a line of Marines stood with their backs to it, facing the hall. A mob of people was trying to press through. Press cards were being waved.

"Colonel, I told you to clear the hall!" Tiborough barked.

The colonel ran to the barrier. "Use your bayonets if you have to!" he shouted.

The disturbance subsided at the sound of his voice. More uniformed men could be seen moving in along the barrier. Presently, the noise receded.

Tiborough turned back to Custer. "You make Benedict Arnold look like the greatest friend the United States ever had," he said.

"Cursing me isn't going to help you," Custer said. "You are going to have to live with this thing; so you'd better try understanding it."

"That appears to be simple," Tiborough said. "All I have to do is send twenty-five cents to the Patent office for the schematics and then write you a letter."

"The world already was headed toward suicide," Custer said. "Only fools failed to realize..."

"So you decided to give us a little push," Tiborough said.

"H. G. Wells warned us," Custer said. "That's how far back it goes, but nobody listened. 'Human history becomes more and more a race between education and catastrophe,' Wells said. But those were just words. Many scientists have remarked the growth curve on the amount of raw energy becoming available to humans—and the diminishing curve on the number of persons required to use that energy. For a long time now, more and more violent power was being made available to fewer and fewer people. It was only a matter of time until total destruction was put into the hands of single individuals.".

"And you didn't think you could take your government into your confidence."

"The government already was committed to a political course diametrically opposite the one this device requires," Custer said. "Virtually every man in the government has a vested interest in not reversing that course."

"So you set yourself above the government?"

"I'm probably wasting my time," Custer said, "but I'll try to explain it. Virtually every government in the world is dedicated to manipulating something called the 'mass man.' That's how governments have stayed in power. But there is no such man. When you elevate the non-existent 'mass man' you degrade the individual. And obviously it was only a matter of time until all of us were at the mercy of the individual holding power."

"You talk like a commie!"

"They'll say I'm a goddamn' capitalist pawn," Custer said. "Let me ask you, Senator, to visualize a poor radio technician in a South American country. Brazil, for example. He lives a hand-to-mouth existence, ground down by an overbearing, unimaginative, essentially uncouth ruling oligarchy. What is he going to do when this device comes into his hands?"

"Murder, robbery and anarchy."

"You could be right," Custer said. "But we might

reach an understanding out of ultimate necessity—that each of us must cooperate in maintaining the dignity of all."

Tiborough stared at him, began to speak musingly: "We'll have to control the essential materials for constructing this thing . . . and there may be trouble for a while, but . . ."

"You're a vicious fool."

In the cold silence that followed, Custer said: "It was too late to try that ten years ago. I'm telling you this thing can be patchworked out of a wide variety of materials that are already scattered over the earth. It can be made in basements and mud huts, in palaces and shacks. The key item is the crystals, but other crystals will work, too. That's obvious. A patient man can grow crystals . . . and this world is full of patient men."

"I'm going to place you under arrest," Tiborough said. "You have outraged every rule—"

"You're living in a dream world," Custer said. "I refuse to threaten you, but I'll defend myself from any attempt to oppress or degrade me. If I cannot defend myself, my friends will defend me. No man who understands what this device means will permit his dignity to be taken from him."

Custer allowed a moment for his words to sink in, then: "And don't twist those words to imply a threat. Refusal to threaten a fellow human is an absolute requirement in the day that has just dawned on us."

"You haven't changed a thing!" Tiborough raged. "If one man is powerful with that thing, a hundred are . . ."

"All previous insults aside," Custer said, "I think you are a highly intelligent man, Senator. I ask you to think long and hard about this device. Use of power is no longer the deciding factor because one man is as powerful as a million. Restraint—*self*-restraint is now the key to survival. Each of us is at the mercy of his neighbor's good will. Each of us, Senator—the man in the palace and the man in the shack. We'd better do all we can to increase that good will—not attempting to buy it, but simply recognizing that individual dignity is the one inalienable right of..."

"Don't you preach at me, you commie traitor!" Tiborough rasped. "You're a living example of..."

"Senator!"

It was one of the TV cameramen in the left rear of the room.

"Let's stop insulting Mr. Custer and hear him out," the cameraman said.

"Get that man's name," Tiborough told an aide. "If he..."

"I'm an expert electronic technician, Senator," the man said. "You can't threaten me now."

Custer smiled, turned to face Tiborough.

"The revolution begins," Custer said. He waved a hand as the senator started to whirl away. "Sit down, Senator."

Wallace, watching the senator obey, saw how the balance of control had changed in this room.

"Ideas are in the wind," Custer said. "There comes a time for a thing to develop. It comes into being. The spinning jenny came into being because that was its time. It was based on countless ideas that had preceded it."

"And this is the age of the laser?" Tiborough asked.

"It was bound to come," Custer said. "But the number of people in the world who're filled with hate and frustration and violence has been growing with terrible speed. You add to that the enormous danger that this might fall into the hands of just one group or

96

nation or..." Custer shrugged. "This is too much power to be confined to one man or group with the hope they'll administer wisely. I didn't dare delay. That's why I spread this thing now and announced it as broadly as I could."

Tiborough leaned back in his chair, his hands in his lap. His face was pale and beads of perspiration stood out on his forehead.

"We won't make it."

"I hope you're wrong, Senator," Custer said. "But the only thing I know for sure is that we'd have had less chance of making it tomorrow than we have today."

# MATING CALL

"If you get caught we'll have to throw you to the wolves," said Dr. Fladdis. "You understand, of course."

Laoconia Wilkinson, senior field agent of the Social Anthropological Service, nodded her narrow head. "Of course," she barked. She rustled the travel and order papers in her lap.

"It was very difficult to get High Council approval for this expedition after the...ah...unfortunate incident on Monligol," said Dr. Fladdis. "That's why your operating restrictions are so severe."

"I'm permitted to take only this—" she glanced at her papers—"Marie Medill?"

"Well, the basic plan of action was her idea," said Dr. Fladdis. "And we have no one else in the department with her qualifications in music."

"I'm not sure I approve of her plan," muttered Laoconia.

"Ah," said Dr. Fladdis, "but it goes right to the heart of the situation on Rukuchp, and the beauty of it is that it breaks no law. That's a legal quibble, I agree. But what I mean is you'll be within the letter of the law."

"And outside its intent," muttered Laoconia. "Not that I agree with the law. Still—" she shrugged— "music!"

Dr. Fladdis chose to misunderstand. "Miss Medill has her doctorate in music, yes," he said. "A highly educated young woman."

"If it weren't for the fact that this may be our last opportunity to discover how those creatures reproduce—" said Laoconia. She shook her head. "What we really should be doing is going in there with a full staff, capturing representative specimens, putting them through—"

"You will note the prohibition in Section D of the High Council's mandate," said Dr. Fladdis. *"'The Field Agent may not enclose, restrain or otherwise restrict the freedom of any Rukuchp native.'"*

"How bad is their birthrate situation?" asked Laoconia.

"We have only the word of the Rukuchp special spokesman. This Grafka. He said it was critical. That, of course, was the determining factor with the High Council. Rukuchp appealed to *us* for help."

Laoconia got to her feet. "You know what I think of this music idea. But if that's the way we're going to attack it, why don't we just break the law all the way—take in musical recordings, players ..."

"Please!" snapped Dr. Fladdis.

Laoconia stared at him. She had never before seen the Area Director so agitated.

"The Rukuchp natives say that introduction of *foreign* music has disrupted some valence of their reproductive cycle," said Dr. Fladdis. "At least, that's how we've translated their explanation. This is the reason for the law prohibiting any traffic in music devices."

"I'm not a child!" snapped Laoconia. "You don't have to explain all ..."

"We cannot be too careful," said Dr. Fladdis. "With

the memory of Monligol still fresh in all minds." He shuddered. "We must return to the spirit of the SocAnth motto: *'For the Greater Good of the Universe.'* We've been warned."

"I don't see how music can be anything but a secondary stimulant," said Laoconia. "However, I shall keep an open mind."

Laoconia Wilkinson looked up from her notes, said: "Marie, was that a noise outside?" She pushed a strand of gray hair from her forehead.

Marie Medill stood at the opposite side of the field hut, staring out of one of the two windows. "I only hear the leaves," she said. "They're awfully loud in that wind."

"You're sure it wasn't Gafka?"

Marie sighed and said, "No, it wasn't his namesong."

"Stop calling that monster a him!" snapped Laoconia.

Marie's shoulders stiffened.

Laoconia observed the reflex and thought how wise the Service had been to put a mature, veteran anthropologist in command here. A hex-dome hut was too small to confine brittle tempers. And the two women had been confined here for 25 weeks already. Laoconia stared at her companion—such a young romantic, that one.

Marie's pose reflected boredom...worry...

Laoconia glanced around the hut's crowded interior. Servo-recorders, night cameras, field computers, mealmech, collapsible floaters, a desk, two chairs, folding bunks, three wall sections taken up by the transceiver linking them with the mother ship circling in satellite orbit overhead. Everything in its place and a place for everything.

"Somehow, I just can't help calling Gafka a him," said Marie. She shrugged. "I know it's nonsense. Still . . . when Gafka sings . . ."

Laoconia studied the younger woman. A blonde girl in a one-piece green uniform; heavy peasant figure, good strong legs, an oval face with high forehead and dreaming blue eyes.

"Speaking of singing," said Laoconia, "I don't know what I shall do if Gafka doesn't bring permission for us to attend their Big Sing. We can't solve this mess without the facts."

"No doubt," said Marie. She spoke snappishly, trying to keep her attention away from Laoconia. The older woman just sat there. She was always just sitting there—so efficient, so driving, a tall gawk with windburned face, nose too big, mouth too big, chin too big, eyes too small.

Marie turned away.

"With every day that passes I'm more convinced that this music thing is a blind alley," said Laoconia. "The Rukuchp birthrate keeps going down no matter how much of our music you teach them."

"But Gafka agrees," protested Marie. "Everything points to it. Our discovery of this planet brought the Rukuchps into contact with the first alien music they've ever known. Somehow, that's disrupted their breeding cycle. I'm sure of it."

"Breeding cycle," sniffed Laoconia. "For all we know, these creatures could be ambulatory vegetables without even the most rudimentary . . ."

"I'm so worried," said Marie. "It's music at the root of the problem, I'm sure, but if it ever got out that we smuggled in those education tapes and taught Gafka all our musical forms . . ."

"We did *not* smuggle anything!" barked Laoconia.

101

"The law is quite clear. It only prohibits any form of *mechanical* reproducer of actual musical sounds. Our tapes are all completely visual."

"I keep thinking of Monligol," said Marie. "I couldn't live with the knowledge that I'd contributed to the extinction of a sentient species. Even indirectly. If our *foreign* music really has disrupted..."

"We don't even know if they breed!"

"But Gafka says..."

"Gafka says! A dumb vegetable. Gafka says!"

"Not so dumb," countered Marie. "He learned to speak our language in less than three weeks, but *we* have only the barest rudiments of songspeech."

"Gafka's an idiot-savant," said Laoconia. "And I'm not certain I'd call what that creature does *speaking*."

"It is too bad that you're tone deaf," said Marie sweetly.

Laoconia frowned. She leveled a finger at Marie. "The thing I note is that we only have their word that their birthrate is declining. They called on us for help, and now they obstruct every attempt at field observation."

"They're so shy," said Marie.

"They're going to be shy one SocAnth field expedition if they don't invite us to that Big Sing," said Laoconia. "Oh! If the Council had only authorized a *full* field expedition with armed support!"

"They couldn't!" protested Marie. "After Monligol, practically every sentient race in the universe is looking on Rukuchp as a final test case. If we mess up another race with our meddling..."

"Meddling!" barked Laoconia. "Young woman, the Social Anthropological Service is a holy calling! Erasing ignorance, helping the backward races!"

"And we're the only judges of what's backward,"

said Marie. "How convenient. Now, you take Monligol. Everyone knows that insects carry disease. So we move in with our insecticides and kill off the symbiotic partner essential to Monligolian reproduction. How uplifting."

"They should have told us," said Laoconia.

"They couldn't," said Marie. "It was a social taboo."

"Well..." Laoconia shrugged. "That doesn't apply here."

"How do you know?"

"I've had enough of this silly argument," barked Laoconia. "See if Gafka's coming. He's overdue."

Marie inhaled a trembling breath, stamped across to the field hut's lone door and banged it open. Immediately the tinkle of glazeforest leaves grew louder. The wind brought an odor of peppermint from the stubble plain to her left.

She looked across the plain at the orange ball of Almac sinking toward a flat horizon, swung her glance to the right where the wall of glazeforest loomed overhead. Rainbow-streaked batwing leaves clashed in the wind, shifting in subtle competition for the last of the day's orange light.

"Do you see *it?*" demanded Laoconia.

Marie shook her head, setting blonde curls dancing across her uniform collar. "It'll be dark soon," she said. "He said he'd return before it got fully dark."

Laoconia scowled, pushed aside her notes. *Always calling it a him! They're nothing but animated Easter eggs! If only...* She broke the train of thought, attention caught by a distant sound.

"There!" Marie peered down the length of glazeforest wall.

A fluting passage of melody hung on the air. It was the meister-song of a delicate wind instrument. As they

103

listened, the tones deepened to an organ throb while a section of cello strings held the melody. Glazeforest leaves began to tinkle in sympathetic harmony. Slowly, the music faded.

"It's Gafka," whispered Marie. She cleared her throat, spoke louder, self-consciously: "He's coming out of the forest quite a ways down."

"I can't tell one from the other," said Laoconia. "They all look alike and sound alike. Monsters."

"They do look alike," agreed Marie, "but the sound is quite individual."

"Let's not harp on my tone deafness!" snapped Laoconia. She joined Marie at the door. "If they'll only let us attend their Sing..."

A six-foot Easter egg ambled toward them on four of its five prehensile feet.

The crystal glistening of its vision cap, tipped slightly toward the field hut, was semi-lidded by inner cloud pigment in the direction of the setting sun. Blue and white greeting colors edged a great bellows muscle around the torso. The bell extension of a mouth/ear—normally visible in a red-yellow body beneath the vision cap—had been retracted to a multi-creased pucker.

"What ugly brutes," said Laoconia.

"Shhhh!" said Marie. "You don't know how far away he can hear you." She waved an arm. "Gaaaf-kaa!" Then: "Damn!"

"What's wrong?"

"I only made eight notes out of his name instead of nine."

Gafka came up to the door, picking a way through the stubble spikes. The orange mouth/ear extended, sang a 22-note harmonica passage: "Maarrriee Mmmmmmedillll." Then a 10-second concerto:

"Laoconnnnia Wiiilkinnnsonnnn!"

"How lovely!" said Marie.

"I wish you'd talk straight out the way we taught you," said Laoconia. "That singing is difficult to follow."

Gafka's vision cap tipped toward her. The voice shifted to a sing-song waver: "But polite sing greeting."

"Of course," said Laoconia. "Now." She took a deep breath. "Do we have permission to attend your Big Sing?"

Gafka's vision cap tipped toward Marie, back to Laoconia.

"Please, Gafka?" said Marie.

"Difficulty," wavered Gafka. "Not know how say. Not have knowledge your kind people. Is subject not want for talking."

"I see," said Laoconia, recognizing the metaphorical formula. "It has to do with your breeding habits."

Gafka's vision cap clouded over with milky pigment, a sign that the two women had come to recognize as embarrassment.

"Now, Gafka," said Laoconia. "None of that. We've explained about science and professional ethics, the desire to be of real help to one another. You must understand that both Marie and I are here for the good of your people."

A crystal moon unclouded in the part of the vision cap facing Laoconia.

"If we could only get them to speak straight out," said Laoconia.

Marie said: "Please, Gafka. We only want to help."

"Understand I," said Gafka. "How else talk this I?" More of the vision cap unclouded. "But must ask question. Friends perhaps not like."

"We are scientists," said Laoconia. "You may ask

any question you wish."

"You are too old for...breeding?" asked Gafka. Again the vision cap clouded over, sparing Gafka the sight of Laoconia shocked speechless.

Marie stepped into the breech. "Gafka! Your people and my people are ...well, we're just too different. We couldn't. There's no way...that is..."

"Impossible!" barked Laoconia. "Are you implying that we might be sexually attacked if we attended your Big Sing?"

Gafka's vision cap unclouded, tipped toward Laoconia. Purple color bands ran up and down the bellows muscle, a sign of confusion.

"Not understand I about sex thing," said Gafka. "My people never hurt other creature." The purple bands slowed their upward-downward chasing, relaxed into an indecisive green. The vision cap tipped toward Marie. "Is true all life kinds start egg young same?" This time the clouding of the vision cap was only a momentary glimmerwhite.

"Essentially, that is so," agreed Laoconia. "We all *do* start with an egg. However, the fertilization process is different with different peoples." Aside to Marie, she said: "Make a note of that point about eggs. It bears out that they may be oviparian as I suspected." Then: "Now, I must know what you meant by your question."

Gafka's vision cap rocked left, right, settled on a point between the two women. The sing-song voice intoned: "Not understand I about different ways. But know I you see many thing my people not see. If breeding (glimmerwhite) different, or you too old for breeding (glimmerwhite) my people say you come Big Sing. Not want we make embarrass for you."

"We are scientists," said Laoconia. "It's quite all

right. Now, may we bring our cameras and recording equipment?"

"Bring you much of things?" asked Gafka.

"We'll only be taking one large floater to carry our equipment," said Laoconia. "How long must we be prepared to stay?"

"One night," said Gafka. "I bring worker friends to help with floater. Go I now. Soon be dark. Come moonrise I return, take to Big Sing place you." The trumpet mouth fluted three minor notes of farewell, pulled back to an orange pucker. Gafka turned, glided into the forest. Soon he had vanished among reflections of glasswood boles.

"A break at last!" barked Laoconia. She strode into the hut, speaking over her shoulder. "Call the ship. Have them monitor our equipment. Tell them to get duplicate recordings. While we're starting to analyze the sound-sight record down here they can be transmitting a copy to the master computers at Kampichi. We want as many minds on this as possible. We may never get another chance like this one!"

Marie said: "I don't—"

"Snap to it!" barked Laoconia.

"Shall I talk to Dr. Baxter?" asked Marie.

"Talk to Helen?" demanded Laoconia. "Why would you want to bother Helen with a routine question like this?"

"I just want to discuss..."

"That transceiver is for official use only," said Laoconia. "Transmit the message as I've directed. We're here to solve the Rukuchp breeding problem, not to chitchat."

"I feel suddenly so uneasy," said Marie. "There's something about this situation that worries me."

"Uneasy?"

"I think we've missed the point of Gafka's warning."

"Stop worrying," said Laoconia. "The natives won't give us any trouble. Gafka was looking for a last excuse to keep us from attending their Big Sing. You've seen how stupidly shy they are."

"But what if—"

"I've had a great deal of experience in handling native peoples," said Laoconia. "You never have trouble as long as you keep a firm, calm grip on the situation at all times."

"Maybe so. But . . ."

"Think of it!" said Laoconia. "The first humans ever to attend a Rukuchp Big Sing. Unique! You mustn't let the magnitude of our achievement dull your mind. Stay cool and detached as I do. Now get that call off to the ship!"

It was a circular clearing perhaps two kilometers in diameter, dark with moonshadows under the giant glaze trees. High up around the rim of the clearing, moonlight painted prismatic rainbows along every leaf edge. A glint of silver far above the center of the open area betrayed the presence of a tiny remote-control floater carrying night cameras and microphones.

Except for a space near the forest edge occupied by Laoconia and Marie, the clearing was packed with silent shadowy humps of Rukuchp natives. Vision caps glinted like inverted bowls in the moonlight.

Seated on a portable chair beside the big pack-floater, Laoconia adjusted the position of the tiny remote unit high above them. In the monitor screen before her she could see what the floater lenses covered—the clearing with its sequin glitter of Rukuchp vision caps and the faintest gleam of red and green instrument lights between herself and Marie seated on the other side of the floater. Marie was monitoring the night lenses that would make the scene appear as bright as day on the recording wire.

Marie straightened, rubbed the small of her back. "This clearing must be at least two kilometers across," she whispered, impressed.

Laoconia adjusted her earphones, tested a relay. Her feet ached. It had been at least a four-hour walk in here to this clearing. She began to feel latent qualms about what might be ahead in the nine hours left of the Rukuchp night. That stupid warning...

"I said it's a big clearing," whispered Marie.

Laoconia cast an apprehensive glance at the silent Rukuchp figures packed closely around. "I didn't realize there'd be so many," she whispered. "It doesn't look to me as though they're dying out. What does your monitor screen show?"

"They fill the clearing," whispered Marie. "And I think they extend back under the trees. I wish I knew which one was Gafka. I should've watched when he left us."

"Didn't he say where he was going?"

"He just asked if this spot was all right for us and if we were ready to help them."

"Well, I'm sure everything's going to be all right," said Laoconia. She didn't sound very convincing, even to herself.

"Isn't it time to contact the ship?" asked Marie.

"They'll be calling any—" A light flashed red on the panel in front of Laoconia. "Here they are now."

She flipped a switch, spoke into her cheek microphone. "Yes?"

The metallic chattering in Laoconia's earphones only made Marie feel more lonely. The ship was so far away above them.

"That's right," said Laoconia. "Transmit your record immediately and ask Kampichi to make an independent study. We'll compare notes later." Silence while she listened, then: "I'm sure there's no danger. You can keep an eye on us through the overhead lenses. But there's never been a report of a Rukuchp native offering violence to anyone . . . Well, I don't see what we can do about it now. We're here and that's that. I'm signing off now." She flipped the switch.

"Was that Dr. Baxter?" asked Marie.

"Yes. Helen's monitoring us herself, though I don't see what she can do. Medical people are very peculiar sometimes. Has the situation changed with the natives?"

"They haven't moved that I can see."

"Why couldn't Gafka have given us a preliminary briefing?" asked Laoconia. "I detest this flying blind."

"I think it still embarrasses him to talk about breeding," said Marie.

"Everything's too quiet," hissed Laoconia. "I don't like it."

"They're sure to do something soon," whispered Marie.

As though her words were the signal, an almost inaudible vibration began to throb in the clearing. Glaze leaves started their sympathetic tinkle-chiming. The vibration grew, became an organ rumble with abrupt piping obbligato that danced along its edges. A cello insertion pulled a melody from the sound, swung it over the clearing while the glazeforest chimed louder and louder.

"How exquisite," breathed Marie. She forced her attention onto the instruments in front of her. Everything was functioning.

The melody broke to a single clear high note of

harmonic brilliance—a flute sound that shifted to a second phase with expanded orchestration. The music picked up element after element while low-register tympani built a stately rhythm into it, and zither tinkles laid a counterpoint on the rhythm.

"Pay attention to your instruments," hissed Laoconia.

Marie nodded, swallowing. The music was like a song heard before, but never before played with this perfection. She wanted to close her eyes; she wanted to submit entirely to the ecstasy of sound.

Around them, the Rukuchp natives remained stationary, a rhythmic expansion and contraction of bellows muscles their only movement.

And the rapture of music intensified.

Marie moved her head from side to side, mouth open. The sound was an infinity of angel choirs—every sublimity of music ever conceived—now concentrated into one exquisite distillation. She felt that it could not possibly grow more beautiful.

But it did.

There came a lifting-expanding-floating...a long gliding suspenseful timelessness.

Silence.

Marie felt herself drifting back to awareness, found her hands limply fumbling with dials. Some element of habit assured her that she had carried out her part of the job, but that music...She shivered.

"They sang for 47 minutes," hissed Laoconia. She glanced around. "Now what happens?"

Marie rubbed her throat, forced her attention onto the luminous dials, the floater, the clearing. A suspicion was forming in the back of her mind.

"I wish I knew which one of these creatures was Gafka," whispered Laoconia. "Do we dare arouse one

111

of them, ask after Gafka?"

"We'd better not," said Marie.

"These creatures did nothing but sing," said Laoconia. "I'm more certain than ever that the music is stimulative and nothing more."

"I hope you're right," whispered Marie. Her suspicion was taking on more definite shape... *music, controlled sound, ecstasy of controlled sound...* Thoughts tumbled over each other in her mind.

Time dragged out in silence.

"What do you suppose they're doing?" hissed Laoconia. "They've been sitting like this for 25 minutes."

Marie glanced around at the ring of Rukuchp natives hemming in the little open space, black mounds topped by dim silver. The stillness was like a charged vacuum.

More time passed.

"Forty minutes!" whispered Laoconia. "Do they expect us to sit here all night?"

Marie chewed her lower lip. *Ecstasy of sound,* she thought. And she thought of sea urchins and the parthenogenetic rabbits of Calibeau.

A stirring movement passed through the Rukuchp ranks. Presently, shadowy forms began moving away into the glazeforest's blackness.

"Where are they going?" hissed Laoconia. "Do you see Gafka?"

"No."

The transmission-receive light flashed in front of Laoconia. She flipped the switch, pressed an earphone against her head. "They just seem to be leaving," she whispered into the cheek microphone. "You see the same thing we do. There's been no movement against

112

us. Let me call you back later. I want to observe this."

A Rukuchp figure came up beside Marie.

"Gafka?" said Marie.

"Gafka," intoned the figure. The voice sounded sleepy.

Laoconia leaned across the instrument-packed floater. "What are they doing now, Gafka?" she demanded.

"All new song we make from music you give," said Gafka.

"Is the sing all ended?" asked Marie.

"Same," breathed Gafka.

"What's this about a new song?" demanded Laoconia.

"Not have your kind song before correct," said Gafka. "In it too much new. Not understand we how song make you. But now you teach, make right you."

"What is all this nonsense?" asked Laoconia. "Gafka, where are your people all going?"

"Going," sighed Gafka.

Laoconia looked around her. "But they're departing singly . . . or . . . well, there don't seem to be any mated pairs. What *are* they doing?"

"Go each to wait," said Gafka.

And Marie thought of caryocinesis and daughter nuclei.

"I don't understand," complained Laoconia.

"You teach how new song sing," sighed Gafka. "New song best all time. We keep this song. Better much than old song. Make better—" the women detected the faint glimmer-haze lidding of Gafka's vision cap—"make better young. Strong more."

"Gafka," said Marie, "is the song all you do? I mean, there isn't anything else?"

113

"All," breathed Gafka. "Best song ever."

Laoconia said: "I think we'd better follow some of these..."

"That's not necessary," said Marie. "Did you enjoy their music, Dr. Wilkinson?"

"Well..." There appeared to be embarrassment in the way the older woman turned her head away. "It was very beautiful."

"And you *enjoyed* it?" persisted Marie.

"I don't see what..."

"You're tone deaf," said Marie.

"It's obviously a stimulant of some sort!" snapped Laoconia. "I don't understand now why they won't let us..."

"They let us," said Marie.

Laoconia turned to Gafka. "I must insist, Gafka, that we be permitted to study all phases of your breeding process. Otherwise we can be of no help to you."

"You best help ever," said Gafka. "Birthrate all good now. You teach way out from mixing of music." A shudder passed upward through Gafka's bellows muscles.

"Do you make sense out of this?" demanded Laoconia.

"I'm afraid I do," said Marie. "Aren't you tired, Gafka?"

"Same," sighed Gafka.

"Laoconia, Dr. Wilkinson, we'd better get back to the hut," said Marie. "We can improvise what we'll need for the Schafter test."

"But the Schafter's for determining *human* pregnancy!" protested Laoconia.

The red light glowed in front of Laoconia. She flipped the switch. "Yes?"

Scratching sounds from the earphones broke the

silence. Marie felt that she did not want to hear the voice from the ship.

Laoconia said: "Of course I know you're monitoring the test of . . . Why should I tell Marie you've already given Schafter tests to yourself . . ." Laoconia's voice climbed. "WHAT? You can't be ser . . . That's impossible! But, Helen, we . . . they . . . you . . . we . . . Of course I . . . Where could we have . . . Every woman on the ship . . ."

There was a long silence while Marie watched Laoconia listening to the earphones, nodding. Presently, Laoconia lifted the earphones off her head and put them down gently. Her voice came out listlessly. "Dr. Bax . . . Helen suspect d that . . . she administered Schafter tests to herself and some to the others."

"She listened to that music?" asked Marie.

"The whole universe listened to that music," said Laoconia. "Some smuggler monitored the ship's official transmission of our recordings. Rebroadcast stations took it. Everyone's going crazy about our *beautiful* music."

"Oh, no," breathed Marie.

Laconia said: "Everyone on the ship listened to our recordings. Helen said she suspected immediately after the broadcast, but she waited the full half hour before giving the Schafter test." Laoconia glanced at the silent hump of Gafka standing beside Marie. "Every woman on that ship who could become pregnant is pregnant."

"It's obvious, isn't it?" asked Marie. "Gafka's people have developed a form of group parthenogenesis. Their Big Sing sets off the blastomeric reactions."

"But we're humans!" protested Laoconia. "How can . . ."

"And parts of us are still very primitive," said Marie. "This shouldn't surprise us. Sound's been used before

115

to induce the first mitotic cleavage in an egg. Gafka's people merely have this as their sole breeding method—with corresponding perfection of technique."

Laoconia blinked, said: "I wonder how this ever got started?"

"And when they first encountered our *foreign* music," said Marie, "it confused them, mixed up their musical relationships. They were fascinated by the new musical forms. They experimented for new sensations ... and their birthrate fell off. Naturally."

"Then you came along," said Laoconia, "and taught them how to master the new music."

"Exactly."

"Marie!" hissed Laoconia.

"Yes?"

"We were right here during that entire ... You don't suppose that we ... that I ..."

"I don't know about you," said Marie, "but I've never felt more certain of anything in my life."

She chewed at her lower lip, fought back tears. "I'm going to have a baby. Female. It'll have only half the normal number of chromosomes. And it'll be sterile. And I ..."

"Say I to you," chanted Gafka. There was an air of sadness in the singsong voice. "Say I to you: all life kinds start egg young same. Not want I to cause troubles. But you say different you."

"Parthenogenesis," said Laoconia with a show of her old energy. "That means, of course, that the human reproductive process need not ... that is, uh ... we'll not have to ... I mean to say that men won't be ..."

"The babies will be drones," said Marie. "You know that. Unfertile drones. This may have its vogue, but it surely can't last."

"Perhaps," said Laoconia. "But I keep thinking of all those rebroadcasts of our recordings. I wonder if these Rukuchp creatures ever had two sexes?" She turned toward Gafka. "Gafka, do you know if..."

"Sorry cause troubles," intoned Gafka. The singsong voice sounded weaker. "Must say farewell now. Time for birthing me."

"*You* are going to give birth?" asked Laoconia.

"Same," breathed Gafka. "Feel pain on eye-top." Gafka's prehensile legs went into a flurry of digging in the ground beside the floater.

"Well, you were right about one thing, Dr. Wilkinson," said Marie. "She-he is not a *him*."

Gafka's legs bent, lowered the ovoid body into the freshly dug concavity in the ground. Immediately, the legs began to shrink back into the body. A crack appeared across the vision cap, struck vertically down through the bellows muscles.

Presently, there were two Gafkas, each half the size of the original. As the women watched, the two half-sized Gafkas began extruding new legs to regain the normal symmetry.

"Oh, no," whispered Marie.

She had a headache.

# ESCAPE FELICITY

"An escape-proof prison cannot be built," he kept telling himself.

His name was Roger Deirut, five feet tall, one hundred and three pounds, crewcut black hair, a narrow face with long nose and wide mouth and space-bleached eyes that appeared to reflect rather than absorb what they saw.

Deirut knew his prison—the D-Service. He had got himself rooted down in the Service like a remittance man half asleep in a hammock on some palm-shaded tropical beach, telling himself his luck would change some day and he'd get out of there.

He didn't delude himself that a one-man D-ship was a hammock, or that space was a tropical beach. But the sinecure element was there and the ships were solicitous cocoons, each with a climate designed precisely for the lone occupant.

That each pilot carried the prison's bars in his mind had taken Deirut a long time to understand. Out here aimed into the void beyond Capella Base, he could feel the bars where they had been dug into his psyche, cemented and welded there. He blamed the operators of Bu-psych and the deep-sleep hypnotic debriefing after each search trip. He told himself that Bu-psych did something to the helpless pilots then, installed this compulsion they called the *Push*.

Some young pilots managed to escape it for a while—tougher psyches, probably, but sooner or later Bu-psych got them all. It was a common compulsion that limited the time a D-ship pilot could stay out before he turned tail and fled for home.

"This time I'll break away," Deirut told himself. He knew he was talking aloud, but he had his computer's vocoders turned off and his absent mumblings would be ignored.

The gas cloud of Grand Nuage loomed ahead of him, clearly defined on his instruments like a piece of torn fabric thrown across the stars. He'd come out of subspace dangerously close, but that was the gamble he'd taken.

Bingaling Benar, fellow pilot and sometime friend, had called him nuts when Deirut had said he was going to tackle the cloud. "Didn't you do that once before?" Bingaling asked.

"I was going to once, but I changed my mind," Deirut had said.

"You gotta slow down, practically crawl in there," Bingaling had said. "I stood it eighty-one days, man. I had the push for real—couldn't take any more and I came home. Anyway, it's nothing but cloud, all the way through."

Bingaling's *endless* cloud was growing larger in the ship's instruments now.

But the cloud enclosed a mass of space that could hide a thousand suns.

*Eighty-one days,* he thought.

"Eighty, ninety days, that's all anyone can take out there," Bingaling had said. "And I'm telling you, in that cloud it's worse. You get the push practically the minute you go in."

Deirut had his ship down to a safe speed now, nosing into the first tenuous layers. There was no mystery about the cloud's composition, he reminded himself. It was hydrogen, but in a concentration that made swift flight suicidal.

"They got this theory," Bingaling had said, "that it's an embryo star like. One day it's just going to go fwoosh and compress down into one star mass."

Deirut read his instruments. He could sense his ship around him like an extension of his own nerves. She was a pinnace class for which he and his fellow pilots had a simple and obscene nickname—two hundred and fifty meters long, crowded from nose to tubes with the equipment for determining if a planet could support human life. In the sleep-freeze compartment directly behind him were the double-checks—two pairs of rhesus monkeys and ten pairs of white mice.

D-ship pilots contended they'd seeded more planets with rhesus monkeys and white mice than they had with humans.

Deirut switched to his stern instruments. One hour into the cloud and already the familiar stars behind him were beginning to fuzz off. He felt the first stirrings of unease; not the push . . . but disquiet.

He crossed his arms, touching the question-mark insignia at his left shoulder. He could feel the ripe green film of corrosion on the brass threads. *I should polish up,* he thought. But he knew he wouldn't. He looked around him at the pilot compartment, seeing unracked food cannisters, a grease smear across the computer console, dirty fatigues wadded under a dolly seat.

It was a sloppy ship.

Deirut knew what was said about him and his fellow

120

pilots back in the top echelons of the D-Service.

"Rogues make the best searchers."

It was an axiom, but the rogues had their drawbacks. They flouted rules, sneered at protocol, ignored timetables, laughed at vector search plans ...and kept sloppy ships. And when they disappeared—as they often did—the Service could never be sure what had happened or where.

Except that the man had been prevented from returning... because there was always the push.

Deirut shook his head. Every thought seemed to come back to the push. He didn't have it yet, he assured himself. Too soon. But the thought was there, aroused. It was the fault of that cloud.

He reactivated the rear scanners. The familiar stars were gone, swallowed in a blanket of nothingness. Angrily, he turned off the scanner switch.

*I've got to keep busy,* he thought.

For a time he set himself to composing and refining a new stanza for the endless D-ship ballad: "I Left My Love on Lyra in the Hands of Gentle Friends." But his mind kept returning to the fact that the stanza might never be heard ... if his plans succeeded. He wondered then how many such stanzas had been composed never to be heard.

The days went by with an ever-slowing, dragging monotony.

*Eighty-one days,* he reminded himself time and again. *Bingaling turned back at eighty-one days.*

By the seventy-ninth day he could see why. There was no doubt then that he was feeling the first ungentle suasions of the push. His mind kept searching for logical reasons.

*You've done your best. No shame in turning back now. Bingaling's undoubtedly right—it's nothing but cloud all the way through. No stars in here...no planets.*

But he was certain what the Bu-psych people had done to him and this helped. He watched the forward scanners for the first sign of a glow. And this helped, too. He was still going some place.

The eighty-first day passed.

The eighty-second.

On the eighty-sixth day he began to see a triple glow ahead—like lights through fog; only the fog was black and otherwise empty.

By this time it was taking a conscious effort to keep his hands from straying toward the flip-flop controls that would turn the ship one hundred eighty degrees onto its return track.

Three lights in the emptiness.

Ninety-four days—two days longer than he'd ever withstood the push before—and his ship swam free of the cloud into open space with three stars lined out at a one o'clock angle ahead of him—a distant white-blue giant, a nearby orange dwarf and in the center...lovely golden soltype to the fifth decimal of comparison.

Feverishly, Deirut activated his mass-anomaly scanners, probing space around the golden-yellow sun.

The push was terrible now, insisting that he turn around. But this was the final convincer for Deirut. If the thing Bu-psych had done to him insisted he go back now, right after discovering three new suns—then there could be only one answer to the question "Why?" They didn't want a D-Service rogue settling down on his own world. The push was a built-in safeguard to make sure the scout returned.

Deirut forced himself to study his instruments.

Presently the golden star gave up its secret—a single planet with a single moon. He punched for first approximation, watched the results stutter off the feedout tape: planetary mass .998421 of Earth norm... rotation forty plus standard hours... mean orbital distance 243 million kilometers... perturbation nine degrees... orbital variation thirty-eight plus.

Deirut sat bolt upright with surprise.

Thirty-eight plus! A variation percentage in that range could only mean the mother star had another companion—and a big one. He searched space around the star.

Nothing.

Then he saw it.

At first he thought he'd spotted the drive flare of another ship—an alien. He swallowed, the push momentarily subdued, and did a quick mental review of the alien-space contact routine worked out by Earth's bigdomes and which, so far as anyone knew, had never been put to the test.

The flare grew until it resolved itself into the gaseous glow of another astronomical body circling the golden sun.

Again, Deirut bent to his instruments. My God, how the thing moved! More than forty kilometers per second. Tape began spewing from the feedout: Mass 321.64... rotation nine standard hours... mean orbital distance 58 million kilometers... perturbation blank (insufficient data)...

Deirut shifted to the filtered visual scanners, watched the companion sweep across the face of its star and curve out of sight around the other side. The thing looked oddly familiar, but he knew he could never have seen it before. He wondered if he should activate the computer's vocoder system and talk to it through the speaker embedded in his neck, but the computer annoyed him with its obscene logic.

The astronomical data went into the banks, though, for the experts to whistle and marvel over later.

Deirut shifted his scanners back to the planet. Shadowline measurement gave it an atmosphere that reached fade-off at an altitude of about a hundred and twenty-five kilometers. The radiation index indicated a whopping tropical belt, almost sixty degrees.

With a shock of awareness, Deirut found his hands groping toward the flip-flop controls. He jerked back, trembling. If he once turned the ship over, he knew he wouldn't have the strength of purpose to bring her back around. The push had reached terrifying intensity.

Deirut forced his attention onto the landing problem, began feeding data into the computer for the shortest possible space-to-ground course. The computer offered a few objections "for his own good," but he insisted. Presently, a landing tape appeared and he fed it into the control console, strapped down, kicked the ship onto automatic and sat back perspiring. His hands held a death grip on the sides of his crashpad.

The D-ship began to buck with the first skipping-flat entrance into the planet's atmosphere. The bucking stopped, returned, stopped—was repeated many times. The D-ship's cooling system whined. Hull plates creaked. Darkside, lightside, darkside—they repeated themselves in his viewer. The automatic equipment began reeling out atmospheric data: oxygen 23.9, nitrogen 74.8, argon 0.8, carbon dioxide 0.04 ... By the time it got into the trace elements, Deirut was gasping with the similarity to the atmosphere of Mother Earth.

The spectrum analyzer produced the datum that the atmosphere was essentially transparent from 3,000 angstroms to $6 \times 10^4$ angstroms. It was a confirmation and he ignored the instruments when they began producing hydromagnetic data and water vapor impingements. There was only one important factor here: he could breathe the stuff out there.

Instead of filling him with a sense of joyful discovery—as it might have thirty or forty days earlier—this turned on a new spasm of the push. He had to consciously restrain himself from clawing at the instrument panel.

Deirut's teeth began to chatter.

The viewer showed him an island appearing over the horizon. The D-ship swept over it. Deirut gasped at sight of an alabaster ring of tall buildings hugging the curve of a bay. Dots on the water resolved into sailboats as he neared. How oddly familiar it all looked.

Then he was past and headed for a mainland with a low range of hills—more buildings, roads, the patchwork of fenced lands. Then he was over a wide range of prairie with herds of moving animals on it.

Deirut's fingers curled into claws. His skin trembled.

The landing jets cut in and his seat reversed itself. The ship nosed up and the seat adjusted to the new altitude. There came a roaring as the ship lowered itself on its tail jets. The proximity cut-off killed all engines.

The D-ship settled with a slight jolt.

Blue smoke and clouds of whirling ashes lifted past Deirut's scanners from the scorched landing circle. Orange flames swept through dry forage on his right, but the chemical automatics from the ship's nose sent a borate shower onto the fire and extinguished it. Deirut saw the backs of animals fleeing through the smoke haze beyond the fire. Amplification showed them to be four-legged, furred and with tiny flat heads. They ran like bouncing balls.

A tight band of fear cinched on Deirut's chest. This place was too earthlike. His teeth chattered with the unconscious demands of the push.

His instruments informed him they were picking up modulated radio signals—FM and AM. A light showing that the Probe-Test-Watch circuits were activated came alive. Computer response circuit telltales began flickering. Abruptly, the PTW bell rang, telling him: "Something approaches!"

The viewer showed a self-propelled vehicle rolling over a low hill to the north supported by what appeared to be five monstrous penumatic bladders. It headed directly toward the D-ship belching pale white smoke from a rear stack with the rhythm of steam power. External microphones picking up the confirming "chuff-chuff-chuff" and his computer announced that it was a double-action engine with sounds that indicated five opposed pairs of pistons.

A five-sided dun brown cab with dark blue-violet windows overhung the front of the thing.

In his fascination with the machine, Deirut almost forgot the wild urge pushing at him from within. The machine pulled up about fifty meters beyond the charred landing circle, extruded a muzzle that belched a puff of smoke at him. The external microphones picked up a loud explosion and the D-ship rocked on its extended tripods.

Deirut clutched the arms of his chair then sprang to the controls of the ship's automatic defenses, poised a hand over the disconnect switch.

The crawling device outside whirled away, headed east toward a herd of the bouncing animals.

Deirut punched the "Warning Only" button.

A giant gout of earth leaped up ahead of the crawler, brought it to a lurching halt at the brink of a smoking hole. Another gout of earth bounced skyward at the left of the machine; another at the right.

Deirut punched "Standby" on the defense mechanisms, turned to assess the damage. Any new threat from the machine out there and the D-ship's formidable arsenal would blast it out of existence. That was always a step to be avoided, though, and he kept one eye on the screen showing the thing out there. It sat unmoving but still chuffing on the small patch of earth left by the three blast-shots from the ship.

Less than ten seconds later, the computer outchewed a strip of tape that said the ship's nose section had been blasted open, all proximity detectors destroyed. Deirut was down on this planet until he could make repairs.

Oddly, this eased the pressures of the push within him. It was still there and he could sense it, but the compulsive drive lay temporarily idle as though it, too, had a standby switch.

Deirut returned his attention to the crawler.

The damage had been done, and there was no helping it. A ship could land with its arsenal set on "Destroy," but deciding what needed destruction was a delicate proposition. Wise counsel said you let the other side get in a first shot if their technology appeared sufficiently primitive. Otherwise, you might make yourself decidedly unwelcome.

*Who'd have thought they'd have a cannon and fire the thing without warning?* he asked himself. And the reply stood there accusingly in his mind: *You should've thought of it, stupid. Gunpowder and steampower are almost always concurrent.*

*Well, I was too upset by the push,* he thought. *Besides, why'd they fire without warning?*

Again, the crawler's cab extruded the cannon muzzle and the cab started to turn to bring the weapon to bear on the ship. A warning blast sent earth cascading into the hole at the left of the crawler. The cab stopped turning.

"That's-a-baby," Deirut said. "Easy does it, fellows. Let's be friends." He flicked a blue switch at the left side of his board. His external microphones damped out as a klaxon sent its bull roar toward the crawler. It was a special sound capable of intimidating almost any creature that heard it. The sound had an astonishing effect on the crawler. A hatch in the middle of the cab popped open and five creatures boiled out of it to stand on the deck of their machine.

Deirut keyed the microphone beside him into the central computer, raised amplification on his view of the five creatures from the machine. He began reading off his own reactions. The human assessment always helped the computer's sensors.

"Humanoid," he said. "Upright tubular bodies about a meter and a half tall with two legs encased in some kind of boot. Sack-like garments belted at the waist. Each has five pouches dangling from the belt. Number five is significant here. Flesh color is pale blue-violet. Two arms; articulation—humanoid, but very long forearm. Wide hands with six fingers; looks like two opposable thumbs, one to each side of the hand. Heads—squarish, domed, covered with what appears to be a dark blue-violet beret. Eyes semi-stalked, yellow and just inside the front *corners* of the head. Those heads are very blocky. I suspect the eyes can be twisted to look behind without turning the head."

The creatures began climbing down off their machine.

Deirut went on with his description: "Large mouth orifice centered beneath the eyes. There appears to be a chin articulation on a short hinge. Orifice lipless, ovoid, no apparent teeth ... correction: there's a dark line inside that may be the local equivalent. Separate small orifices below each eye stalk—possibly for breathing. One just turned its head. I see a slight indentation centered on the side of the head—purpose unknown. It doesn't appear to be an ear."

The five were advancing on the ship now; Deirut backed off the scanner to keep them in view, said: "They carry bows and arrows. That's odd, considering the cannon. Each has a back quiver with...five arrows. That five again. Bows slung on the string over left shoulder. Each has a short lance in a back harness, a blue-violet pennant just below the lance head. Some kind of figure on the pennant—looks like an upside down "U" in orange. Same figures repeated on the front of their tunics which are also blue-violet. Blue-violet and five. What's the prognosis?"

Deirut waited for the computer's answer to come to him through the speaker grafted into his neck. Relays clicked and the vocoder whispered through the bones of his head: "Probable religious association with color and number five. Extreme caution is indicated on religious matters. Body armor and hand weapon mandatory."

*That's the trouble with computers,* Deirut thought. *Too logical.*

The five natives had stopped just outside the fire-blackened landing circle. They raised their arms to the ship, chanted something that sounded like "Toogayala-toogayala-toogayala." The sound came from the oval central orifice.

"We'll toogayala in just a minute," Deirut muttered. He brought out a Borgen machine pistol, donned body armor, aimed two of the ship's bombards directly at the steam wagon and set them on a dead-man switch keyed to a fifteen-second stoppage of his heart. He rigged the stern port to the PTW system, keyed to blow up any unauthorized intruders. Into various pockets he stuffed a lingua pack receptor tuned to his implanted speaker through the computer, a standard contact kit for sampling whatever interested him, a half dozen minigrenades, energy tablets, food analyzer, a throwing knife in a sheath, a miniscanner linked to the ship computer and a slingshot. With a final, grim sensation, he stuffed a medikit under the armor next to his heart.

One more glance around the familiar control center and he slid down the tube to the stern port, opened it and stepped out.

The five natives threw themselves flat on the ground, arms extended toward him.

Deirut took a moment to study them and his surroundings. There was a freshness to the air that even his nose filters could not diminish. It was morning here yet and the sun threw flat light against the low hills and clumps of scrub. They stood out with a clean chiaroscuro dominated by the long blue spear of the ship's shadow wavering across the prairie.

Deirut looked up at his D-ship. She was a red and white striped tower on his side with a gaping hole where the nose should have been. Her number—1107—stenciled in luminous green beneath the nose had just escaped the damage area. He returned his attention to the natives.

They remained stretched out on the grass, their stalked eyes stretched out and peering up at him.

"Let's hope you have a good metal-working industry, friends," Deirut said. "Otherwise, I'm going to be an extremely unhappy visitor."

At the sound of his voice, the five grunted in unison: "Toogayala ung-ung."

"Ung-ung?" Deirut asked. "I thought we were going

to toogayala." He brought out the lingua pack, hung it on his chest with the mike aimed at the natives, moved toward them out of the ship's shadow. As an afterthought, he raised his right hand, palm out and empty in the universal human gesture of peace, but kept his left hand on the Borgen.

"Toogayala!" the five screamed.

His lingua pack remained silent. Toogayala and ung-ung were hardly sufficient for breaking down a language.

Deirut took another step toward them.

The five rocked back to their knees and arose, crouching and apparently poised for flight. Five pairs of stalked eyes pointed toward him. Deirut had the curious feeling then that the five appeared familiar. They looked a little like giant grasshoppers that had been crossed with an ape. They looked like bug-eyed monsters from a work of science fantasy he had read in his youth, which he saw as clear evidence that what the imagination of man could conceive, nature could produce.

Deirut took another step toward the natives, said: "Well, let's talk a little, friends. Say something. Make language, huh?"

The five backed up two steps. Their feet made a dry rustling sound in the grass.

Deirut swallowed. Their silence was a bit unnerving.

Abruptly, something emitted a buzzing sound. It seemed to come from a native on Deirut's right. The creature clutched for its tunic, gabbled: "s'Chareecha! s'Chareecha!" It pulled a small object from a pocket as the others gathered around.

Deirut tensed, lifted the Borgen.

The natives ignored him to concentrate on the object in the one creature's hands.

"What's doing?" Deirut asked. He felt tense, uneasy. This wasn't going at all the way the books said it should.

The five straightened suddenly and without a backward look, returned to their steam wagon and climbed into the cab.

*What test did I fail?* Deirut wondered.

Silence settled over the scene.

In the course of becoming a D-ship pilot, Deirut had gained fame for a certain pungency of speech. He paused a moment to practice some of his more famed selections, then took stock of his situation—standing here exposed at the foot of the ship while the unpredictable natives remained in their steam wagon. He clambered back through the port, sealed it, and jacked into the local computer outlet for a heart-to-heart conference.

"The buzzing item was likely a timepiece," the computer said. "The creature in possession of it was approximately two millimeters taller than his tallest companion. There are indications this one is the leader of the group."

"Leader schmeader," Deirut said. "What's this toogayala they keep yelling?"

From long association with Deirut, the computer had adopted a response pattern to meet the rhetorical question or the question for which there obviously was no answer. "Tut, tut," it said.

"You sound like my old Aunt Martha," Deirut said. "They screamed that toogayala. It's obviously important."

"When they noted your hand, that is when they raised their voices to the highest decibel level thus far recorded here," the computer said.

"But why?"

"Possible answer," the computer said. "You have five fingers."

"Five," Deirut said. "Five...five...five..."

"We detect only five heavenly bodies here," the computer said. "You have noted that the skies are otherwise devoid of stars. The rapid companion is overhead right now, you know."

"Five," Deirut said.

"This planet," the computer said, "the three hot gaseous and plasma bodies and the other companion to this planet's sun."

Deirut looked at his hand, flexed the fingers.

"They may think you are a deity," the computer said. "They have six fingers; you have five."

"Empty skies except for three suns," Deirut said.

"Do not forget this planet and the other companion," the computer said.

Deirut thought about living on such a planet—no banks of stars across the heavens...all that hidden behind the enclosing hydrogen cloud.

He began to tremble unaccountably with an attack of the *push*.

"What'll it take to fix the nose of the ship?" Deirut asked. He tried to still his trembling.

"A sophisticated machine shop and the work of electronics technicians of at least grade five. The repair data is available in my banks."

"What're they doing in that machine?" Deirut demanded. "Why don't they talk?"

"Tut, tut," the computer said.

Thirty-eight minutes later, the natives again emerged from their steam wagon, took up stations standing at the edge of the charred ground.

133

Deirut repeated his precautionary measures, went out to join them. He moved slowly, warily, the Borgen ready in his left hand.

The five awaited him this time without retreating. They appeared more relaxed, chattering in low voices among themselves, watching him with those stalked eyes. The word sounds remained pure gibberish to Deirut, but he had the lingua pack trained on them and knew the computer would have the language in a matter of time.

Deirut stopped about eight paces from the natives, said: "Glad to see you, boys. Have a nice nap in your car?"

The tallest one nodded, said: "What's doing?"

Deirut gaped, speechless.

A native on the left said: "Let's hope you have a good metal-working industry, friends. Otherwise, I'm going to be an extremely unhappy visitor."

The tallest one said: "Glad to see you, boys. Have a nice nap in your car?"

"They're mimicking me!" Deirut gasped.

"Confirmed," the computer said.

Deirut overcame an urge to laugh, said: "You're the crummiest looking herd of no-good animals I ever saw. It's a wonder your mothers could stand the sight of you."

The tall native repeated it for him without an error.

"Reference to mothers cannot be accepted at this time," the computer said. "Local propagation customs unknown. There are indications these may be part vegetable—part animal."

"Oh, shut up," Deirut said.

"Oh, shut up," said a native on his left.

"Suggest silence on your part," the computer said. "They are displaying signs of trying to break down

134

your language. Better we get their language, reveal less of ourselves."

Deirut saw the wisdom in it, spoke subvocally for the speaker in his throat: "You're so right."

He clamped his lips into a thin line, stared at the natives. Silence dragged on and on.

Presently, the tall one said: "Augroop somilican."

"Toogayala," said the one on the left.

"Cardinal number," the computer said. "Probable position five. Hold up your five fingers and say toogayala."

Deirut obeyed.

"Toogayala, toogayala," the natives agreed. One detached himself, went to the steam wagon and returned with a black metal figurine about half a meter tall, extended it toward Deirut.

Cautiously, Deirut moved forward, accepted the thing. It felt heavy and cold in his hand. It was a beautifully stylized figure of one of the natives, the eye stalks drooping into inverted U-shapes, mouth open.

Deirut brought out his contact kit, pressed it against the metal. The kit went "ping" as it took a sample.

The natives stared at him.

"Iron-magnesium-nickel alloy," the computer said. "Figure achieved by casting. Approximate age of figure twenty-five million standard years."

Deirut felt his throat go dry. He spoke subvocally: "That can't be!"

"Dating accurate to plus or minus six thousand years," the computer said. "You will note the figures carved on the casting. The inverted U on the chest is probably the figure five. Beneath that is writing. Pattern too consistent for different interpretation."

"Civilization for twenty-five million years," Deirut said.

"Plus or minus six thousand years," the computer said.

Again, Deirut felt a surge of the *push*, fought it down. He wanted to return to the crippled ship, flee this place in spite of the dangers. His knees shook.

The native who had given him the figurine, stepped forward, reclaimed it. "Toogayala," the native said. It pointed to the inverted U on the figure and then to the symbol on its own chest.

"But they only have a steam engine," Deirut protested.

"Very sophisticated steam engines," the computer said. "Cannon is retractable, gyroscopically mounted, self-tracking."

"They can fix the ship!" Deirut said.

"If they will," the computer said.

The tall native stepped forward now, touched a finger to the lingua pack, said: "s'Chareecha" with a falling inflection. Deirut watched the hand carefully. It was six-fingered, definitely, the skin a mauve-blue. The fingers were horn-tipped and double-knuckled.

"Try ung-ung," the computer suggested.

"Ung-ung," Deirut said.

The tall one jumped backward and all five sent their eye stalks peering toward the sky. They set up an excited chattering among themselves in which Deirut caught several repeated sounds: "Yau-bron ... s'Chareecha ... Autoga ... Sreese-sreese ..."

"We have an approximation for entry now," the computer said. "The tall one is called Autoga. Address him by name."

"Autoga," Deirut said.

The tall one turned, tipped his eye stalks toward Deirut.

"Say *Ai-Yaubron ung sreese s'Chareecha,*" the computer said.

Deirut obeyed.

The natives faced each other, returned their attention to Deirut. Presently, they began grunting almost uncontrollably. Autoga sat down on the ground, pounded it with his hands, all the while keeping up the grunting.

"What the devil?" Deirut said.

"They're laughing," the computer said. "Go sit beside Autoga."

"On the ground?" Deirut asked.

"Yes."

"Is it safe?"

"Of course."

"Why're they laughing?"

"They're laughing at themselves. You tricked them, made them jump. This is definitely laughter."

Hesitantly, Deirut moved to Autoga's side, sat down.

Autoga stopped grunting, put a hand on Deirut's shoulder, spoke to his companions. With a millisecond delay, the computer began translating: "This god-self-creation is a good Joe, boys. His accent is lousy, but he has a sense of humor."

"Are you sure of that translation?" Deirut asked.

"Reasonably so," the computer said. "Without greater morphological grounding, a cultural investigation in depth and series comparisons of vocal evolution, you get only a gross literal approximation, of course. We'll refine it while we go along. We're ready to put your subvocals through the lingua pack."

"Let's talk," Deirut said.

Out of the lingua pack on his chest came a series of

sounds approximating "Ai-ing-eeya."

Computer translation of Autoga's reply was: "That's a good idea. It's open sky."

Deirut shook his head. It didn't sound right. Open sky?

"Sorry we damaged your vehicle," Autoga said. "We thought you were one of our youths playing with danger."

Deirut swallowed. "You thought my ship...you people can make ships of this kind?"

"Oh, we made a few about ten million *klurch* ago," Autoga said.

"It was at least fifteen million *klurch*," said the wrinkle-faced native on Deirut's left.

"Now, Choon, there you go exaggerating again," Autoga said. He looked at Deirut. "You'll have to forgive Choon. He wants everything to be bigger, better and greater than it is."

"What's a klurch?" Deirut asked.

The computer answered for his ears alone: "Probable answer—the local year, about one and one-third standards."

"I'm glad you decided to be peaceful," Deirut said.

The lingua pack rendered this into a variety of sounds and the natives stared at Deirut's chest.

"He is speaking from his chest," Choon said.

Autoga looked up at the ship. "There are more of you?"

"Don't answer that," the computer said. "Suggest the ship is a source of mystical powers."

Deirut digested this, shook his head. Stupid computer! "These are sharp cookies," he said speaking aloud.

"What a delightful arrangement of noises," Autoga said. "Do it again."

138

"You thought I was one of your youths," Deirut said. "Now who do you think I am?"

The lingua pack remained silent. His ear speaker said: "Suggest that question not be asked."

"Ask it!" Deirut said.

A gabble of sound came from the lingua pack.

"We debated that during the presence of s'Chareecha," Autoga said. "We hid in the purple darkness, you understand, because we have no wish to seed under the influence of s'Chareecha. A majority among us decided you are the personification of our design for a deity. I dissented. My thought is that you are an unknown, although I grant you temporarily the majority title."

Deirut wet his lips with his tongue.

"He has five fingers," Choon said.

"This was the argument you used to convince Tura and Lecky," Autoga said. "This argument still doesn't answer Spispi's objection that the five fingers could be the product of genetic manipulation or that plus amputation."

"But the eyes," Choon said. "Who could conceive of such eyes? Not in our wildest imaginations..."

"Perhaps you offend our visitor," Autoga said. He glanced at Deirut, the stalked eyes bending outward quizzically.

"And the articulation of the legs and arms," one of the other natives ventured.

"You're repeating old arguments, Tura," Autoga said.

Deirut suddenly had a picture of himself as he must appear to these natives. Their eyes had obvious advantages over his. He had seen them look behind themselves without turning their heads. The double thumb arrangement looked useful. They must think one thumb an odd limitation. He began to chuckle.

"What is this noise?" Autoga asked.

"I'm laughing," Deirut said.

"I will render that: 'I'm laughing at myself,'" the computer said. Sounds issued from the lingua pack.

"A person who can laugh at himself has taken a major step toward the highest civilization," Autoga said. "No offense intended."

"The theories of Picheck that the concerted wish for a deity must produce same are here demonstrated," Choon said. "It's not quite the shape of entity I had envisioned, however, but we..."

"Why don't we inquire?" Autoga asked and turned to Deirut. "Are you a deity?"

"I'm a mortal human being, nothing more," Deirut said.

The lingua pack remained silent.

"Translate that!" Deirut blared.

The computer spoke for him alone: "The experience, training and memory banks available suggest that it would be safer for you to pose as a deity. Their natural awe would enable you to..."

"We're not going to fool these characters for five minutes," Deirut said. "They've built spaceships. They have advanced electronic techniques. You heard their radio. They've had a civilization for more than twenty-five million years." He paused. "Haven't they?"

"Definitely. The cast figure was an advanced form and technique."

"Then translate my words!"

Deirut grew conscious that he had been speaking aloud and the natives were following his words and the movements of his mouth with a rapt intensity.

"Translate," Autoga said. "That would be *chtsuyop*, no?"

"You must speak subvocally," the computer said.

"They are beginning to break down your language."

"They're doing it in their heads, you stupid pile of electronic junk," Deirut said. "I have to use you! And you think I can pose as a god with these people?"

"I will translate because you command it and my override circuits cannot circumvent your command," the computer said.

"A computer!" Autoga said. "He has a translating computer in his vehicle! How quaint."

"Translate," Deirut said.

Sounds issued from the lingua pack.

"I am vindicated," Autoga said. "And you will note that I did it on nothing more than the design of the vehicle and the cut of his clothing plus the artifacts, of course."

"This is why you are in command," Choon said. "I suffer your correction and instruction abysmally."

Autoga looked at Deirut. "What will you require other than the repair of your vehicle?"

"Don't you want to know where I'm from?" Deirut asked.

"You are from somewhere," Autoga said. "It has been theorized that other suns and worlds might exist beyond the hydrogen cloud from which we were formed. Your presence suggests this theory is true."

"But ... but don't you want contact with us ... trade, exchange ideas?"

"It is not apparent," Autoga said, "that the empty universe theory has been disproved. However, a primitive such as yourself, even you must realize such interchange would be pointless."

"But we ..."

"We well know that the enclosure of our universe has forced us in upon ourselves," Choon said. "If that's what you were going to say?"

"He was going into boring detail about what he has to offer us," Autoga said. "I suggest we get about doing what has to be done. Spispi, you and Tura take care of the computer in his vehicle. Choon and I will..."

"What're you doing?" Deirut asked. He leaped to his feet. At least, he thought he leaped to his feet, but in a moment he grew conscious that he was still sitting on the ground, the five natives facing him, staring.

"They are erasing some of my circuits!" the computer wailed. "A magneto-gravitic field encloses me and the... aroo, tut-tut, jingle bells, jingle bells."

"This is very interesting," Autoga said presently. "He has made contact with a civilization of our level at some previous time. You will note the residual inhibition against lengthy travel away from his home. We'll make the inhibition stronger this time."

Deirut stared at the chattering natives with a sense of deja vu. The speaker in his neck remained silent. His lingua pack made no sound. He felt movement in his mind like spiders crawling along his nerves.

"Who do you suppose he could've contacted?" Choon asked.

"Not one of our groups, of course," Autoga said. "Before we stay out in the light of s'Chareecha and plant ourselves for the next seeding, we must start a flow of inquiry."

"Who will talk to us about such things?" Choon asked. "We are mere herdsmen."

"Perhaps we should listen more often to the entertainment broadcasts," Spispi said. "Something may have been said."

"We may be simple herdsmen whose inquiry will not go very far," Autoga said, "but this has been an experience to afford us many hours of conversation. Imagine having the empty universe theory refuted!"

Deirut awoke in the control seat of his ship, smelled in the stink of the place his own sweat touched by the chemistry of fear. A glance at the instrument panel showed that he had succumbed to the push and turned ship. He was headed back out of the cloud without having found anything in it.

An odd sadness came over Deirut.

*I'll find my planet some day,* he thought. *It'll have alabaster buildings and sheltered waters for sailing and long stretches of prairie for game animals.*

The automatic log showed turning-around at ninety-four days.

*I stood it longer than Bingaling,* he thought.

He remembered the conversation with Bingaling then and the curious reference to a previous attempt at the cloud. *Maybe I did,* he thought. *Maybe I forgot because the push got so tough.*

Presently, his mind turned to thoughts of Capella Base, of going home. Just the thought of it eased the pressures of the push which was still faintly with him. The push . . . the push—it had beaten him again. Next trip out, he decided, he'd head the opposite direction, see what was to be found out there.

Almost idly then Deirut wondered about the push. *Why do we call it the push?* he wondered. *Why don't we call it the pull?*

The question interested him enough to put it to the computer.

"Tut-tut," the computer said.

# THE GM EFFECT

It was a balmy fall evening and as Dr. Valeric Sabantoce seated himself at the long table in Meade Hall's basement seminar room, he thought of how the weather would be sensationalized tomorrow by the newspapers and wire services. They would be sure to remark on the general clemency of the elements, pointing out how Nature's smiling aspect made the night's tragedy so much more horrible.

Sabantoce was a short, rotund man with a wild shock of black hair that looked as though it had never known a comb. His round face with its look of infant innocence invariably led strangers to an incorrect impression—unless they were at once exposed to his ribald wit or caught the weighted stare of his deeply-socketed brown eyes.

Fourteen people sat around the long table now—nine students and five faculty—with Professor Joshua Latchley in the chairman's seat at the head.

"Now that we're all here," Latchley said, "I can tell you the purpose of tonight's meeting. We are faced with a most terrible decision. We ... ahhh—"

Latchley fell silent, chewed at his lower lip. He was conscious of the figure he cut here—a tall, ungainly bald man in thick-lensed glasses ... the constant air of apology he wore as though it were a shield. Tonight, he felt that this appearance was a disguise. Who could guess—except Sabantoce, of course—at the daring exposed by this seemingly innocent gathering?

"Don't leave 'em hanging there, Josh," Sabantoce said.

"Yes . . . ahh, yes," Latchley said. "It has occurred to me that Dr. Sabantoce and I have a special demonstration to present here tonight, but before we expose you to that experiment, as it were, perhaps we should recapitulate somewhat."

Sabantoce, wondering what had diverted Latchley, glanced around the table—saw that they were *not* all there. Dr. Richard Marmon was missing.

*Did he suspect and make a break for it?* Sabantoce wondered. He realized then that Latchley was stalling for time while Marmon was being hunted out and brought in here.

Latchley rubbed his shiny pate. He had no desire to be here, he thought. But this had to be done. He knew that outside on the campus the special 9:00 P.M. hush had fallen over Yankton Technical Institute and this was his favorite hour for strolling—perhaps up to the fresh pond to listen to the frogs and the couples and to think on the etymological derivations of—

He became conscious of restless coughing and shuffling around the table, realized he had permitted his mind to wander. He was infamous for it, Latchley knew. He cleared his throat. *Where the devil was that Marmon? Couldn't they find him?*

"As you know," Latchley said, "we've made no particular efforts to keep our discovery secret, although we've tried to discourage wild speculation and outside discussion. Our intention was to conduct thorough tests before publishing. All of you—both the

145

student . . . ahh, 'guinea pigs' and you professors of the faculty committee—have been most cooperative. But inevitably news of what we are doing here has spread—sometimes in a very hysterical and distorted manner."

"What Professor Latchley is saying," Sabantoce interrupted, "is that the fat's in the fire."

Expressions of curiosity appeared on the faces of the students who, up to this moment, had been trying to conceal their boredom. Old Dr. Inkton had a fit of coughing.

"There's an old Malay expression," Sabantoce said, "that when one plays Bumps-a-Daisy with a porcupine, one is necessarily jumpy. Now, all of us should've known this porcupine was loaded.'"

"Thank you, Dr. Sabantoce," Latchely said. "I feel . . . and I know this is a most unusual course . . . that all of you should share in the decision that must be made here tonight. Each of you, by participating in this project, has become involved far more deeply here than is the usual case with scientific experiments of this general type. And since you student *assistants* have been kept somewhat in the dark, perhaps Dr. Sabantoce, as original discoverer of the GM effect should fill you in on some of the background."

*Stall it is,* Sabantoce thought.

"Discovery of the genetic memory, or GM effect, was an accident," Sabantoce said picking up his cue. "Dr. Marmon and I were looking for a hormonal method of removing fat from the body. Our Compound 105 had given excellent results on mice and hamsters. We had six generations without apparent side effects and that morning I had decided to try 105 on myself."

Sabantoce allowed himself a self-deprecating grin,

said: "You may remember I had a few excess pounds then."

The responsive laughter told him he had successfully lightened the mood which had grown a bit heavy after Latchley's portentous tone.

*Josh is a damn' fool,* Sabantoce told himself. *I warned him to keep it light. This is a dangerous business.*

"It was eight minutes after ten A.M. when I took that first dosage," Sabantoce said. "I remember it was a very pleasant spring morning and I could hear Carl Kychre's class down the hall reciting a Greek ode. In a few minutes I began to feel somewhat euphoric — almost drunk, but very gently so—and I sat down on a lab stool. Presently, I began reciting with Kychre's class, swinging my arm to the rhythm of it. The next thing I knew, there was Carl in the lab door with some students peering in behind him and I realized I might have been a bit loud."

"'That's magnificent archaic Greek but it *is* disturbing my class,' Carl said."

Sabantoce waited for laughter to subside.

"I suddenly realized I was two people," Sabantoce said. "I was perfectly aware of where I was and who I was, but I also knew quite certainly that I was a Hoplite soldier named Zagreut recently returned from a mercenary venture on Kyrene. It was the *double-exposure* effect that so many of you have remarked. I had all the memories and thoughts of this Hoplite, including his very particular and earthy inclinations toward a female who was uppermost in his/my awareness. And there was this other thing we've all noticed: I was thinking his/my thoughts in Greek, but they were cross-linked to my dominant present and its

English-based awareness. I could translate at will. It was a very heady experience, this realization that I was two people."

One of the graduate students said: "You were a whole mob, Doctor."

Again, there was laughter. Even old Inkton joined in.

"I must've looked a bit peculiar to poor Carl," Sabantoce said. "He came into the lab and said: 'Are you all right?' I told him to get Dr. Marmon down there fast... which he did. And speaking of Marmon, do any of you know where he is?"

Silence greeted the question; then Latchley said: "He's being... summoned."

"So," Sabantoce said. "Well, to get on: Marmon and I locked ourselves in the lab and began exploring this thing. Within a few minutes we found out you could direct the subject's awareness into any stratum of his genetic inheritance, there to be *illuminated* by an ancestor of his choice; and we were caught immediately by the realization that this discovery gave an entirely new interpretation to the concept of instinct and to theories of memory storage. When I say we were excited, that's the understatement of the century."

The talkative graduate student said: "Did the effect fade the way it does with the rest of us?"

"In about an hour," Sabantoce said. "Of course, it didn't fade completely, as you know. That old Hoplite's right here with me, so to speak—along with the rest of the *mob*. A touch of 105 and I have him full on—all his direct memories up to the conception-moment of my next ancestor in his line. I have some overlaps, too, and later memories of his through parallel ancestry and later siblings. I'm also linked to his maternal line, of course—and two of you are tied into this same fabric, as you know. The big thing here is that the remarkably accurate memories of that Hoplite play hob with several accepted histories of the period. In fact, he was our first intimation that much recorded history is a crock."

Old Inkton leaned forward, coughed hoarsely, said: "Isn't it about time, doctor, that we did something about that?"

"In a way, that's why we're here tonight," Sabantoce said. And he thought: *Still no sign of Marmon. I hope Josh knows what he's talking about. But we have to stall some more.*

"Since only a few of us know the full story on some of our more sensational discoveries, we're going to give you a brief outline of those discoveries," Sabantoce said. He put on his most disarming smile, gestured to Latchley. "Professor Latchley, as historian-coordinator of that phase in our investigations, can carry on from here."

Latchley cleared his throat, exchanged a knowing look with Sabantoce. *Did Marmon suspect?* Latchley asked himself. *He couldn't possibly know . . . but he might have suspected.*

"Several obvious aspects of this research method confront one immediately," Latchley said, breaking his attention away from Sabantoce and the worry about Marmon. "As regards any major incident of history—say, a battle—we find a broad selection of subjects on the victorious side and, sometimes, no selection at all on the defeated side. Through the numerous cross references found within even this small group, for example, we find remarkably few *adjacent* and incidental memories within the Troy quadrant of the Trojan wars—some female subjects, of course, but few males. The male bloodlines were virtually wiped out."

Again, Latchley sensed restlessness in his audience and felt a moment of jealousy. Their attention didn't wander when Sabantoce was speaking. The reason was obvious: Sabantoce gave them the dirt, so to speak.

Latchley forced his apologetic smile, said: "Perhaps you'd like a little of the real dirt."

*They did perk up, by heaven!*

"As many have suspected," Latchley said, "our evidence makes it conclusive that Henry Tudor did order the murder of the two princes in the Tower ... at the same time he set into motion the propaganda against Richard III. Henry proves to've been a most vile sort—devious, cruel, cowardly, murderous—political murder was an accepted part of his regime." Latchley shuddered. "And thanks to his sex drive, he's an ancestor of many of us."

"Tell 'em about Honest Abe," Sabantoce said.

Latchley adjusted his glasses, touched the corner of his mouth with a finger, then: "Abraham Lincoln."

He said it as though announcing a visitor and there was a long pause.

Presently, Latchley said: "I found this most distressing. Lincoln was my particular hero in childhood. As some of you know, General Butler was one of my ancestors and ... well, this was *most* distressing."

Latchley fumbled in his pocket, brought up a scrap of paper, studied it, then: "In a debate with Judge Douglas, Lincoln said: 'I tell you very frankly that I am not in favor of Negro citizenship. I am not, nor ever have been, in favor of bringing about in any way the social and political equality of the white and black races; that I am not nor ever have been, in favor of making voters or jurors of Negroes, nor of qualifying them to hold office, nor to inter-marry with white people. I will say in addition that there is a physical difference between the white and black races, which, I suppose, will forever forbid the two races living together upon terms of social and political equality; and in as much as they cannot so live—while they do remain together—there must be the position of the superiors and the inferiors; and that I, as much as any other man, am in favor of the superior being assigned to the white man.'"

Latchley sighed, stuffed the paper into a pocket. "Most distressing," he said. "Once, in a conversation with Butler, Lincoln suggested that all Negroes should be deported to Africa. Another time, talking about the Emancipation Proclamation, he said: 'If it helps preserve the Union, that's enough. But it's as clear to me as it is to any thinking man in the Republic that this proclamation will be declared unconstitutional by the Supreme Court following the cessation of hostilities.'"

Sabantoce interrupted: "How many of you realize what hot potatoes these are?"

The faces around the table turned toward him then back to Latchley.

"Once you have the clue of an on-the-scene observer," Latchley said, "you even find correspondence and other records of corroboration. It's amazing how people used to hide their papers."

The talkative graduate student leaned his elbows on the table, said: "The hotter the potato, the more people will notice it, isn't that right, Professor Latchley?"

*Poor fellow's bucking for a better grade even now,* Sabantoce thought. And he answered for Latchley: "The hottest potatoes are the most difficult to swallow, too."

151

The inane exchange between Sabantoce and the student left a hollow silence behind it and a deepening sense of uneasiness.

Another student said: "Where's Dr. Marmon? I understand he has a theory that the more GM we bring into contact with consciousness, the more we're controlled by the dominant brutality of our ancestors. You know, he says the most brutal ones survived to have children and we kind of gloss that over in our present awareness ... or something like that."

Old Inkton stirred out of his semidaze, turned his sour milk eyes on Latchley. "Pilgrims," he said.

"Ah, yes," Latchley said.

Sabantoce said: "We have eyewitness accounts of Puritans and Pilgrims robbing and raping Indians. Brutality. Some of my ancestors, I'm afraid."

"Tea party," Old Inkton said.

*Why doesn't the old fool shut up?* Latchley wondered. And he found himself increasingly uneasy about Marmon's absence. *Could there have been a double double-cross?* he asked himself.

"Why not outline the Boston Tea Party?" Sabantoce asked. "There're a few here who weren't in on that phase."

"Yes ... ahhh-mmmm," Latchley said. "Massachusetts had a smuggling governor then, of course. Everybody of consequence in the Colonies was smuggling. Navigation Acts and all that. The governor and his cronies were getting their tea from the Dutch. Had warehouses full of it. The British East India Company was on the verge of bankruptcy when the British Government voted a subsidy—equivalent to more than twenty million dollars in current exchange. Because of this ... ahh, subsidy, the East India Company's tea could be sent in at about half the price

152

of the smuggled tea—even including the tax. The governor and his henchmen faced ruin. So they hired brigands to wear Indian disguise and dump the East India Company's tea into the harbor—about a half million dollars worth of tea. And the interesting thing is it was better tea than the smugglers had. Another item to note is that the governor and his cronies then added the cost of the hired brigands onto the price charged for their smuggled tea."

"Hot potatoes," Sabantoce said. "And we haven't even gone into the religious issues—Moses and his aides drafting the Ten Commandments...the argument between Pilate and the religious fanatic."

"Or the present United States southern senator whose grandfather was a light-skinned Negro," Latchley said.

Again, that air of suspenseful uneasiness came over the room. People turned and looked at their companions, twisted in their chairs.

Sabantoce felt it and thought: *We can't let them start asking the wrong questions. Maybe this was a bad tack to take. We should've stalled them some other way...perhaps in some other place. Where is Marmon?*

"Our problem is complicated by accuracy, strangely enough," Latchley said. "When you know where to look, the corroborating evidence is easy to find. The records of that southern senator's ancestry couldn't be disputed."

A student at the opposite end of the table said: "Well, if we have the evidence then nothing can stop us."

"Ahh . . . mmmm," Latchley said. "Well ...ahh..the financial base for our own school is involv..."

153

He was interrupted by a disturbance at the door. Two uniformed men pushed a tall blond young man in a rumpled dark suit into the room. The door was closed and there came the click of a lock. It was an ominous sound.

Sabantoce rubbed his throat.

The young man steadied himself with a hand against the wall, worked his way up the room to a point opposite Latchley, lurched across to an empty chair and collapsed into it. A thick odor of whisky accompanied him.

Latchley stared at him, feeling both relief and uneasiness. They were *really* all here now. The newcomer stared back out of deep-set blue eyes. His mouth was a straight, in-curving line in a long face that appeared even longer because of an extremely high forehead.

"What's going on here, Josh?" he demanded.

Latchley put on his apologetic smile, said: "Now, Dick, I'm sorry we had to drag you away from wherev..."

"Drag!" The young man glanced at Sabantoce, back to Latchley. "Who are those guys? Said they were campus police, but I never saw 'em before. Said I had to come with them...vital importance!"

"I told you this was an important meeting tonight," Sabantoce said. "You've..."

"Important meeting," the young man sneered.

"We must decide tonight about abandoning the project," Latchley said.

A gasp sounded around the table.

*That was clever,* Sabantoce thought. He looked down the table at the others, said: "Now that Dr. Marmon is here, we can bring the thing out and examine it."

"Aband..." Marmon said and sat up straight in his chair.

A long moment of silence passed. Abruptly, the table erupted to discord—everyone trying to talk at once. The noise subsided only when Sabantoce overrode it, slamming a palm against the table and shouting: "Please!"

Into the sudden silence, Latchley said. "You have no idea how painful this disclosure is to those of us who've already faced the realities of it."

"Realities?" Marmon demanded. He shook his head and the effort he made to overcome the effects of drink was apparent to everyone around the table.

"Let me point out to all of you just one *little* part of our total problem," Sabantoce said. "The inheritance of several major fortunes in this country could be legally attacked—with excellent chances of success—on the basis of knowledge we've uncovered."

Sabantoce gave them a moment to absorb this, then: "We're boat rockers in a world whose motto is "Don't give up the ship.' And we could tip over quite a few ships."

"Let us face it," Latchley said, picking up his cue from Sabantoce. "We are not a very powerful group."

"Just a minute!" Marmon shouted. He hitched his chair closer to the table. "Bunch of crepe hangers. Where's y'r common sense? We got the goods on a whole bunch of bums! Have you any idea how much that's worth?"

From down the table to his left came one explosive word: "Blackmail?"

Latchley looked at Sabantoce with a raised-eyebrows expression that said clearly: "See? I told you so."

"Why not?" Marmon demanded. "These bums have

been blackmailing us f'r centuries. 'B'lieve what I tell y', man, or we'll pull y'r arms outa their sockets!' That's what they been tellin's . . . telling us." He rubbed his lips.

Sabantoce stood up, moved around the table and rested a hand lightly on Marmon's shoulder. "O.K. We'll let Dr. Marmon be the devil's advocate. While he's talking, Dr. Latchley and I will go out and get the film and equipment for the little demonstration we've prepared for you. It should give you a clear under-standing of what we're up against." He nodded to Latchley, who arose and joined him.

They crossed to the door, trying not to move too fast. Sabantoce rapped twice on the panel. The door opened and they slipped out between two uniformed guards, one of whom closed and locked the door behind them.

"This way, please," the other guard said.

They moved up the hall, hearing Marmon's voice fade behind them: "The bums have always controlled the history books and the courts and the coinage and the military and every . . ."

Distance reduced the voice to an unintelligible murmur.

"Damn' Commie," one of the guards muttered.

"It does seem such a waste," Latchley said.

"Let's not kid ourselves," Sabantoce said as he started up the stairs to the building's side exit. "When the ship's sinking, you save what you can. I think the Bishop explained things clearly enough: God's testing all men and this is the ultimate test of faith."

"Ultimate test, certainly," Latchley said, laboring to keep up with Sabantoce. "And I'm afraid I must agree with whoever it was said this would produce only chaos—unsettled times . . . anarchy."

"Obvious," Sabantoce said, as he stepped through the outer door being held by another guard.

Latchley and the escort followed.

At once, Sabantoce noted that all the campus lights had been extinguished. *The contrived power failure,* he thought. *They probably switched Meade to an emergency circuit so we wouldn't notice.*

One of their guards stepped forward, touched Latchley's arm, said: "Take the path directly across the quad to the Medical School. Use the back door into Vance Hall. You'll have to hurry. There isn't much time."

Sabantoce led the way down the steps and onto the dark path away from Meade Hall. The path was only a suggestion of lighter gray in the darkness. Latchley stumbled into Sabantoce as they hurried, said: "Excuse me."

There was an impression of many moving dark shapes in the shadows around them. Once a light was flashed in their faces, immediately extinguished.

A voice came from the dark corner of a building: "Down here. Quickly."

Hands guided them down steps, through a door, past heavy draperies, through another door and into a small, dimly lighted room.

Sabantoce recognized it—a medical storeroom that appeared to have been emptied of its supplies rather quickly. There was a small box of compresses on a shelf at his right.

The room was heavy with tobacco smoke and the odor of perspiration. At least a dozen men loomed up in the gloom around them—some of the men in uniform.

A heavy-jowled man with a brigadier's star on his shoulder confronted Sabantoce, said: "Glad to see you made it safely. Are they all in that building now?"

"Every last one," Sabantoce said. He swallowed.

"What about the formula for your Compound 105?"

"Well," Sabantoce said, and allowed a smirk to touch his lips: "I took a little precaution about that—just to keep you honest. I mailed a few copies around to..."

"We know about those," the brigadier said. "We've had the mails from this place closed off and censored for months. I mean those copies you typed in the bursar's office."

Sabantoce turned white. "Well, they're..."

Latchley interrupted, saying: "Really, what's going on here? I thought we..."

"Be quiet!" the brigadier snapped. He returned his attention to Sabantoce. "Well?"

"I...ahh..."

"Those are the ones we found under the floor of his rooms," said a man by the door. "The typeface is identical, sir."

"But I want to know if he made any other copies," the brigadier said.

It was clear from the expression on Sabantoce's face that he had not. "Well...I..." he began.

Again, Latchley interrupted. "I see no need to..."

The loud cork-popping sound of a silenced revolver cut him off. The noise was repeated.

Latchley and Sabantoce crumpled to the floor, dead before they hit it. The man by the door stepped back, holstering his weapon.

As though punctuating their deaths, the outside night was ripped by an explosion.

Presently, a man leaned into the room, said: "The walls went in the way we planned, sir. Thermite and

158

napalm are finishing it. Won't be a trace of those dirty Commies."

"Good work, captain," the brigadier said. "That will be all. Just keep civilians away from the immediate area until we're sure."

"Very good, sir."

The head retreated and the door was closed.

*Good man,* the brigadier thought. He fingered the lone remaining copy of Compound 105's formula in his pocket. *They were all good men. Hand picked. Have to use a different screening process to pick the men for the next project, though: the investigation of possible military uses in this Compound 105.*

"I want those bodies burned practically to ash," he said, gesturing with a toe at Sabantoce and Latchley. "Deliver them with those you pick up from the building."

From the shadowed rear of the room came a heavy, growling voice: "What'll I tell the senator?"

"Tell him anything you want," the brigadier said. "I'll show him my private report later." And he thought: *There's an immediate use for this compound—we have a senator right in our pockets.*

"Damn' nigger lovers," the growling voice said.

"Speak not unkindly of the dead," said a smooth tenor from the opposite corner of the room.

A man in a black suit pushed himself through to open area around the bodies, knelt and began praying in a soft, mumbling voice.

"Tell me as soon as that fire's out," the brigadier said.

# THE FEATHERBEDDERS

*"Once there was a Slorin with a one-syllable name who is believed to have said: 'niche for every one of us and every one of us in his niche.'"*
—Folk saying of the
*Scattership* People

There must be a streak of madness in a Slorin who'd bring his only offspring, an untrained and untried youth, on a mission as potentially dangerous as this one, Smeg told himself.

The rationale behind his decision remained clear: The colonial nucleus must preserve its elders for their detail memory. The youngest of the group was the logical one to be volunteered for this risk. Still...

Smeg forced such thoughts out of his mind. They weakened him. He concentrated on driving the gray motor-pool Plymouth they'd signed out of the government garage in the state capital that morning. The machine demanded considerable attention.

The Plymouth was only two years old, but this region's red rock roads and potholes had multiplied those years by a factor of at least four. The steering was loose and assorted squeaks arose from front and rear as he negotiated a rutted downgrade. The road took them

160

into a shadowed gulch almost bare of vegetation and across the rattling planks of a wooden bridge that spanned a dry creekbed. They climbed out the other side through ancient erosion gullies, past a zone of scrub cottonwoods and onto the reaching flat land they'd been crossing for two hours.

Smeg risked a glance at Rick, his offspring, riding silently beside him. The youth had come out of the pupal stage with a passable human shape. No doubt Rick would do better next time—provided he had the opportunity. But he was well within the seventy-five percent accuracy limit the Slorin set for themselves. It was a universal fact that the untrained sentience saw what it *thought* it saw. The mind tended to supply the missing elements.

A nudge from the Slorin mindcloud helped, of course, but this carried its own perils. The nudged mind sometimes developed powers of its own—with terrifying results. Siorin had learned long ago to depend on the directional broadcast of the mind's narrow band, and to locate themselves in a network limited by the band's rather short range.

However, Rick had missed none of the essentials for human appearance. He had a gentle, slender face whose contours were difficult to remember. His brown eyes were of a limpid softness that made human females discard all suspicions while the males concentrated on jealousy. Rick's hair was a coarse, but acceptable black. The shoulders were a bit high and the thorax somewhat too heroic, but the total effect aroused no probing questions.

That was the important thing: no probing questions.

Smeg permitted himself a silent sigh. His own shape—that of a middle-aged government official, gray at the temples, slightly paunchy and bent of shoulder, and with weak eyes behind gold-rimmed glasses—was more in the Slorin tradition.

*Live on the margins,* Smeg thought. *Attract no attention.*

In other words, don't do what they were doing today.

Awareness of danger forced Smeg into extreme contact with this body his plastic genes had fashioned. It was a good body, a close enough duplicate to interbreed with the natives, but he felt it now from the inside, as it were, a fabric of newness stretched over the ancient substance of the Slorin. It was familiar, yet bothersomely unfamiliar.

*I am Sumctroxelunsmeg,* he reminded himself. *I am a Slorin of seven syllables, each addition to my name an honor to my family. By the pupa of my jelly-sire whose name took fourteen thousand heartbeats to pronounce, I shall not fail!*

There! That was the spirit he needed—the eternal wanderer, temporarily disciplined, yet without boundaries. "If you want to swim, you must enter the water," he whispered.

"Did you say something, Dad?" Rick asked.

Ahhh, that was very good, Smeg thought. Dad—the easy colloquialism.

"I was girding myself for the ordeal, so to speak," Smeg said. "We must separate in a few minutes." He nodded ahead to where a town was beginning to hump itself out of the horizon.

"I think I should barge right in and start asking about their sheriff," Rick said.

Smeg drew in a sharp breath, a gesture of surprise that fitted this body. "Feel out the situation first," he said.

More and more, he began to question the wisdom of

162

sending Rick in there. Dangerous, damnably dangerous. Rick could get himself irrevocably killed, ruined beyond the pupa's powers to restore. Worse than that, he could be exposed. There was the real danger. Give natives the knowledge of what they were fighting and they tended to develop extremely effective methods.

Slorin memory carried a bagful of horror stories to verify this fact.

"The Slorin must remain ready to take any shape, adapt to any situation," Rick said. "That it?"

Rick spoke the axiom well, Smeg thought, but did he really understand it? How could he? Rick still didn't have full control of the behavior patterns that went with this particular body shape. Again, Smeg sighed. If only they'd saved the infiltration squad, the expendable specialists.

Thoughts such as this always brought the more disquieting question: *Saved them from what?*

There had been five hundred pupae in the *Scattership* before the unknown disaster. Now, there were four secondary ancestors and one new offspring created on this planet. They were shipless castaways on an unregistered world, not knowing even the nature of the disaster which had sent them scooting across the void in an escape capsule with minimum shielding.

Four of them had emerged from the capsule as basic Slorin polymorphs to find themselves in darkness on a steep landscape of rocks and trees. At morning, there'd been four additional trees there—watching, listening, weighing the newness against memories accumulated across a time-span in which billions of planets such as this one could have developed and died.

The capsule had chosen an excellent landing site: no nearby sentient constructions. The Slorin now knew the region's native label—central British Columbia. In that period of awakening, though it had been a place of unknown dangers whose chemistry and organization required the most cautious testing.

In time, four black bears had shambled down out of the mountains. Approaching civilization, they'd hidden and watched—listening, always listening, never daring to use the mindcloud. Who knew what mental powers the natives might have? Four roughly fashioned hunters had been metamorphosed from Slorin pupae in a brush-screened cave. The hunters had been tested, refined.

Finally—the hunters had scattered.

Slorin always scattered.

"When we left Washington you said something about the possibility of a trap," Rick said. "You don't really think—"

"Slorin have been unmasked on some worlds," Smeg said. "Natives have developed situational protective devices. This has some of the characteristics of such a trap."

"Then why investigate? Why not leave it alone until we're stronger?"

"Rick!" Smeg shuddered at the youth's massive ignorance. "Other capsules may have escaped," he said.

"But if it's a Slorin down here, he's acting like a dangerous fool."

"More reason to investigate. We could have a damaged pupa here, one who lost part of the detail memory. Perhaps he doesn't know how to act—except out of instincts."

"Then why not stay out of the town and probe just a little bit with the mindcloud?"

*Rick cannot be trusted with this job,* Smeg thought. *He's too raw, too full of the youthful desire to play with the mindcloud.*

"Why not?" Rick repeated.

Smeg pulled the car to a stop at the side of the dirt road, opened his window. It was getting hot—be noon in about an hour. The landscape was a hardscrabble flatness marked by sparse vegetation and a clump of buildings about two miles ahead. Broken fences lined both sides of the road. Low cottonwoods off to the right betrayed the presence of the dry creekbed. Two scrofulous oaks in the middle distance provided shade for several steers. Away on the rim of the badland, obscured by haze, there was a suggestion of hills.

"You going to try my suggestion?" Risk asked.

"No."

"Then why're we stopping? This as far as you go?"

"No." Smeg sighed. "This is as far as *you* go. I'm changing plans. You will wait. I will go into the village."

"But I'm the younger. I'm—"

"And I'm in command here."

"The others won't like this. They said—"

"The others will understand my decision."

"But Slorin law says—"

"Don't quote Slorin law to me!"

"But—"

"Would you teach your grandfather how to shape a pupa?" Smeg shook his head. Rick must learn how to control the anger which flared in this bodily creation. "The limit of the law is the limit of enforcement—the real limit of organized society. We're not an organized society. We're two Slorin—alone, cut off from our pitiful net. Alone! Two Slorin of widely disparate ability. You are capable of carrying a message. I do not judge you capable of meeting the challenge in this village."

Smeg reached across Rick, opened the door.

"This is a firm decision?" Rick asked.

"It is. You know what to do?"

Rick spoke stiffly: "I take that kit of yours from the back and I play the part of a soil engineer from the Department of Agriculture."

"Not a *part*, Rick. You *are* a soil engineer."

"But—"

"You will make real tests which will go into a real report and be sent to a real office with a real function. In the event of disaster, you will assume my shape and step into my niche."

"I see."

"I truly hope you do. Meanwhile, you will go out across that field. The dry creekbed is out there. See those cottonwoods?"

"I've identified the characteristics of this landscape."

"Excellent. Don't deviate. Remember that you're the offspring of Sumctroxelunsmeg. Your jelly-sire's name took fourteen thousand heartbeats to pronounce. Live with pride."

"I was supposed to go in there, take the risk of it—"

"There are risks and there are risks. Remember, make real tests for a real report. Never betray your niche. When you have made the tests, find a place in that creekbed to secrete yourself. Dig in and wait. Listen on the narrow band at all times. Listen, that is all you do. In the event of disaster, you must get word to the others. In the kit there's a dog collar with a tag bearing a promise of reward and the address of our Chicago drop. Do you know the greyhound shape?"

"I know the plan, Dad."

Rick slid out of the car. He removed a heavy black case from the rear, closed the doors, stared in at his parent.

166

Smeg leaned across the seat, opened the window. It creaked dismally.

"Good luck, Dad," Rick said.

Smeg swallowed. This body carried a burden of attachment to an offspring much stronger than any in previous Slorin experience. He wondered how the offspring felt about the parent, tried to probe his own feelings toward the one who'd created him, trained him, sealed his pupa into the *Scattership*. There was no sense of loss. In some ways, he *was* the parent. As different experiences changed him, he would become more and more the individual, however. Syllables would be added to his name. Perhaps, someday, he might feel an urge to be reunited.

"Don't lose your cool, Dad," Rick said.

"The God of Slorin has no shape," Smeg said. He closed the window, straightened himself behind the steering wheel.

Rick turned, trudged off across the field toward the cottonwoods. A low cloud of dust marked his progress. He carried the black case easily in his right hand.

Smeg put the car in motion, concentrated on driving. That last glimpse of Rick, sturdy and obedient, had pierced him with unexpected emotions. Slorin parted, he told himself. It is natural for Slorin to part. An offspring is merely an offspring.

A Slorin prayer came into his mind. "Lord, let me possess this moment without regrets, and, losing it, gain it forever."

The prayer helped, but Smeg still felt the tug of that parting. He stared at the shabby building of his target town. Someone in this collection of structures Smeg was now entering had not learned a basic Slorin lesson: *There is a reason for living; Slorin must not live in a way that destroys this reason.*

Moderation, that was the key.

A man stood in the dusty sunglare toward the center of the town—one lone man beside the dirt road that ran unchecked toward the distant horizon. For one haunted moment Smeg had the feeling it was not a man, but a dangerous other-shaped enemy he'd met before. The feeling passed as Smeg brought the car to a stop nearby.

Here was the American peasant, Smeg realized—tall, lean, dressed in wash-faded blue bib overalls, a dirty tan shirt and tennis shoes. The shoes were coming apart to reveal bare toes. A ground green painter's hat with green plastic visor did an ineffective job of covering his yellow hair. The visor's rim was cracked. It dripped a fringe of ragged binding that swayed when the man moved his head.

Smeg leaned out his window, smiled: "Howdy."

"How do."

Smeg's sense of hearing, trained in a history of billions of such encounters, detected the xenophobia and reluctant bowing to convention at war in the man's voice.

"Town's pretty quiet," Smeg said.

"Yep."

Purely human accents, Smeg decided. He permitted himself to relax somewhat, asked: "Anything unusual ever happen around here?"

"You fum the gov'ment?"

"That's right." Smeg tapped the motor-pool insignia on his door. "Department of Agriculture."

"Then you ain't part of the gov'ment conspiracy?"

"Conspiracy?" Smeg studied the man for a clue to hidden meanings. Was this one of those southern

168

towns where anything from the government just had to be communist?

"Guess you ain't," the man said.

"Of course not."

"That there was a serious question you asked, then ... about unusual thing happening?"

"I ... yes."

"Depends on what you call unusual."

"What ... do *you* call unusual?" Smeg ventured.

"Can't rightly say. And you?"

Smeg frowned, leaned out his window, looked up and down the street, studied each detail: the dog sniffing under the porch of a building labeled "General Store," the watchful blankness of windows with here and there a twitching curtain to betray someone peering out, the missing boards on the side of a gas station beyond the store—one rusty pump there with its glass chamber empty. Every aspect of the town spoke of heat-addled somnolence ... yet it was wrong. Smeg could feel tensions, transient emotional eddies that irritated his highly tuned senses. He hoped Rick already had a hiding place and was listening.

"This is Wadeville, isn't it?" Smeg asked.

"Yep. Used to be county seat 'fore the war."

He meant the War Between The States, Smeg realized, recalling his studies of regional history. As always, the Slorin were using every spare moment to absorb history, mythology, arts, literature, science— You never knew which might be the valuable piece of information.

"Ever hear about someone could get right into your mind?" the man asked.

Smeg overcame a shock reaction, groped for the proper response. Amused disbelief, he decided, and

169

managed a small chuckle. "That the unusual thing you have around here?"

"Didn't say yes; didn't say no."

"Why'd you ask then?" Smeg knew his voice sounded like crinkling bread wrapper. He pulled his head back into the car's shadows.

"I jes' wondered if you might be hunting fer a teleepath?"

The man turned, hawked a cud of tobacco toward the dirt at his left. A vagrant breeze caught the spittle, draped it across the side of Smeg's car.

"Oh, dang!" the man said. He produced a dirty yellow bandanna, knelt and scrubbed with it at the side of the car.

Smeg leaned out, studied this performance with an air of puzzlement. The man's responses, the vague hints at mental powers—they were confusing, fitted no pattern in Slorin experience.

"You got somebody around here claiming to be a telepath?" Smeg asked.

"Can't say." The man stood up, peered in at Smeg. "Sorry about that there. Wind, y'know. Accident. Didn't mean no harm."

"Certainly."

"Hope you won't say nothing to the sheriff. Got 'er all cleaned off your car now. Can't tell where I hit 'er."

The man's voice carried a definite tone of fear, Smeg realized. He stared at this American peasant with a narrow, searching gaze. *Sheriff*, he'd said. Was it going to be this easy? Smeg wondered how to capitalize on that opening. Sheriff. Here was an element of the mystery they'd come to investigate.

As the silence drew out, the man said: "Got 'er all clean. You can get out and look for yourself."

"I'm sure you did, Mr. . . . ahhh . . ."

"Painter, Josh'a Painter. Most folks call me Josh on account of my first name there, Josh'a Painter."

"Pleased to meet you, Mr. Painter. My name's Smeg, Henry Smeg."

"Smeg," Painter said with a musing tone. "Don't rightly believe I ever heard that name before."

"It used to be much longer," Smeg said. "Hungarian."

"Oh."

"I'm curious, Mr. Painter, why you'd be afraid I might tell the sheriff because the wind blew a little tobacco juice on my car?"

"Never can tell how some folks'll take things," Painter said. He looked from one end of Smeg's car to the other, back to Smeg. "You a gov'ment man, this car an' all, reckoned I'd best be sure, one sensible man to another."

"You've been having trouble with the government around here, is that it?"

"Don't take kindly to most gov'ment men hereabouts, we don't. But the sheriff, he don't allow us to do anything about that. Sheriff is a mean man, a certain mean man sometimes, and he's got my Barton."

"Your barton," Smeg said, drawing back into the car to conceal his puzzlement. *Barton?* This was an entirely new term. Strange that none of them had encountered it before. The study of languages and dialects had been most thorough. Smeg began to feel uneasy about his entire conversation with this Painter. The conversation had never really been under control. He wondered how much of it he'd actually understood. There was in Smeg a longing to venture a mindcloud probe, to nudge the man's motives, make him *want* to explain.

"You one of them survey fellows like we been getting?" Painter asked.

"You might say that," Smeg said. He straightened his shoulders. "I'd like to walk around and look at your town, Mr. Painter. May I leave my car here?"

"'Tain't in the way that I can see," Painter said. He managed to appear both interested and disinterested in Smeg's question. His glance flicked sideways, all around—at the car, the road, at a house behind a privet hedge across the way.

"Fine," Smeg said. He got out, slammed the door, reached into the back for the flat-crowned Western hat he affected in these parts. It tended to break down some barriers.

"You forgetting your papers?" Painter asked.

"Papers?" Smeg turned, looked at the man.

"Them papers full of questions you gov'ment people allus use."

"Oh." Smeg shook his head. "We can forget about papers today."

"You jes' going to wander around?" Painter asked.

"That's right."

"Well, some folks'll talk to you," Painter said. "Got all kinds of different folks here." He turned away, started to walk off.

"Please, just a minute," Smeg said.

Painter stopped as though he'd run into a barrier, spoke without turning. "You want something?"

"Where're you going, Mr. Painter?"

"Jes' down the road a piece."

"I'd...ahhh, hoped you might guide me," Smeg said. "That is if you haven't anything better to do?"

Painter turned, stared at him. "Guide? In Wadeville?" He looked around him, back to Smeg. A tiny smile tugged at his mouth.

"Well, where do I find your sheriff, for instance?" Smeg asked.

172

The smile disappeared. "Why'd you want him?"

"Sheriffs usually know a great deal about an area."

"You sure you actual' want to see him?"

"Sure. Where's his office?"

"Well now, Mr. Smeg..." Painter hesitated, then: "His office is just around the corner here, next the bank."

"Would you show me?" Smeg moved forward, his feet kicking up dust puddles in the street. "Which corner?"

"This'n right here." Painter pointed to a fieldstone building at his left. A weed-grown lane led off past it. The corner of a wooden porch jutted from the stone building into the lane.

Smeg walked past Painter, peered down the lane. Tufts of grass grew in the middle and along both sides, green runners stretching all through the area. Smeg doubted that a wheeled vehicle had been down this way in two years—possibly longer.

A row of objects on the porch caught his attention. He moved closer, studied them, turned back to Painter.

"What're all those bags and packages on that porch?"

"Them?" Painter came up beside Smeg, stood a moment, lips pursed, eyes focused beyond the porch.

"Well, what are they?" Smeg pressed.

"This here's the bank," Painter said. "Them's night deposits."

Smeg turned back to the porch. Night deposits? Paper bags and fabric sacks left out in the open?

"People leaves 'em here if'n the bank ain't open," Painter said. "Bank's a little late opening today. Sheriff had 'em in looking at the books last night."

*Sheriff examining the bank's books?* Smeg wondered. He hoped Rick was missing none of this and

173

could repeat it accurately . . . just in case. The situation here appeared far more mysterious than the reports had indicated. Smeg didn't like the feeling of this place at all.

"Makes it convenient for people who got to get up early and them that collects their money at night," Painter explained.

"They just leave it right out in the open?" Smeg asked.

"Yep. 'Night deposit' it's called. People don't have to come aound when—"

"I know what it's called! But . . . right out in the open like that . . . without a guard?"

"Bank don't open till ten thirty most days," Painter said. "Even later when the sheriff's had 'em in at night."

"There's a guard," Smeg said. "That's it, isn't it?"

"Guard? What we need a guard fer? Sheriff says leave them things alone, they gets left alone."

*The sheriff again,* Smeg thought. "Who . . . ahh deposits money like this?" he asked.

"Like I said: the people who got to get up early and . . ."

"But *who* are these people?"

"Oh. Well, my cousin Reb: He has the gas station down to the forks. Mr. Seelway at the General Store there. Some farmers with cash crops come back late from the city. Folks work across the line at the mill in Anderson when they get paid late of a Friday. Folks like that."

"They just . . . leave their money out on this porch."

"Why not?"

"Lord knows," Smeg whispered.

"Sheriff says don't touch it, why—it don't get touched."

Smeg looked around him, sensing the strangeness of

this weed-grown street with its wide-open night depository protected only by a sheriff's command. Who was this sheriff? *What* was this sheriff?

"Doesn't seem like there'd be much money in Wadeville," Smeg said. "That gas station down the main street out there looks abandoned, looks like a good wind would blow it over. Most of the other buildings—"

"Station's closed," Painter said. "You need gas, just go out to the forks where my cousin, Reb—"

"Station failed?" Smeg asked.

"Kind of."

"Kind of?"

"Sheriff, he closed it."

"Why?"

"Fire hazard. Sheriff, he got to reading the state Fire Ordinance one day. Next day he told ol' Jamison to dig up the gas tanks and cart 'em away. They was too old and rusty, not deep enough in the ground and didn't have no concrete on 'em. 'Sides that, the building's too old, wood all oily."

"The sheriff ordered it...just like that." Smeg snapped his fingers.

"Yep. Said he had to tear down that station. Ol' Jamison sure was mad."

"But if the sheriff says do it, then it gets done?" Smeg asked.

"Yep. Jamison's tearing it down—one board every day. Sheriff don't seem to pay it no mind long as Jamison takes down that one board every day."

Smeg shook his head. One board every day. What did that signify? Lack of a strong time sense? He looked back at the night deposits on the porch, asked: "How long have people been depositing their money here this way?"

"Been since a week or so after the sheriff come."

"And how long has that been?"

"Ohhhhh . . . four, five years maybe."

Smeg nodded to himself. His little group of Slorin had been on the planet slightly more than five years. This could be . . . this could be—He frowned. But what if it wasn't?

The dull plodding of footsteps sounded from the main street behind Smeg. He turned, saw a tall fat man passing there. The man glanced curiously at Smeg, nodded to Painter.

"Mornin', Josh," the fat man said. It was a rumbling voice.

"Mornin', Jim," Painter said.

The fat man skirted the Plymouth, hesitated to read the emblem on the car door, glanced back at Painter, resumed his plodding course down the street and out of sight.

"That was Jim," Painter said.

"Neighbor?"

"Yep. Been over to the Widow McNabry's again . . . all the whole dang' night. Sheriff's going to be mighty displeasured, believe me."

"He keeps an eye on your morals, too?"

"Morals?" Painter scratched the back of his neck. "Can't rightly say he does."

"Then why would he mind if . . . Jim—"

"Sheriff, he says it's a sin and a crime to take what don't belong to you, but it's a blessing to give. Jim, he stood right up to the sheriff, said he jes' went to the widow's to give. So—" Painter shrugged.

"The sheriff's open to persuasion, then?"

"Some folks seem to think so."

"You don't?"

"He made Jim stop smoking and drinking."

Smeg shook his head sharply, wondering if he'd heard correctly. The conversation kept darting around into seeming irrelevancies. He adjusted his hat brim, looked at his hand. It was a good hand, couldn't be told from the human original. "Smoking and drinking?" he asked.

"Yep."

"But why?"

"Said if Jim was taking on new ree-sponsibilities like the widow he couldn't commit suicide—not even slow like."

Smeg stared at Painter who appeared engrossed with a nonexistent point in the sky. Presently, Smeg managed: "That's the weirdest interpretation of the law I ever heard."

"Don't let the sheriff hear you say that."

"Quick to anger, eh?"

"Wouldn't say that."

"What *would* you say?"

"Like I told Jim: Sheriff get his eye on you, that is it. You going to toe the line. Ain't so bad till the sheriff get his eye on you. When he see you—that is the end."

"Does the sheriff have his eye on you, Mr. Painter?"

Painter made a fist, shook it at the air. His mouth drew back in a fierce, scowling grimace. The expression faded. Presently, he relaxed, sighed.

"Pretty bad, eh?" Smeg asked.

"Dang conspiracy," Painter muttered. "Gov'ment got its nose in things don't concern it."

"Oh?" Smeg watched Painter closely, sensing they were on productive ground. "What does—"

"Dang near a thousand gallons a year!" Painter exploded.

"Uhhh—" Smeg said. He wet his lips with his tongue, a gesture he'd found to denote human uncertainty.

"Don't care if you are part of the conspiracy," Painter said. "Can't do nothing to me now."

"Believe me, Mr. Painter, I have no designs on . . ."

"I made some 'shine when folks wanted," Painter said. "Less'n a thousand gallons a year . . . almost. Ain't much considering the size of some of them stills t'other side of Anderson. But them's across the line! 'Nother county! All I made was enough fer the folks 'round here."

"Sheriff put a stop to it?"

"Made me bust up my still."

"Made *you* bust up your still?"

"Yep. That's when he got my Barton."

"Your . . . ahhh . . . barton?" Smeg ventured.

"Right from under Lilly's nose," Painter muttered. His nostrils dilated, eyes glared. Rage lay close to the surface.

Smeg looked around him, searching the blank windows, the empty doorways. What in the name of all the Slorin furies was a barton?

"Your sheriff seems to hold pretty close to the law," Smeg ventured.

"Hah!"

"No liquor," Smeg said. "No smoking. He rough on speeders?"

"Speeders?" Painter turned his glare on Smeg. "Now, you tell me what we'd speed in, Mr. Smeg."

"Don't you have any cars here?"

"If my cousin Reb didn't have his station over to the forks where he get the city traffic, he'd be bust long ago. State got a law—car got to stop in jes' so many lights. Got to have windshield wiper things. Got to have tires

178

which you can measure the tread on. Got to steer ab-so-lutely jes' right. Car don't do them things, it is *junk*. Junk! Sheriff, he make you sell that car for junk! Ain't but two, three folks in Wadeville can afford a car with all them things."

"He sounds pretty strict," Smeg said.

"Bible-totin' parson with hell fire in his eyes couldn't be worse. I tell you, if that sheriff didn't have my Barton, I'd a run out long ago. I'd a ree-beled like we done in Sixty-one. Same with the rest of the folks here . . . most of 'em."

"He has their . . . ahhh, bartons?" Smeg asked, cocking his head to one side, waiting.

Painter considered this for a moment, then: "Well, now . . . in a manner of speaking, you could call it that way."

Smeg frowned. Did he dare ask what a barton was? No! It might betray too much ignorance. He longed for a proper Slorin net, all the interlocked detail memories, the Slorin spaced out within the limits of the narrow band, ready to relay questions, test hypotheses, offer suggestions. But he was alone except for one inexperienced offspring hiding out there across the fields . . . waiting for disaster. Perhaps Rick had encountered the word, though. Smeg ventured a weak interrogative.

Back came Rick's response, much too loud: "Negative."

So Rick didn't know the word either.

Smeg studied Painter for a sign the man had detected the narrow band exchange. Nothing. Smeg swallowed, a natural fear response he'd noticed in this body, decided to move ahead more strongly.

"Anybody ever tell you you have a most unusual sheriff?" he asked.

179

"Them gov'ment survey fellows, that's what they say. Come here with all them papers and all them questions, say they interested in our crime rate. Got no crime in Wade County, they say. Think they telling us something!"

"That's what I heard about you," Smeg offered. "No crime."

"Hah!"

"But there must be some crime," Smeg said.

"Got no 'shine," Painter muttered. "Got no robbing and stealing, no gambling. Got no drunk drivers 'cepting they come from somewheres else and then they is mighty displeasured they drunk drove in Wade County. Got no *ju*venile dee-linquents like they talk about in the city. Got no patent medicine fellows. Got nothing."

"You must have a mighty full jail, though."

"Jail?"

"All the criminals your sheriff apprehends."

"Hah! Sheriff don't throw folks in jail, Mr. Smeg. Not 'less they is from over the line and needs to sleep off a little ol' spree while they sobers up enough to pay the fine."

"Oh?" Smeg stared out at the empty main street, remembering the fat man—Jim. "He gives the local residents a bit more latitude, eh? Like your friend, Jim."

"Jes' leading Jim along, I say."

"What do you mean?"

"Pretty soon the widow's going to be in the family way. Going to be a quick wedding and a baby and Jim'll be jes' like all the rest of us."

Smeg nodded as though he understood. It was like the reports which had lured him here... but unlike them, too. Painter's "survey fellows" had been amused

180

by Wadeville and Wade County, so amused even their driest governmentese couldn't conceal it. Their amusement had written the area off—"purely a local phenomenon." Tough southern sheriff. Smeg was not amused. He walked slowly out to the main street, looked back along the road he'd traveled.

Rick was out there listening...waiting.

What would the waiting produce?

An abandoned building up the street caught Smeg's attention. Somewhere within it a door creaked with a rhythm that matched the breeze stirring the dust in the street. A "SALOON" sign dangled from the building on a broken guy wire. The sign swayed in the wind—now partly obscured by a porch roof, now revealed: "LOON"..."SALOON"..."LOON"..."SALOON" ...

The mystery of Wadeville was like that sign, Smeg thought. The mystery moved and changed, now one thing, now another. He wondered how he could hold the mystery still long enough to examine it and understand it.

A distant wailing interrupted his reverie.

It grew louder—a siren.

"Here he come," Painter said.

Smeg glanced at Painter. The man was standing beside him glaring in the direction of the siren.

"Here he sure do come," Painter muttered.

Another sound accompanied the siren now—the hungry throbbing of a powerful motor.

Smeg looked toward the sound, saw a dust cloud on the horizon, something vaguely red within it.

"Dad! Dad!" That was Rick on the narrow band.

Before he could send out the questioning thought, Smeg felt it—the growing force of a mindcloud so strong it made him stagger.

181

Painter caught his arm, steadied him.

"Gets some folks that way the first time," Painter said.

Smeg composed himself, disengaged his arm, stood trembling. Another Slorin! It had to be another Slorin. But the fool was broadcasting a signal that could bring down chaos on them all. Smeg looked at Painter. The natives had the potential—his own Slorin group had determined this. Were they in luck here? Was the local strain insensitive? But Painter had spoken of it getting some folks the first time. He'd spoken of telepaths.

Something was very wrong in Wadeville...and the mindcloud was enveloping him like a gray fog. Smeg summoned all his mental energy, fought free of the controlling force. He felt himself standing there then like an island of clarity and calm in the midst of that mental hurricane.

There were sharp sounds all around him now—window blinds snapping up, doors slamming. People began to emerge. They lined the street, a dull-eyed look of expectancy about them, an angry wariness. They appeared to be respectable humans all, Smeg thought, but there was a sameness about them he couldn't quite define. It had something to do with a dowdy, slump-shouldered look.

"You going to see the sheriff," Painter said. "That's for sure."

Smeg faced the oncoming thunder of motor and siren. A long red fire truck with a blonde young woman in green leotards astride its hood emerged from the dust cloud, hurtled down the street toward the narrow passage where Smeg had parked his car.

At the wheel of the truck sat what appeared to be a dark-skinned man in a white suit, dark blue shirt, a white ten-gallon hat. A gold star glittered at his breast.

He clutched the steering wheel like a racing driver, head low, eyes forward.

Smeg, free of the mindcloud, saw the driver for what he was—a Slorin, still in polymorph, his shape approximating the human...but not well enough ...not well enough at all.

Clustered around the driver, on the truck's seat, clinging to the sides and the ladders on top, were some thirty children. As they entered the village, they began yelling and laughing, screaming greetings.

"There's the sheriff," Painter said. "That unusual enough fer you?"

The truck swerved to avoid Smeg's car, skidded to a stop opposite the lane where he stood with Painter. The sheriff stood up, looked back toward the parked car, shouted: "Who parked that *auto*mobile there? You see how I had to swing way out to git past it? Somebody tear down my 'No Parking' sign again? Look out if you did! You know I'll find out who you are! Who did that?"

While the sheriff was shouting, the children were tumbling off the truck in a cacophony of greetings— "Hi, Mama!" "Daddy, you see me?" "We been all the way to Commanche Lake swimming." "You see the way we come, Pa?" "You make a pie for me, Mama? Sheriff says I kin have a pie."

Smeg shook his head at the confusion. All were off the truck now except the sheriff and the blonde on the hood. The mindcloud pervaded the mental atmosphere like a strong odor, but it stopped none of the outcry.

Abruptly, there came the loud, spitting crack of a rifle shot. A plume of dust burst from the sheriff's white suit just below the golden star.

Silence settled over the street.

Slowly, the sheriff turned, the only moving figure in
183

the frozen tableaux. He looked straight up the street toward an open window in the second story of a house beyond the abandoned service station. His hand came up; a finger extruded. He shook his finger, a man admonishing a naughty child.

"I warned you," he said.

Smeg uttered a Slorin curse under his breath. The fool! No wonder he was staying in polymorph and relying on the mindcloud—the whole village was in arms against him. Smeg searched through his accumulated Slorin experience for a clue on how to resolve this situation. A whole village aware of Slorin powers! Oh, that sinful fool!

The sheriff looked down at the crowd of silent children, staring first at one and then another. Presently, he pointed to a barefoot girl of about eleven, her yellow hair tied in pigtails, a soiled blue and white dress on her gangling frame.

"You there, Molly Mae," the sheriff said. "You see what your daddy done?"

The girl lowered her head and began to cry.

The blonde on the truck's hood leaped down with a lithe grace, tugged at the sheriff's sleeve.

"Don't interrupt the law in the carrying out of its duties," the sheriff said.

The blonde put her hands on her hips, stamped a foot. "Tad, you hurt that child and I won't never speak to you, never again," she said.

Painter began muttering half under his breath: "No...no...no...no—"

"Hurt Molly Mae?" the sheriff asked. "Now, you know I won't hurt her. But she's got to go away, never see her kin again as long as she lives. You know that."

"But Molly Mae didn't do you no hurt," the young

184

woman said. "It were her daddy. Why can't you send him away?"

"There's some things you just can't understand," the sheriff said. "Grown up adult can only be taken from sinful, criminal ways a slow bit at a time 'less'n you make a little child of him. Now, I'd be doing the crime if I made a little child out of a grown-up adult. Little girl like Molly Mae, she's a child right now. Don't make much difference."

So that was it, Smeg thought. That was the sheriff's real hold on this community. Smeg suddenly felt that a barton had to mean—a hostage.

"It's cruel," the blonde young woman said.

"Law's got to be cruel sometimes," the sheriff said. "Law got to eliminate crime. Almost got it done. Only crimes we had hereabouts for months are crimes 'gainst me. Now, you all know you can't get away with crimes like that. But when you show that *dis*regard for the majesty of the law, you got to be punished. You got to remember, all of you, that every part of a family is ree-sponsible for the whole entire family."

*Pure Slorin thinking,* Smeg thought. He wondered if he could make his move without exposing his own alien origins. Something had to be done here and soon. Did he dare venture a probe of greeting into the fool's mind? No. The sheriff probably wouldn't even receive the greeting through that mindcloud noise.

"Maybe you're doing something wrong then," the young woman said. "Seems awful funny to me when the only crimes are put right on the law itself."

*A very pertinent observation,* Smeg thought.

Abruptly, Painter heaved himself into motion, lurched through the crowd of children toward the sheriff.

The blonde young woman turned, said: "Daddy! You stay out'n this."

"You be still now, you hear, Barton Marie?" Painter growled.

"You know you can't do anything," she wailed. "He'll only send me away."

"Good! I say good!" Painter barked. He pushed in front of the young woman, stood glaring up at the sheriff.

"Now, Josh," the sheriff said, his voice mild.

They fell silent, measuring each other.

In this moment, Smeg's attention was caught by a figure walking toward them on the road into the village. The figure emerged from the dust—a young man carrying a large black case.

*Rick!*

Smeg stared at his offspring. The young man walked like a puppet, loose at the knees. His eyes stared ahead with a blank seeking.

*The mindcloud,* Smeg thought. *Rick was young, weak. He'd been calling out, wide open when the mindcloud struck. The force that had staggered a secondary ancestor had stunned the young Slorin. He was coming now blindly toward the irritation source.*

"Who that coming there?" the sheriff called. "That the one parked this car illegal?"

"Rick!" Smeg shouted.

Rick stopped.

"Stay where you are!" Smeg called. This time, he sent an awakening probe into the youth.

Rick stared around him, awareness creeping into his eyes. He focused on Smeg, mouth falling open.

"Dad!"

"Who're you?" the sheriff demanded, staring at Smeg. A jolt from the mindcloud jarred Smeg.

There was only one way to do this, Smeg realized. Fight fire with fire. The natives already had felt the mindcloud.

Smeg began opening the enclosing mental shields, dropped them abruptly and lashed out at the sheriff. The Slorin polymorph staggered back, slumped onto the truck seat. His human shape twisted, writhed.

"Who're you?" the sheriff gasped.

Shifting to the Slorin gutturals, Smeg said: "I will ask the questions here. Identify yourself."

Smeg moved forward, a path through the children opening for him. Gently, he moved Painter and the young woman aside.

"Do you understand me?" Smeg demanded.

"I... understand you." The Slorin gutturals were rough and halting, but recognizable.

In a softer tone, Smeg said: "The universe has many crossroads where friends can meet. Identify yourself."

"Min... I think. Pzilimin." The sheriff straightened himself on the seat, restored some of his human shape to its previous form. "Who are you?"

"I am Sumctroxelunsmeg, secondary ancestor."

"What's a secondary ancestor?"

Smeg sighed. It was pretty much as he had feared. The name, Pzilimin, that was the primary clue—a tertiary ancestor from the *Scattership*. But this poor Slorin had been damaged, somehow, lost part of his detail memory. In the process, he had created a situation here that might be impossible to rectify. The extent of the local mess had to be examined now, though.

"I will answer your questions later," Smeg said. "Meanwhile—"

"You know this critter?" Painter asked. "You part of the conspiracy?"

Shifting to English, Smeg said: "Mr. Painter, let the government handle its own problems. This man is one of our problems."

"Well, he sure is a problem and that's the truth."

"Will you let me handle him?"

"You sure you can do it?"

"I . . . think so."

"I sure hope so."

Smeg nodded, turned back to the sheriff. "Have you any idea what you've done here?" he asked in basic Slorin.

"I . . . found myself a suitable official position and filled it to the best of my ability. Never betray your niche. I remember that. Never betray your niche."

"Do you know what you are?"

"I'm . . . a Slorin?"

"Correct. A Slorin tertiary ancestor. Have you any idea how you were injured?"

"I . . . no. Injured?" He looked around at the people drawing closer, all staring curiously. "I . . . woke up out there in the . . . field. Couldn't . . . remember—"

"Very well, we'll—"

"I remembered one thing! We were supposed to lower the crime rate, prepare a suitable society in which . . . in which . . . I . . . don't know."

Smeg stared across the children's heads at Rick who had come to a stop behind the truck, returned his attention to Pzilimin.

"I have the crime rate here almost down to an irreducible minimum," the Slorin sheriff said.

Smeg passed a hand across his eyes. Irreducible minimum! He dropped his hand, glared up at the poor fool. "You have made these people aware of Slorin," he accused. "You've made them aware of themselves, which is worse. You've started them thinking about

188

what's behind the law. Something every native law enforcement offical on this planet knows by instinct, and you, a Slorin—injured or not—couldn't see it."

"See what?" Pzilimin asked.

"Without crime there's no need for law enforcement officers! We are here to prepare niches in which Slorin can thrive. And you begin by doing yourself out of a job! The first rule in any position is to maintain enough of the required activity for that job to insure your continued employment. Not only that, you must increase your scope, open more such positions. This is what is meant by not betraying your niche."

"But...we're supposed to create a society in which...in which—"

"You were supposed to reduce the incident of violence, you fool! You must channel the crime into more easily manageable patterns. You left them violence! One of them shot at you."

"Oh...they've tried worse than that."

Smeg looked to his right, met Painter's questioning gaze.

"He another Hungarian?" Painter asked.

"Ah-h-h, yes!" Smeg said, leaping at this opportunity.

"Thought so, you two talking that foreign language there." Painter glared up at Pzilimin. "He oughta be dee-ported."

"That's the very thing," Smeg agreed. "That's why I'm here."

"Well, by gollies!" Painter said. He sobered. "I better warn you, though. Sheriff, he got some kind of machine sort of that scrambles your mind. Can't hardly think when he turns it on. Carries it in his pocket, I suspect."

"We know all about that," Smeg said. "I have a

189

machine of the same kind myself. It's a defense secret and he had no right to use it."

"I'll bet you ain't Department of Agriculture at all," Painter said. "I bet you're with the CIA."

"We won't talk about that," Smeg said. "I trust, however, that you and your friends won't mention what has happened here."

"We're true blue Americans, all of us, Mr. Smeg. You don't have to worry about us."

"Excellent," Smeg said. And he thought: *How convenient. Do they think me an utter fool?* Smoothly, he turned back to Pzilimin, asked: "Did you follow all that?"

"They think you're a secret agent."

"So it seems. Our task of extracting you from this situation has been facilitated. Now tell me, what have done about their children?"

"Their children?"

"You heard me."

"Well... I just erased all those little tracks in their little minds and put 'em on a train headed north, the ones I sent away to punish their folks. These creatures have a very strong protective instinct toward the young. Don't have to worry about their—"

"I know about their instincts, Pzilimin. We'll have to find those children, restore them and return them."

"How'll we find them?"

"Very simple. We'll travel back and forth across this continent, listening on the narrow band. We will listen for you, Pzilimin. You cannot erase a mind without putting your own patterns in it."

"Is that what happened when I tried to change the adult?"

Smeg goggled at him, senses reeling. Pzilmin couldn't have done that, Smeg told himself. He

190

couldn't have converted a native into a Slorin-patterned, full-power broadcast unit and turned it loose on this planet. No Slorin could be that stupid! "Who?" he managed.

"Mr. McNabry."

*McNabry? McNabry?* Smeg knew he'd heard the name somewhere. *McNabry? Widow McNabry!*

"Sheriff, he say something about Widow McNabry?" Painter asked. "I thought I heard him—"

"What happened to the late Mr. McNabry?" Smeg demanded, whirling on Painter.

"Oh, he drowned down south of here. In the river. Never did find his body."

Smeg rounded on Pzilimin. "Did you—"

"Oh, no! He just ran off. We had this report he drowned and I just—"

"In effect, you killed a native."

"I didn't do it on purpose."

"Pzilimin, get down off that vehicle and into the rear seat of my machine over here. We will forget that I'm illegally parked, shall we?"

"What're you going to do?"

"I'm going to take you away from here. Now, get down off of there!"

"Yes, sir." Pzilimin moved to obey. There was a suggestion of rubbery, nonhuman action to his knees that made Smeg shudder.

"Rick," Smeg called. "You will drive."

"Yes, Dad."

Smeg turned to Painter. "I hope you all realize the serious consequences to yourselves if any of this should get out?"

"We sure do, Mr. Smeg. Depend on it."

"I am depending on it," Smeg said. And he thought: *Let them analyze that little statement . . . after we're*

191

*gone.* More and more he was thanking the Slorin god who'd prompted him to change places with Rick. One wrong move and this could've been a disaster. With a curt nod to Painter, he strode to his car, climbed into the rear beside Pzilimin. "Let's go, Rick."

Presently, they were turned around, headed back toward the state capital. Rick instinctively was pressing the Plymouth to the limit of its speed on this dirt road. Without turning, he spoke over his shoulder to Smeg:

"That was real cool, Dad, the way you handled that. We go right back to the garage now?"

"We disappear at the first opportunity," Smeg said.

"Disappear?" Pzilimin asked.

"We're going pupa, all of us, and come out into new niches."

"Why?" Rick said.

"Don't argue with me! That village back there wasn't what it seemed."

Pzilimin stared at him. "But you said we'd have to find their children and—"

"That was for their benefit, playing the game of ignorance. I suspect they've already found their children. Faster, Rick."

"I'm going as fast as I dare right now, Dad."

"No matter. They're not going to chase us." Smeg took off his Western hat, scratched where the band had pressed into his temples.

"I'm not sure," Smeg said. "But they made it too easy for us to get Pzilimin out of there. I suspect they are the source of the disaster which set us down here without our ship."

"Then why didn't they just...eliminate Pzilimin and—"

"Why didn't Pzilimin simply eliminate those who opposed him?" Smeg asked. "Violence begets violence,

192

Rick. This is a lesson many sentient beings have learned. They had their own good reasons for handling it this way."

"What'll we do?" Rick asked.

"We'll go to earth, like foxes, Rick. We will employ the utmost caution and investigate this situation. That is what we'll do."

"Don't they know that . . . back there?"

"Indeed, they must. This should be very interesting."

Painter stood in the street staring after the retreating car until it was lost in a dust cloud. He nodded to himself once.

A tall fat man came up beside him, said: "Well, Josh, it worked."

"Told you it would," Painter said. "I knew dang well another capsule of them Slorin got away from us when we took their ship."

The blonde young woman moved around in front of them, said: "My dad sure is smart."

"You listen to me now, Barton Marie," Painter said. "Next time you find a blob of something jes' lyin' in a field, you leave it alone, hear?"

"How was I to know it'd be so strong?" she asked.

"That's jes' it!" Painter snapped. "You never know. That's why you leaves such things alone. It was you made him so gol dang strong, pokin' him that way. Slorin aren't all that strong 'less'n you ignite 'em, hear?"

"Yes, Dad."

"Dang near five years of him," the fat man said. "I don't think I coulda stood another year. He was gettin' worse all the time."

"They always do," Painter said.

"What about that Smeg?" the fat man asked.

"That was a wise ol' Slorin," Painter agreed. "Seven

193

syllables if I heard his full name rightly."

"Think he suspects?"

"Pretty sure he does."

"What we gonna do?"

"What we allus do. We got their ship. We're gonna move out for a spell."

"Oh-h-h, not again!" the fat man complained.

Painter slapped the man's paunch. "What you howling about, Jim? You changed from McNabry into this when you had to. That's the way life is. You change when you have to."

"I was just beginning to get used to this place."

Barton Marie stamped her foot. "But this is such a nice body!"

"There's other bodies, child," Painter said. "Jes' as nice."

"How long do you think we got?" Jim asked.

"Oh, we got us several months. One thing you can depend on with Slorin, they are cautious. They don't do much of anything very fast."

"I don't want to leave," Barton Marie said.

"It won't be forever, child," Painter said. "Once they give up hunting for us, we'll come back. Slorin make a planet pretty nice for our kind. That's why we tolerates 'em. Course, they're pretty stupid. They work too hard. Even make their own ships ... for which we can be thankful. They haven't learned how to blend into anything but a bureaucratic society. But that's their misfortune and none of our own."

"What did you do about the government survey people?" Smeg asked Pzilimin, bracing himself as the car lurched in a particularly deep rut.

"I interviewed them in my office, kept it pretty shadowy, wore dark glasses," Pzilimin said. "Didn't use the ... mindcloud."

"That's a blessing," Smeg said. He fell silent for a space, then: "A damn poem keeps going through my head. Over and over, it just keeps going around in my head."

"A poem, you said?" Rick asked.

"Yes. It's by a native wit ... Jonathan Swift, I believe his name was. Read it during my first studies of their literature. It goes something like this—'A flea hath smaller fleas that on him prey; and these have smaller still to bite 'em; and so proceed ad infinitum.'"

# OLD RAMBLING HOUSE

On his last night on Earth, Ted Graham stepped out of a glass-walled telephone booth, ducked to avoid a swooping moth that battered itself in a frenzy against a bare globe above the booth.

Ted Graham was a long-necked man with a head of pronounced egg shape topped by prematurely balding sandy hair. Something about his lanky, intense appearance suggested his occupation: certified public accountant.

He stopped behind his wife, who was studying a newspaper classified page, and frowned. "They said to wait here. They'll come get us. Said the place is hard to find at night."

Martha Graham looked up from the newspaper. She was a doll-faced woman, heavily pregnant, a kind of pink prettiness about her. The yellow glow from the light above the booth subdued the red auburn cast of her ponytail hair.

"I just *have* to be in a house when the baby's born," she said. "What'd they sound like?"

"I dunno. There was a funny kind of interruption—like an argument in some foreign language."

"Did they sound foreign?"

"In a way." He motioned along the night-shrouded

196

line of trailers toward one with two windows glowing amber. "Let's wait inside. These bugs out here are fierce."

"Did you tell them which trailer is ours?"

"Yes. They didn't sound at all anxious to look at it. That's odd—them wanting to trade their house for a trailer."

"There's nothing odd about it. They've probably just got itchy feet like we did."

He appeared not to hear her. "Funniest-sounding language you ever heard when that argument started—like a squirt of noise."

Inside the trailer, Ted Graham sat down on the green couch that opened into a double bed for company.

"They could use a good tax accountant around here," he said. "When I first saw the place, I got that definite feeling. The valley looks prosperous. It's a wonder nobody's opened an office here before."

His wife took a straight chair by the counter separating kitchen and living area, folded her hands across her heavy stomach.

"I'm just continental tired of wheels going around under me," she said. "I want to sit and stare at the same view for the rest of my life. I don't know how a trailer ever seemed glamorous when—"

"It was the inheritance gave us itchy feet," he said.

Tires gritted on gravel outside.

Martha Graham straightened. "Could that be them?"

"Awful quick, if it is." He went to the door, opened it, stared down at the man who was just raising a hand to knock.

"Are you Mr. Graham?" asked the man.

"Yes." He found himself staring at the caller.

"I'm Clint Rush. You called about the house?" The

man moved farther into the light. At first, he'd appeared an old man, fine wrinkle lines in his face, a tired leather look to his skin. But as he moved his head in the light, the wrinkles seemed to dissolve—and with them, the years lifted from him.

"Yes, we called," said Ted Graham. He stood aside. "Do you want to look at the trailer now?"

Martha Graham crossed to stand beside her husband. "We've kept it in awfully good shape," she said. "We've never let anything get seriously wrong with it."

*She sounds too anxious,* though Ted Graham. *I wish she'd let me do the talking for the two of us.*

"We can come back and look at your trailer tomorrow in daylight," said Rush. "My car's right out here, if you'd like to see our house."

Ted Graham hesitated. He felt a nagging worry tug at his mind, tried to fix his attention on what bothered him.

"Hadn't we better take our car?" he asked. "We could follow you."

"No need," said Rush. "We're coming back into town tonight anyway. We can drop you off then."

Ted Graham nodded. "Be right with you as soon as I lock up."

Inside the car, Rush mumbled introductions. His wife was a dark shadow in the front seat, her hair drawn back in a severe bun. Her features suggested gypsy blood. He called her Raimee.

*Odd name,* thought Graham. And he noticed that she, too, gave the strange first impression of age that melted in a shift of light.

Mrs. Rush turned her gypsy features toward Martha Graham. "You are going to have a baby?"

198

It came out as an odd, veiled statement.

Abruptly, the car rolled forward.

Martha Graham said, "It's supposed to be born in about two months. We hope it's a boy."

Mrs. Rush looked at her husband. "I have changed my mind," she said.

Rush spoke without taking his attention from the road. "It is too . . ." He broke off, spoke in a tumble of strange sounds.

Ted Graham recognized it as the language he'd heard on the telephone.

Mrs. Rush answered in the same tongue, anger showing in the intensity of her voice. Her husband replied, his voice calmer.

Presently, Mrs. Rush fell moodily silent.

Rush tipped his head toward the rear of the car. "My wife has moments when she does not want to get rid of the old house. It has been with her for many years."

Ted Graham said, "Oh." Then: "Are you Spanish?"

Rush hesitated. "No. We are Basque."

He turned the car down a well-lighted avenue that merged into a highway. They turned onto a side road. There followed more turns—left, right, right.

Ted Graham lost track.

They hit a jolting bump that made Martha gasp.

"I hope that wasn't too rough on you," said Rush. "We're almost there."

The car swung into a lane, its lights picking out the skeleton outlines of trees: peculiar trees—tall, gaunt, leafless. They added to Ted Graham's feeling of uneasiness.

The lane dipped, ended at a low wall of a house—red brick with clerestory windows beneath overhanging eaves. The effect of the wall and a wide-beamed door they could see to the left was ultra-modern.

Ted Graham helped his wife out of the car, followed the Rushes to the door.

"I thought you told me it was an old house," he said.

"It was designed by one of the first modernists," said Rush. He fumbled with an odd curved key. The wide door swung open onto a hallway equally wide, carpeted by a deep pile rug. They could glimpse floor-to-ceiling view windows at the end of the hall, city lights beyond.

Martha Graham gasped, entered the hall as though in a trance. Ted Graham followed, heard the door close behind them.

"It's so—so—so *big*," exclaimed Martha Graham.

"You want to trade this for our trailer?" asked Ted Graham.

"It's too inconvenient for us," said Rush. "My work is over the mountains on the coast." He shrugged. "We cannot sell it."

Ted Graham looked at him sharply. "Isn't there any money around here?" He had a sudden vision of a tax accountant with no customers.

"Plenty of money, but no real estate customers."

They entered the living room. Sectional divans lined the walls. Subdued lighting glowed from the corners. Two paintings hung on the opposite walls—oblongs of odd lines and twists that made Ted Graham dizzy.

Warning bells clamored in his mind.

Martha Graham crossed to the windows, looked at the lights far away below. "I had no idea we'd climbed that far," she said. "It's like a fairy city."

Mrs. Rush emitted a short, nervous laugh.

Ted Graham glanced around the room, thought: *If the rest of the house is like this, it's worth fifty or sixty thousand.* He thought of the trailer: *A good one, but not worth more than seven thousand.*

Uneasiness was like a neon sign flashing in his mind. "This seems so . . ." He shook his head.

"Would you like to see the rest of the house?" asked Rush.

Martha Graham turned from the window. "Oh, yes."

Ted Graham shrugged. *No harm in looking,* he thought.

When they returned to the living room, Ted Graham had doubled his previous estimate on the house's value. His brain reeled with the summing of it: a solarium with an entire ceiling covered by sun lamps, an automatic laundry where you dropped soiled clothing down a chute, took it washed and ironed from the other end . . .

"Perhaps you and your wife would like to discuss it in private," said Rush. "We will leave you for a moment."

And they were gone before Ted Graham could protest.

Martha Graham said, "Ted, I honestly never in my life dreamed—"

"Something's very wrong, honey."

"But, Ted—"

"This house is worth at least a hundred thousand dollars. Maybe more. And they want to trade *this*"—he looked around him—"for a seven-thousand-dollar trailer?"

"Ted, they're foreigners. And if they're so foolish they don't know the value of this place, then why should—"

"I don't like it," he said. Again he looked around the room, recalled the fantastic equipment of the house. "But maybe you're right."

201

He stared out at the city lights. They had a lacelike quality: tall buildings linked by lines of flickering incandescence. Something like a Roman candle shot skyward in the distance.

"Okay!" he said. "If they want to trade, let's go push the deal..."

Abruptly, the house shuddered. The city lights blinked out. A humming sound filled the air.

Martha Graham clutched her husband's arm. "Ted! Wha—what was that?"

"I dunno." He turned. "Mr. Rush!"

No answer. Only the humming.

The door at the end of the room opened. A strange man came through it. He wore a short togalike garment of gray, metallic cloth belted at the waist by something that glittered and shimmered through every color of the spectrum. An aura of coldness and power emanated from him—a sense of untouchable hauteur.

He glanced around the room, spoke in the same tongue the Rushes had used.

Ted Graham said, "I don't understand you, mister."

The man put a hand to his flickering belt. Both Ted and Martha Graham felt themselves rooted to the floor, a tingling sensation vibrating along every nerve.

Again the strange language rolled from the man's tongue, but now the words were understood.

"Who are you?"

"My name's Graham. This is my wife. What's going—"

"How did you get here?"

"The Rushes—they wanted to trade us this house for our trailer. They brought us. Now look, we—"

"What is your talent—your occupation?"

"Tax accountant. Say! Why all these—"

"That was to be expected," said the man. "Clever!

Oh, excessively clever!" His hand moved again to the belt. "Now be very quiet. This may confuse you momentarily."

Colored lights filled both the Grahams' minds. They staggered.

"You are qualified," said the man. "You will serve."

"Where are we?" demanded Martha Graham.

"The coordinates would not be intelligible to you," he said. "I am of the Rojac. It is sufficient for you to know that you are under Rojac sovereignty."

Ted Graham said, "But—"

"You have, in a way, been kidnapped. And the Raimees have fled to your planet—an unregistered planet."

"I'm afraid," Martha Graham said shakily.

"You have nothing to fear," said the man. "You are no longer on the planet of your birth—nor even in the same galaxy." He glanced at Ted Graham's wrist. "That device on your wrist—it tells your local time?"

"Yes."

"That will help in the search. And your sun—can you describe its atomic cycle?"

Ted Graham groped in his mind for his science memories from school, from the Sunday supplements. "I can recall that our galaxy is a spiral like—"

"Most galaxies are spiral."

"Is this some kind of a practical joke?" asked Ted Graham.

The man smiled, a cold, superior smile. "It is no joke. Now I will make you a proposition."

Ted nodded warily. "All right, let's have the stinger."

"The people who brought you here were tax collectors we Rojac recruited from a subject planet. They were conditioned to make it impossible for them to leave their job untended. Unfortunately, they were

203

clever enough to realize that if they brought someone else in who could do their job, they were released from their mental bonds. Very clever."

"But—"

"You may have their job," said the man. "Normally, you would be put to work in the lower echelons, but we believe in meting out justice wherever possible. The Raimees undoubtedly stumbled on your planet by accident and lured you into this position without—"

"How do you know I can do your job?"

"That moment of brilliance was an aptitude test. You passed. Well, do you accept?"

"What about our baby?" Martha Graham worriedly wanted to know.

"You will be allowed to keep it until it reaches the age of decision—about the time it will take the child to reach adult stature."

"Then what?" insisted Martha Graham.

"The child will take its position in society— according to its ability."

"Will we ever see our child after that?"

"Possibly."

Ted Graham said, "What's the joker in this?"

Again the cold, superior smile. "You will receive conditioning similar to that which we gave the Raimees. And we will want to examine your memories to aid us in our search for your planet. It would be good to find a new inhabitable place."

"Why did they trap us like this?" asked Martha Graham.

"It's lonely work," the man explained. "Your house is actually a type of space conveyance that travels along your collection route—and there is much travel to the job. And then—you will not have friends, nor time for much other than work. Our methods are necessarily severe at times."

*"Travel?"* Martha Graham repeated in dismay.

"Almost constantly."

Ted Graham felt his mind whirling. And behind him, he heard his wife sobbing.

The Raimees sat in what had been the Grahams' trailer.

"For a few moments, I feared he would not succumb to the bait," she said. "I knew you could never overcome the mental compulsion enough to leave them there without their first agreeing."

Raimee chuckled. "Yes. And now I'm going to indulge in everything the Rojac never permitted. I'm going to write ballads and poems."

"And I'm going to paint," she said. "Oh, the delicious freedom!"

"Greed won this for us," he said. "The long study of the Grahams paid off. They couldn't refuse to trade."

"I knew they'd agree. The looks in their eyes when they saw the house! They both had . . ." She broke off, a look of horror coming into her eyes. "One of them did not agree!"

"They both did. You heard them."

"The baby?"

He stared at his wife. "But—but it is not at the age of decision!"

"In perhaps eighteen of this planet's years, it *will* be at the age of decision. What then?"

His shoulders sagged. He shuddered. "I will not be able to fight it off. I will have to build a transmitter, call the Rojac and confess!"

"And they will collect another inhabitable place," she said, her voice flat and toneless.

"I've spoiled it," he said. "I've spoiled it!"

# A-W-F UNLIMITED

The morning the space armor problem fell into the agency's lap, Gwen Everest had breakfast at her regular restaurant, an automated single-niche place catering to bachelor girls. Her order popped out of the slot onto her table, and immediately the tabletop projecta-menu switched to selling Interdorma's newest Interpretive Telelog.

"You own private dream translator! The secret companion to every neurosis!"

Gwen stared at the inch-high words doing a skitter dance above her fried eggs. She had written that copy. Her food beneath the ad looked suddenly tasteless. She pushed the plate away.

Along the speedwalk into Manhattan a *you-seeker*, its roboflier senses programmed to her susceptibilities, flew beside her ear. It was selling a year's supply of Geramyl—"the breakfast drink that helps you LIVE longer!"

The selling hook this morning was a Gwen Everest idea: a life insurance policy with the first year's premiums paid—"absolutely FREE if you accept this offer now!"

In sudden anger, she turned on the roboflier, whispered a code phrase she had wheedled from an

206

engineer who serviced the things. The roboflier darted upward in sudden erratic flight, crashed into the side of a building.

A small break in her control. A beginning.

Waiting for Gwen along the private corridor to the Singlemaster, Hucksting and Battlemont executive offices were displays from the recent Religion of the Month Club campaign. She ran a gamut of adecals, layouts, slogans, projos, quartersheets, skinnies. The works.

"Subscribe now and get these religions absolutely FREE! Complete text of the Black Mass plus Abridged Mysticism!"

She was forced to walk through an adecal announcing: "Don't be Half Safe! Believe in Everything! Are you sure that African Bantu Witchcraft is not the True Way?"

At the turn of the corridor stood a male-female graphic with flesh-stimulant skinnies and supered voices, "Find peace through Tantrism."

The skinnies made her flesh crawl.

Gwen fled into her office, slumped into her desk chair. With mounting horror, she realized that she had either written or supervised the writing of every word, produced every selling idea along that corridor.

The interphon on her desk emitted its fluted "Good morning." She slapped the blackout switch to keep the instrument from producing an image. The last thing she wanted now was to see one of her co-workers.

"Who is it?" she barked.

"Gwen?" No mistaking that voice: André Battlemont, bottom name on the agency totem.

"What do you want?" she demanded.

"Our Gwenny is feeling nasty this morning, isn't she?"

"Oh, Freud!" She slapped the disconnect, leaned forward with elbows on the desk, put her face in her hands. *Let's face it,* she thought. *I'm 48, unmarried, and a prime mover in an industry that's strangling the universe. I'm a professional strangler.*

"Good morning," fluted the interphon.

She ignored it.

"A strangler," she said.

Gwen recognized the basic problem here. She had known it since childhood. Her universe was a continual replaying of "The Emperor's New Suit." She saw the nakedness.

"Good morning," fluted the interphon.

She dropped her right hand away from her face, flicked the switch. "Now what?"

"Did you cut me off, Gwen?"

"What if I did?"

"Gwen, please! We have a problem."

"We always have problems."

Battlemont's voice dropped one octave. "Gwen. This is a Big problem."

*Uncanny the way he can speak capital letters,* she thought. She said: "Go away."

"You've been leaving your Interdorma turned off!" accused Battlemont. "You mustn't. Neurosis can creep up on you."

"Is that why you called me?" she asked.

"Of course not."

"Then go away."

Battlemont did a thing then that everyone from Singlemaster on down knew was dangerous to try with Gwen Everest. He pushed the override to send his image dancing above her interphon.

After the momentary flash of anger, Gwen correctly interpreted the act as one of desperation. She found herself intrigued. She stared at the round face, the pale eyes (definitely too small, those eyes), the pug nose and wide gash of mouth above almost no chin at all.

Plus the hairline in full retreat.

"André, you are a mess," she said.

He ignored the insult. Still speaking in the urgency octave, he said: "I have called a full staff meeting. You must attend at once."

"Why?"

"There are two military people in there, Gwen." He gulped. "It's desperate. Either we solve their problem or they will ruin us. They will draft every man in the agency!"

"Even you?"

"Yes!"

She moved her right hand toward the interphon's emergency disconnect. "Good-by, André."

"Gwen! My God! You can't let me down at a time like this!"

"Why not?"

He spoke in breathless haste. "We'll raise your salary. A bonus. A bigger office. More help."

"You can't afford me now," she said.

"I'm begging you, Gwen. Must you abuse me?"

She closed her eyes, thought: *The insects! The damned little insects with their crummy emotions! Why can't I tell them all to go to composite hell?* She opened her eyes, said: "What's the military's flap?"

Battlemont mopped his forehead with a pastel blue handkerchief. "It's the Space Service," he said. "The female branch. The WOMS. Enlistments have fallen to almost nothing."

She was interested in spite of herself. "What's happened?"

"Something to do with the space armor. I don't

know. I'm so upset."

"Why have they tossed it into our laps like this? The ultimatum, I mean."

Battlemont glanced left and right, leaned forward. "The grapevine has it they're testing a new theory that creative people work better under extreme stress."

"The Psychological Branch again," she said. "Those jackasses!"

"But what can we do?"

"Hoist 'em," she said. "You run along to the conference."

"And you'll be there, Gwen?"

"In a few minutes."

"Don't delay too long, Gwen." Again he mopped his forehead with the blue handkerchief. "Gwen, I'm frightened."

"And with good reason." She squinted at him. "I can see you now: Nothing on but a lead loincloth, dumping fuel into a radioactive furnace. Freud, what a picture!"

"This is no joke, Gwen!"

"I know."

"You *are* going to help?"

"In my own peculiar way, André." She hit the emergency disconnect.

André Battlemont turned away from his interphon, crossed his office to a genuine Moslem prayer rug. He sat down on it facing the floor-to-ceiling windows that looked eastward across midtown Manhattan. This was the 1479th floor of the Stars of Space building, and it was quite a view out there whenever the clouds lifted. But the city remained hidden beneath a low ceiling this morning.

Up here it was sunny, though—except in Battlemont's mood. A fear-cycle ululated along his nerves.

What he was doing on the prayer rug was practicing

210

Yoga breathing to calm those nerves. The military could wait. They *had* to wait. The fact that he faced the general direction of Mecca was left over from two months before. Yoga was a month old. There was always some carry-over.

Battlemont had joined the Religion of the Month Club almost a year ago—seduced by his own agency's deep motivation campaign plus the Brotherhood Council's seal of approval.

This month it was the Reinspired Neo-Cult of St. Freud.

A test adecal superimposed itself on the cloud-floor view beneath him. It began playing the latest Gwen-Everest-inspired pitch of the IBMausoleum. Giant rainbow letters danced across the fleecy background.

"Make your advice immortal! Let us store your voice and thought patterns in everlasting electronic memory circuits! When you are gone, your loved ones may listen to your voice as you answer their questions exactly the way you would most likely have answered them in Life!"

Battlemont shook his head. The agency, fearful of its dependence on the live Gwen Everest, had secretly recorded her at a staff conference once. Very illegal. The unions were death on it. But the IBMausoleum had broken down with the first question put to Gwen's ghost-voice.

"Some people have thought patterns that are too complex to permit accurate psyche-record," the engineer explained.

Battlemont did not delude himself. The sole genius of the agency's three owners lay in recognizing the genius of Gwen Everest. She *was* the agency.

It was like riding the tiger to have such an employee. Singlemaster, Hucksting and Battlemont had ridden

211

this tiger for 22 years. Battlemont closed his eyes, pitched her in his mind: a tall, lean woman, but with a certain grace. Her face was long, dominated by cold blue eyes, framed in waves of auburn hair. She had a wit that could slash you to ribbons, and that priceless commodity: the genius to pull selling sense out of utter confusion.

Battlemont sighed.

He was in love with Gwen Everest. Had been for 22 years. It was the reason he had never married. His Interdorma explained that it was because he wanted to be dominated by a strong woman.

But that only explained. It didn't help.

For a moment, he thought wistfully of Singlemaster and Hucksting, both taking their annual three-month vacation at the geriatrics center on Oahu. Battlemont wondered if he dared ask Gwen to take her vacation with him. Just once.

No.

He realized what a pitiful figure he made on the prayer rug. Pudgy little man in a rather unattractive blue suit.

Tailors did things for him that they called "improving your good points." But except when he viewed himself in a Vesta-Mirror to see the sample clothes projected back onto his own idealized image, he could never pin down what those "good points" were.

Gwen would certainly turn him down.

He feared that more than anything. As long as there remained the possibility . . .

Memory of the waiting. Space Service deputation intruded. Battlemont trembled, broke the Yoga breathing pattern. The exercise was having its usual effect: a feeling of vertigo. He heaved himself to his feet.

"One cannot run away from fate," he muttered.

That was a carry-over from the Karma month.

According to Gwen, the agency's conference room had been copied from a Florentine bordello's Emperor Room. It was a gigantic space. The corners were all flossy curlicues in heavy gilding, an effect carried over into deep carvings on the wall panels. The ceiling was a mating of Cellini cupids with Dali landscapes.

Period stuff. Antique.

Into this baroque setting had been forced a one-piece table 6 feet wide and 42 feet long. It was an enlarged bit of Twentieth Century Wallstreetiana fenced in by heavy wooden chairs. Beanbag paper-weights and golden wheel ashtrays graced every place.

The air of the room was blue with the smoke of mood-cigs. ("It rhymes with Good Bigs!") The staff seated around the table was fighting off the depressant effect of the two Space Service generals, one male and one female, seated in flanking positions beside Battlemont's empty chair. There was a surprising lack of small talk and paper rustling.

All staff members had learned of the ultimatum via the office grapevine.

Battlemont slipped in his side door, crossed to his chair at the end of the table, dropped into it before his knees gave out. He stared from one frowning military face to the other.

No response.

He cleared his throat. "Sorry I'm...ah...Pressing business. Unavoidable." He cast a frantic glance around the table. No sign of Gwen. He smiled at one officer, the other.

No response.

On his right sat Brigadier General Sonnet Finnister of the WOMS (Women of Space). Battlemont had been appalled to see her walk. Drill-sergeant stride. No nonsense. She wore a self-designed uniform: straight pleated skirt to conceal bony hips, a loose blouse to camouflage lack of upper development, and a long cape to confuse the whole issue. Atop her head sat a duck-billed, flat-fronted cap that had been fashioned for the single purpose of hiding the Sonnet Finnister forehead, which went too high and too wide.

She seldom removed the hat.

(This particular hat, Battlemont's hurried private investigations had revealed, looked hideous on every other member of the WOMS. To a woman, they called it "the Sonnet Bonnet." There had been the additional information that the general herself was referred to by underlings as "Sinister Finnister"—partly because of the swirling cape.)

On Battlemont's left sat General Nathan Owling of the Space Engineers. Better known as "Howling Owling" because of a characteristic evidenced when he became angry. He appeared to have been shaped in the officer caste's current mold of lean, blond athlete. The blue eyes reminded Battlemont of Gwen's eyes, except that the man's appeared colder.

If that were possible.

Beyond Owling sat Leo Prim, the agency's art director. He was a thin young man, thin to a point that vibrated across the edge of emaciation. His black hair, worn long, held a natural wave. He had a narrow Roman nose, soulful brown eyes, strong cleft in the chin, generous mouth with large lips. A mood-cig dangled from the lips.

If Battlemont could have chosen his own appearance, he would have liked to look like Leo Prim. Romantic. Battlemont caught Prim's attention, ventured a smile of camaraderie.

214

No response.

General Sonnet Finnister tapped a thin finger on the tabletop. It sounded to Battlemont like the slack drum of a death march.

"Hadn't we better get started?" demanded Finnister.

"Are we all here—finally?" asked Owling.

Battlemont swallowed past a lump in his throat. "Well...ah...no...ah..."

Owling opened a briefcase in his lap, glanced at an intelligence report, looked around the table. "Miss Everest is missing," he announced.

Finnister said: "Couldn't we go ahead without her?"

"We'll wait," said Owling. He was enjoying himself. *Damned parasites need a touch of the whip now and then!* he thought. *Shows 'em where they stand.*

Finnister glared at Owling, a hawk stare that had reduced full colonels (male) to trembling. The stare rolled off Owling without effect. *Trust the high command to pair me with a male supremacy type like Owling!* she thought.

"Is this place safe from snooping?" asked Owling.

Battlemont turned his own low-wattage glare on the staff seated in the mood smoke haze around the table. No glance met his. "That's all anybody ever does around here!" he snapped.

"What?" Owling started to rise.

"Busybodies!" blared Battlemont. "My whole staff!"

"Ohhh." Owling sank back into his chair. "I meant a different kind of snooping."

"Oh, that." Battlemont shrugged, suppressed an urge to glance up at the conference room's concealed recorder lenses. "We cannot have our ideas pirated by other agencies, you know. Absolutely safe here."

Gwen Everest chose this moment for her entrance. All eyes followed her as she came through the end door, strode down the length of the room.

Battlemont admired her grace. Such a feminine woman in spite of her strength. So different from the female general.

Gwen found a spare chair against the side wall, crowded it in between Battlemont and Finnister.

The commander of the WOMS glared at the intruder. "Who are *you?*"

Battlemont leaned forward. "This is Miss Everest, our...ah..." He hesitated, confused. Gwen had never had an official title with the agency. Never needed it. Everyone in the place knew she was the boss. "Ahh...Miss Everest is our...ah...director of coordination," said Battlemont.

"Why! That's a wonderful title!" said Gwen. "I must get it printed on my stationery." She patted Battlemont's hand, faced him and, in her best undercover-agent-going-into-action voice, said: "Let's have it, Chief. Who are these people? What's going on?"

General Owling nodded to Gwen. "I'm Owling, General, Space Engineers." He gestured to the rocket splash insignia on his shoulder. "My companion is General Finnister, WOMS."

Gwen had recognized the famous Finnister face. She smiled brightly, said: "General Woms!"

"Finnister!" snapped the female general.

"Yes, of course," said Gwen. "General Finnister Woms. Must not go too informal, you know."

Finnister spoke in slow cadence: "I...am... General...Sonnet...Finnister...of... of...the...Women...of...Space! The WOMS!"

"Oh, how stupid of me," said Gwen. "Of course you are." She patted the general's hand, smiled at Battlemont.

Battlemont, who well knew the falsity of this mood
216

in Gwen Everest, was trying to scrunch down out of sight in his chair.

In that moment, Gwen realized with a twinge of fear that she had reached a psychic point of no return. Something slipped a cog in her mind. She glanced around the table. Familiar faces leaped at her with unreal clarity. Staring eyes. (The best part of a conference was to watch Gwen in action.) *I can't take any more of this,* thought Gwen. *I have to declare myself.*

She focused on the military. The rest of the people in this room owned little pieces of her, but not these two. Owling and Finnister. Space generals. Symbols. Targets!

*Let the chips fall where they may! Fire when ready, Gridley. Shoot if you must this old gray head ... Wait until you see the whites of their eyes.*

Gwen nodded to herself.

One misstep and the agency was ruined.

*Who cares?*

It all passed in a split second, but the decision was made.

*Rebellion!*

Gwen turned her attention on Owling. "Would you be kind enough to end this stalling around and get the meeting under way?"

"Stall..." Owling broke it off. The intelligence report had said Gwen Everest was fond of shock tactics. He gave her a curt nod, passed the nod to Finnister.

The female general addressed Battlemont. "Your agency, as we explained to you earlier, has been chosen for a vital task, Mr. Battlefield."

"Battlemont," said Gwen.

Finnister stopped short. "What?"

217

"His name is Battle*mont*, not Battle*field*," said Gwen.

"What of it?"

"Names are important," said Gwen. "I'm sure you appreciate this."

The Finnister cheeks flushed. "Quite!"

Owling stepped into the breach. "We are authorized to pay this agency double the usual fee for perform-ance," he said. "However, if you fail us we'll draft every male employee here into the Space Service!"

"What an asinine idea!" said Gwen. "Our people would destroy the Space Service. From within." Again she smiled at Battlemont. "André here could do it all by himself. Couldn't you, ducky?" She patted Battle-mont's cheek.

Battlemont tried to crouch farther down into the chair. He avoided the eyes of the space brass, said: "Gwen . . . please . . ."

"What do you mean, destroy the Space Service?" demanded Finnister.

Gwen ignored her, addressed Owling. "This is another one of the Psych Branch's brainstorms," she said. "I can smell the stench of 'em in every word."

Owling frowned. As a matter of fact, he had the practical builder's suspicion of everything subjective. This Everest woman made a good point there. But the military had to stand shoulder to shoulder against outsiders. He said: "I don't believe you are properly equipped to fathom military tactics. Let's get on to the problem we . . ."

"Military tactics yet!" Gwen rapped the table. "Destroy your forces, men. This is it! Synchronize your watches. Over the top!"

"Gwen!" said Battlemont.

"Of course," said Gwen. She faced Finnister. "Would you mind awfully outlining your problem in simple terms that our unmilitarized minds could understand?"

A pause, a glare. Finnister spewed her words through stiff lips. "Enlistments in the WOMS have fallen to an alarming degree. *You* are going to correct this."

Behind Gwen, Battlemont nodded vigorously.

"Women can release men for the more strenuous tasks," said Owling.

"And there are many things women can do that men cannot do," said Finnister.

"Absolutely essential," said Owling.

"Absolutely," agreed Finnister.

"Can't draft women, I suppose," said Gwen.

"Tried to get a bill through," said Owling. "Damned committee's headed by an anti-military woman."

"Good for her," said Gwen.

"You do *not* sound like the person for this job," said Owling. "Perhaps..."

"Oh, simmer down," said Gwen.

"Miss Everest is the best in the business," said Battlemont.

Gwen said: "Why are enlistments down? You've run the usual surveys, I suppose."

"It's the space armor," said Finnister. "Women don't like it."

"Too mechanical," said Owling. "Too practical."

"We need...ah...glamour," said Finnister. She adjusted the brim of her cap.

Gwen frowned at the cap, cast a glance up and down the Finnister uniform. "I've seen the usual news pictures of the armor," she said. "What do they wear underneath it? Something like your uniform?"

Finnister suppressed a surge of anger. "No. They wear special fatigues."

"The armor cannot be removed while they are in space," said Owling.

"Oh?" said Gwen. "What about physical functions, that sort of thing?"

"Armor takes care of everything," said Owling.

"Apparently not *quite* everything," murmured Gwen. She nodded to herself, mulling tactics.

Battlemont straightened, sniffed the atmosphere of the conference room. Staff all alert, quiet, attentive. Mood had lightened somewhat. Gwen appeared to be taking over. Good old Gwen. Wonderful Gwen. No telling what she was up to. As usual. She'd solve this thing, though. Always did. Unless...

He blinked. Could she be toying with them? He tried to imagine Gwen's thought patterns. Impossible. IBMausoleum couldn't even do it. Unpredictable. All Battlemont could be certain of was that Gwen would get a gigantic belly laugh from the picture of the agency's male staff members drafted, slaving away on space freighters.

Battlemont trembled.

General Finnister was saying: "The problem is not one of getting women to enlist for Earth-based service. We need them in the ships, the asteroid stations, the..."

"Let's get this straight," said Gwen. "My great-great-grandmother was in some kind of armed service. I read her diary once. She called it the 'whackies' or something like that."

"WACS," said Finnister.

"Yes," said Gwen. "It was during the war with Spain."

220

"Japan," said Owling.

"What I'm driving at is, why all the sudden interest in women? My great-great-grandmother had one merry old time running away from some colonel who wanted... Well, you know. Is this some kind of a dodge to provide women for your space colonels?"

Finnister scowled her blackest.

Quickly suppressed chuckles sounded around the table.

Owling decided to try a new tack. "My dear lady, our motives are of the highest. We need the abilities of women so that mankind can march side by side to the stars."

Gwen stared at him in open admiration. "Go-wan!" she said.

"I mean it," said Owling.

"You're a poet!" said Gwen. "Oh... and I've wronged you. Here I was—dirty-minded me—thinking you wanted women for base purposes. And all the time you wanted *companions*. Someone to share this glorious new adventure."

Again, Battlemont recognized the danger signals. He tried to squeeze himself into as small a target as possible. Most of the staff around the table saw the same signals, but they were intent, fascinated.

"Exactly!" boomed Finnister.

Gwen's voice erupted in an angry snarl: "And we name all the little bastards after the stars in Virgo, ehhh?"

It took a long moment for Finnister and Owling to see that they had been gulled. Finnister started to rise.

"Siddown!" barked Gwen. She grinned. She was having a magnificent time. Rebellion carried a sense of euphoria.

Owling opened his mouth, closed it without a howl.

221

Finnister sank back into her chair.

"Shall we get down to business?" snapped Gwen. "Let's look at this glorified hunk of tin you want us to glamourize."

Finnister found something she could focus her shocked attention on. "Space armor is mostly plastic, not tin."

"Plastic-schmastic," said Gwen. "I want to see your Iron Gertie."

General Owling took two deep breaths to calm his nerves, snapped open the briefcase, extracted a folder of design sketches. He pushed them toward Gwen—a hesitant motion as though he feared she might take his hand with them. He now recognized that the incredible intelligence report was correct: this astonishing female was the actual head of the agency.

"Here's—Iron Gertie," he said, and forced a chuckle.

Gwen leafed through the folder while the others watched.

Battlemont stared at her. He realized something the rest of the staff did not: Gwen Everest was not being the usual Gwen Everest. There was a subtle difference. An abandon. Something was *very* wrong!

Without looking up from the drawings, Gwen addressed herself to Finnister. "That uniform you're wearing, General Finnister. You design that yourself?"

"What? Oh, yes. I did."

Battlemont trembled.

Gwen reached out, rapped one of Finnister's hips. "Bony," she said. She turned a page in the folder, shook her head.

"Well!" exploded Finnister.

Still without looking up, Gwen said: "Simmer down. How about the hat? You design that, too?"

"Yesss!" It was a sibilant explosion.

Gwen lifted her attention to the hat, spoke in a reasonable tone: "Possibly the most hideous thing I've ever seen."

"Well of all the—"

"Are you a fashion designer?" asked Gwen politely.

Finnister shook her head as though to clear it of cobwebs.

"You are *not* a fashion designer?" pressed Gwen.

Finnister bit the words off. "I have had *some* experience in choosing—"

"The answer is no, then," said Gwen. "Thought so." She brought her attention back to the folder, turned a page.

Finnister glared at her in open-mouthed rage.

Gwen glanced up at Owling. "Why'd you put the finger on this agency?"

Owling appeared to have trouble focusing his attention on Gwen's question. Presently, he said: "You were . . . it was pointed out that this agency was one of the most successful in . . . if not the most successful . . ."

"We were classified as experts, eh?"

"Yes. If you want to put it that way."

"I want to put it that way." She glanced at Finnister. "So we let the experts do the designing, is that clear? You people keep your greasy fingers off. Understood?" She shot a hard stare at Owling, back to Finnister.

"I don't know about you!" Finnister snapped at Owling, "but I've had all—"

"If you value your military career you'll just sit down and listen," said Gwen. Again, she glared at Owling. "Do you understand?"

Owling shook his head from side to side. Amazement dominated him. Abruptly, he realized that his head shaking could be interpreted as negative. He bobbed his head up and down, decided in mid-motion that this was undignified. He stopped, cleared his throat.

*What an astonishing female!* he thought.

Gwen pushed the folder of design sketches uptable to Leo Prim, the art director. "Tell me, General Owling," she said, "why is the armor so bulky?"

Leo Prim, who had opened the folder, began to chuckle.

"Marvelous, isn't it?" said Gwen.

Someone farther uptable asked: "What is?"

Gwen kept her attention on Owling. "Some jassack engineer in the Space Service designed a test model suit of armor like a gigantic woman—breasts and all." She glanced at Finnister. "You ran a survey on the stupid thing, of course?"

Finnister nodded. She was shocked speechless.

"I could've saved you the trouble," said Gwen. "One of the reasons you'd better listen carefully to what *expert me* has to say. No woman in her right mind would get into that thing. She'd feel big—and she'd feel naked." Gwen shook her head. "Freud! What a combination!"

Owling wet his lips with his tongue. "Ah, the armor has to provide sufficient shielding against radiation, and it must remain articulate under extremes of pressure and temperature," he said. "It can't be made any smaller and still permit a human being to fit into it."

"Okay," said Gwen. "I have the beginnings of an idea."

She closed her eyes, thought: *These military jerks are a couple of sitting ducks. Almost a shame to pot them.* She opened her eyes, glanced at Battlemont. His eyes were closed. He appeared to be praying. *Could be the ruination of poor André and his lovely people, too,* she thought. *What a marvelous collection of professional stranglers! Well, can't be helped. When Gwen Everest goes out, she goes out in a blaze of glory! All flags flying! Full speed ahead! Damn the torpedoes!*

"Well?" said Owling.

*Fire one!* thought Gwen. She said: "Presumably, you have specialists, experts who can advise us on technical details."

"At your beck and call whenever you say the word," said Owling.

Battlemont opened his eyes, stared at the back of Gwen's neck. A ray of hope stabbed through his panic. Was it possible that Gwen was really taking over?

"I'll also want all the dope on which psychological types make the best WOMS," said Gwen. "If there is such a thing as a best WOM."

Battlemont closed his eyes, shuddered.

"I don't believe I've ever been treated this high-handedly in my entire career!" blurted Finnister. "I'm not entirely sure that—"

"Just a moment, please," said Owling. He studied Gwen, who was smiling at him. The intelligence report said this woman was "probable genius" and should be handled delicately.

"I'm only sorry the law doesn't give us the right to draft women, too!" barked Finnister.

"Then you wouldn't really have this problem, would you?" asked Gwen. She turned her smile on Finnister. It was full of beatitudes.

Owling said: "I know we have full authority to handle this at our own discretion, General Finnister, and I agree that we've been subjected to some abuse but..."

"Abuse!" Finnister said.

225

"And high time, too," said Gwen.

A violent shudder passed through Battlemont. He thought: *We are doomed!*

"However," said Owling, "we mustn't let our personal feelings cloud a decision for the good of the service."

"I hear the bugles blowing," murmured Gwen.

"This agency *was* chosen as the one most likely to solve the problem," said Owling.

"There *could* have been a mistake!" said Finnister.

"Not likely."

"You are determined to turn this thing over to . . . to . . ." Finnister broke off, tapped her palms on the tabletop.

"It's advisable," said Owling. He thought: *This Gwen Everest will solve our problem. No problem could resist her. No problem would dare!*

General Owling had become a Gwenophile.

"Very well, then," snarled Finnister. "I will reserve my judgment."

General Finnister had become a Gwenophobe.

Which was part of Gwen Everest's program.

"I presume you two will be available for technical consultations from time to time," said Gwen.

"Our subordinates take care of details," said Owling. "All General Finnister and I are interested in is the big picture, the key to the puzzle."

"Big picture, key to puzzle," mused Gwen. "Wonderful idea."

"What?" Owling stared at her, puzzled.

"Nothing," said Gwen. "Just thinking out loud."

Owling stood up, looked at Finnister. "Shall we be going?"

Finnister also stood up, turned toward the door at the end of the room. "Yesss!"

226

Together, one on each side of the table, they marched the length of the room: tump-a-thump-a-tump-a-thump-a-tump...Just as they reached the door and Owling opened it, Gwen jumped to her feet. "Charrrrge!" she shouted.

The two officers froze, almost turned, thought better of it. They left, slamming the door.

Battlemont spoke plaintively into the silence. "Gwen, why do you destroy us?"

"Destroy you? Don't be silly!"

"But, Gwen..."

"Please be quiet, André; you're interrupting my train of thought." She turned to Leo Prim. "Leo, take those sketches and things of that big-breasted Bertha they designed. I want adecal workups on them, full projos, the entire campaign outlay."

"Big Bertha adecals, projos, the outlay," said Prim. "Right!"

Gwen, what are you doing?" asked Battlemont. "You said yourself that—"

"You're babbling, André," said Gwen. She glanced up at the ceiling. An eye in one of the Cellini cupids winked at her. "We got the usual solid recordings of this conference, I presume?"

"Of course," said Battlemont.

"Take those recordings, Leo," said Gwen. "Do a sequence out of them featuring only General Sinister Sonnet Bonnet Finnister."

"What'd you call her?" asked Prim.

Gwen explained about the Finnister nicknames. "The fashion trade knows all about her," she finished. "A living horror."

"Yeah, okay," said Prim. "A solid sequence of nothing but Finnister. What do you want it to show?"

"Every angle of that uniform," said Gwen. "And the

hat. Freud! Don't forget that hat!"

Battlemont spoke plaintively. "I don't understand."

"Good," said Gwen. "Leo, send me Restivo and Jim Spark...a couple more of your best design people. Include yourself. We'll..."

"And, lo! Ben Adam's name led all the rest," said Battlemont.

Gwen turned, stared down at him. For one of the rare times in their association, Battlemont had surprised her with something he said.

*I wonder if our dear André could be human?* she mused.

*No! I must be going soft in the head.* She said: "André, go take a meditation break until time to call our next conference. Eh? There's a good fellow."

*Always before when she abused me it was like a joke between us,* thought Battlemont dolefully. *But now she is trying to hurt.* His concern now was for Gwen, not for the agency. *My Gwen needs help. And I don't know what to do.*

"Meditation break time," said Gwen. "Or you could go to a mood bar. Why don't you try the new Interdorma mediniche? A niche in time saves the mind!"

"I prefer to remain awake for our last hours together," said Battlemont. A sob clutched at his throat. He stood up to cover the moment, drew himself to attention, fixed Gwen with a despairing glare. "I feel the future crouching over us alike a great beast!" He turned his back on her, strode out through his private door.

"I wonder what the devil he meant by that?" mused Gwen.

Prim said: "This is the month of St. Freud. They go

for prescience, extrasensory perception, that sort of thing."

"Oh, certainly," she said. "I wrote the brochure." But she found herself disturbed by Battlemont's departure. *He looked so pitiful,* she thought. *What if this little caper backfires and he gets drafted? It could happen. Leo and the rest of these stranglers could take it. But André . . .* She gave a mental shrug. *Too late to turn back now.*

Department heads began pressing toward Gwen along the table. "Say, Gwen, what about the production on . . ." "If I'm going to meet any deadlines I'll need more . . ." "Will we have to drop our other . . ."

"Shaddup!" bellowed Gwen.

She smiled sweetly into the shocked silence. "I will meet with each of you privately, just as soon as I get in a fresh stock of crying towels. First things first, though. Number one problem: we get the monkey off our backs. Eh?"

And she thought: *You poor oafs! You aren't even aware how close you are to disaster. You think Gwen is taking over as usual. But Gwen doesn't care. Gwen doesn't give a damn any more. Gwen is resigning in a blaze of glory! Into the valley of death rode the 600! Or was it 400? No matter. War is hell! I only regret that I have but one life to give for my agency. Give me liberty or give me to the WOMS.*

Leo Prim said: "You're going for the throat on these two military types, is that it?"

"Military tactics," said Gwen. "No survivors! Take no prisoners! Death to the White Eyes!"

"Huh?" said Prim.

"Get right on that assignment I gave you," she said.

"Uhh . . ." Prim looked down at the folder Owling

had left. "Workups on this Big Bertha thing ... a solido on Finnister. Okay." He shook his head. "You know, this business could shape up into a Complete Flap."

"It could be worse than that," Gwen cautioned.

Someone else said: "It's absolutely the worst I've ever seen. Drafted!"

And Gwen thought: *Ooooh! Someone has trepidations!* Abruptly, she said: "Absolutely worst flap." She brightened. "That's wonderful! One moment, all you lovely people."

There was sudden stillness in the preparations for departure.

"It has been moved that we label this business the Absolutely Worst Flap," she said.

Chuckles from the staff.

"You will note," said Gwen, "that the initials A-W-F are the first three letters in the word *awful*."

Laughter.

"Up to now," said Gwen, "we've only had to contend with Minor, Medium and Complete Flaps. Now I give you the AWF! It rhymes with the grunt of someone being slugged in the stomach!"

Into the laughter that filled the room, Prim said: "How about the U and L in awful? Can't let them go to waste."

"Un*Limited!*" snapped Gwen. "Absolutely Worst Flap UnLimited!" She began to laugh, had to choke it off as the laughter edged into hysteria. *Whatinell's wrong with me?* she wondered. She glared at Prim. "Let's get cracking, men! Isn't a damn one of you would look good in uniform."

The laughter shaded down into nervous gutterings. "That Gwen!"

Gwen had to get out of there. It was like a feeling of nausea. She pushed her way down the side of the room.

The sparkle had gone out of her rebellion. She felt that all of these people were pulling at her, taking bits of herself that she could never recapture. It made her angry. She wanted to kick, bite, claw. Instead, she smiled fixedly. "Excuse me. May I get through here? Sorry. Thank you. Excuse me."

And an image of André Battlemont kept intruding on her consciousness. *Such a pitiful little fellow. So...well...sweet. Dammit! Sweet! In a despicable sort of way.*

Twenty-five days slipped off the calendar. Twenty-five days of splashing in a pool of confusion. Gwen's element. She hurled herself into the problem. This one had to be just right. A tagline for her exit. A Gwen Everest signature at the bottom of the page.

Technical experts from the military swarmed all through the agency. Experts on suit articulation. Experts on shielding. Pressure coefficients. Artificial atmosphere. Waste reclamation. Subminiature power elements. A locksmith. An expert on the new mutable plastics. (*He* had to be flown in from the West Coast.)

Plus the fashion experts seen only by Gwen.

It was quite a job making sure that each military expert saw only what his small technical world required.

Came the day of the Big Picture. The very morning.

Adjacent to her office Gwen maintained a special room about 20 feet square. She called it "my intimidation room." It was almost Louis XV: insubstantial chairs, teetery little tables, glass gimcracks on the light fixtures, pastel cherubs on the wall panels.

The chairs looked as though they might smash flat under the weight of a medium-sized man. Each (with the exception of a padded throne chair that slid from behind a wall panel for Gwen) had a seat that canted

231

forward. The sitters kept sliding off, gently, imperceptibly.

None of the tables had a top large enough for a note pad *and* an ashtray. One of these items had to be balanced in the lap or placed underfoot. That forced an occasional look at the carpet.

The carpet had been produced with alarming psychological triggers. The uninitiated felt they were standing upside down in a fishbowl.

General Owling occupied one of the trick chairs. He tried to keep from staring at the cherub centered in a wall panel directly across from him, slightly to the right of the seated figure of André Battlemont. Battlemont looked ill. Owling pushed himself backward in the chair. His knees felt exposed. He glanced at General Finnister. She sat to his right beyond a spindly table. She pulled her skirt down as he watched. He wondered why she sat so forward on the chair.

*Damned uncomfortable little chairs!*

He noted that Battlemont had brought in one of the big conference room chairs for himself. Owling wondered why they all couldn't have those big, square, solid, secure chairs. For that matter, why wasn't this meeting being held in the big conference room? Full staff. The Big Picture! He glanced up at the wall panel opposite. *Stupid damned cherub!* He looked down at the rug, grimaced, tore his gaze away.

Finnister had looked at the rug when she came into the room, had almost lost her balance. Now, she tried to keep her attention off it. Her mind seethed with disquieting rumors. Individual reports from the technical experts failed to reveal a total image. It was like a jigsaw puzzle with pieces from separate puzzles all thrown together. She pushed herself backward in the chair. *What an uncomfortable room.* Intuition told her the place was subtly deliberate. Her latent anger at Gwen Everest flared. *Where is that woman?*

Battlemont cleared his throat, glanced at the door to his right through which Gwen was expected momentarily. *Must she always be late?* Gwen had avoided him for weeks. Too busy. Suddenly this morning she had to have André Battlemont front and center. A figurehead. A prop for her little show. He knew pretty much what she was doing, too. In the outward, physical sense. She might be able to keep things from some of the people around here, but André Battlemont ran his own intelligence system. As to what was going on in her mind, though, he couldn't be sure. All he knew was that it didn't fit. Not even for Gwen.

Finnister said: "Our technical people inform us that you've been pretty interested—" she pushed herself back in the chair—"in the charactristics of some of the newer mutable plastics."

"That is true," said Battlemont.

"Why?" asked Owling.

"Ahhh, perhaps we'd better wait for Miss Everest," said Battlemont. "She is bringing a solido projector."

"You have mockups already?" asked Owling.

"Yes."

"Good! How many models?"

"One. Our receptionist. Beautiful girl."

"What?" Finnister and Owling in unison.

"Oh! You mean . . . that is, we have the one to show you. It is really two . . . but only one of . . ." He shrugged, suppressed a shudder.

Finnister and Owling looked at each other.

Battlemont closed his eyes. *Gwen, please hurry.* He thought about her solution to the military problem, began to tremble. Her basic idea was sound, of course. Good psychological roots. But the military would never go for it. Especially that female general who walked like a sergeant. Battlemont's eyes snapped open as he heard a door open.

Gwen came in pushing a portable display projector. A glance of mutual dislike passed between Gwen and Finnister, was masked by mutual bright smiles immediately.

"Good morning, everybody," chirped Gwen.

*Danger signal!* thought Battlemont. *She's mad! She's . . .* He stopped the thought, focused on it. *Maybe she is. We work her so hard.*

"Anxious to see what you have there," said Owling. "Just getting ready to ask for a progress report when you called this meeting."

"We wanted to have something first that you could appreciate as an engineer," said Gwen.

Owling nodded.

Finnister said: "Our people report that you've been very secretive about your work. Why?"

"The very walls have ears. Loose lips lose the Peace! Don't be half safe!" Gwen positioned the projector in the center of the room, took the remote control, crossed to a panel which swung out to disgorge her chair. She sat down facing Finnister and Owling.

Seconds dragged past while she stared in fascination at Finnister's knees.

"Gwen?" said Battlemont.

Finnister tugged down on the hem of her skirt.

"What do you have to show us?" demanded Owling. He pushed himself back in the chair.

"First," said Gwen, "let us examine the perimeters of the problem. You must ask yourself: What do young women want when they enter the service?"

"Sounds sensible," said Owling.

Finnister nodded, her dislike of Gwen submerged in attention to the words.

"They want several things," said Gwen. "They want travel . . . adventure . . . the knight errant sort of thing. Tally-ho!"

Battlemont, Finnister and Owling snapped to shocked attention.

"Gives you pause when you think about it," murmured Gwen. "All those women looking for something. Looking for the free ride. The brass ring. The pot at the end of the rainbow."

She had them nodding again, Gwen noted. She raised her voice: "The old carrousel! The jingle-dingle joy journey!"

Battlemont looked at her sadly. *Mad. Ohhh, my poor, poor Gwenny.*

Owling said: "I . . . uh . . ."

"But they all want one commodity!" snapped Gwen. "And what's that? Romance! That's what's that. And in the unconscious mind what's that romance? That romance is sex!"

"I believe I've heard enough," said Finnister.

"No," said Owling. "Let's . . . uh . . . this is all, I'm sure, preliminary. I want to know where . . . after all, the model . . . models they've developed . . ."

"What's with sex when you get all the folderol off it?" demanded Gwen. "The psychological roots. What's down there?"

Owling scratched his throat, stared at her. He had a basic distrust of subjective ideas, but he always came smack up against the fear that maybe (just maybe now) they were correct. Some of them appeared (and it could be appearance *only*) to work.

"I'll tell you what's down there," muttered Gwen.

"Motherhood. Home. Security with a man. The flag."

Owling thought: *It all sounds so sensible . . . except . . .*

"And what does your armor do?" asked Gwen. "Armor equals no amour! They're locked up in desexed chunks of metal and plastic where no men can get at them. Great Freud! Men can't even see them in there!"

"Women don't really *want* men to get at them!" barked Finnister. "Of all the disgusting ideas I've ever—"

"Just a minute!" said Gwen. "A *normal* woman always wants the *possibility*. That's what she wants. And she wants it under *her* control. You've eliminated the possibility. You've taken all control out of their hands, put your women at the mercy of the elements, separated from cold, masculine, angular ABRUPT AND FINAL DEATH! by only a thin layer of plastic and metal."

Battlemont stared at her helplessly. *Poor Gwen. Doomed. And she won't even sell this idea. We're all doomed with her.*

Finnister glared at Gwen, still smarting under the implied dig of the word *normal.*

"How do you propose to get around these, ah, objections?" asked Owling.

"You'll see," said Gwen. "Let's go in from the perimeter now. Remember, the basic idea is to be able to run away with the assurance that she will be caught. She wants a certain amount of exposure as a female without being too bare-ahhh-faced about it."

"Mmmmph!" said Finnister.

Gwen smiled at her.

*Gwen is deliberately destroying herself and us with her,* thought Battlemont.

"Do you see what is lacking?" asked Gwen.

"Hmmmm-ahhhhh-hmmmmm," said Owling.

"A universal symbol," said Gwen. "A bold symbol. A symbol!"

"What do you propose?" asked Owling.

"That's it!" said Gwen. "A proposal! Plus—" she hesitated—"the symbol! The key is very simple." She sat up, perky, grinning at them. "In fact, it's a key!"

Finnister and Owling spoke in unison: "A key?"

"Yes. Two keys, actually. Symbolism's obvious." She produced two keys from her jacket pocket, held them up. "As you can see, one key is hard, angular . . . a masculine key. The other has fancy curves. It's daintier, more the . . ."

"Do you mean to tell me," howled Owling, "that you people have spent all these weeks, all those consultations with our experts and come up with . . . with . . . with . . ." He pointed, unable to continue.

Gwen shook her head from side to side. "Oh, no. Remember, these are just symbols. They're important, of course. One might even say they were vital. Each key will be inscribed with the name of the person who gets it."

"What are they keys to?" asked Finnister. She was fascinated in spite of herself.

"To the space armor, naturally," said Gwen. "These keys lock your people in their armor—both men *and* women."

"Lock them?" protested Finnister. "But you said . . ."

"I know," said Gwen. "But, you see, a key that will lock people into something will also let them out. As a matter of fact, any one of these keys will open any suit. That's for the safety factor."

"But they can't get *out* of their suits when they're in space!" howled Owling. "Of all the . . ."

"That's right!" said Gwen. "They can't *really* get out. So we give them the *symbol* of getting out. For exchanging."

"Exchanging?" asked Finnister.

"Certainly. A male astronaut sees a girl astronaut he likes. He asks her to trade keys. Very romantic. Symbolic of things that *may* happen when they return to Earth or get to a base where they can get out of the suits."

"Miss Everest," said Finnister, "as you so aptly pointed out earlier, no astronaut can see one of our women in this armor. And even if he could, I don't believe that I'd..."

She froze, staring, shocked speechless.

Gwen had pushed a stud on the solido projector's remote control. A suit of space armor appeared to be hanging in the center of the room. In the suit, wearing a form-fitting jacket, stood the agency's busty receptionist. The suit of armor around her was transparent from the waist up.

"The bottom half remains opaque at all times," said Gwen. "For reasons of modesty... the connections. However, the top half..."

Gwen pushed another stud. The transparent upper half faded through gray to black until it concealed the model.

"For privacy when desired," said Gwen. "That's how we've used the new mutable plastic. Gives the girl some control over her environment."

Again, Gwen pushed the first stud. The upper half of the model reappeared.

Finnister gaped at the form-fitting uniform.

Gwen stood up, took a pointer, gestured in through the projection. "This uniform was designed by a leading couturier. It is made to reveal while concealing.

238

A woman with only a fair figure will appear to good advantage in it. A woman with an excellent figure appears stunning, as you can see. Poor figures—" Gwen shrugged—"there *are* exercises for developing them. Or so I am told."

Finnister interrupted in a cold voice. "And what do you propose to do with that . . . that uni . . . clothing?"

"This will be the regulation uniform for the WOMS," said Gwen. "There's a cute little hat goes with it. Very sexy."

Battlemont said: "Perhaps the changeover could be made slowly so as to . . ."

"What changeover?" demanded Finnister. She leaped to her feet. "General Owling?"

Owling tore his attention from the model. "Yes?"

"Completely impractical! I will put up with no more!" barked Finnister.

Battlemont thought: *I knew it. Oh, my poor Gwenny! They will destroy her, too. I knew it.*

"We can't waste any more time with this agency," said Finnister. "Come, General."

"Wait!" yelped Battlemont. He leaped to his feet. "Gwen, I told you . . ."

Finnister said: "It's regrettable, but . . ."

"Perhaps we're being a little hasty," said Owling. "There may be something to salvage from this . . ."

"Yes!" said Battlemont. "Just a little more time is all we need to get a fresh . . ."

"I think not," said Finnister.

Gwen smiled from one to the other, thought: *What a prize lot of gooney birds!* She felt a little drunk, as euphoric as if she had just come from a mood bar. *Rebellion, it's wonderful! Up the Irish! Or something.*

Owling shrugged, thought: *We have to stand together against civilians. General Finnister is right.*

*Too bad, though.* He got to his feet.

"Just a little more time," pleaded Battlemont.

*Too bad about André,* thought Gwen. She had an inspiration, said: "One moment, please."

Three pairs of eyes focused on her.

Finnister said: "If you think you can stop me from going through with our threat, dissuade yourself. I'm perfectly aware that you had that uni...that *clothing* designed to make *me* look hideous!"

"Why not?" asked Gwen. "I was only doing to you what you did to virtually every other woman in the WOMS."

"Gwen!" pleaded Battlemont in horror.

"Be still, André," said Gwen. "It's just a matter of timing, anyway. Today. Tomorrow. Next week. Not really important."

"Oh, my poor Gwenny," sobbed Battlemont.

"I was going to wait," said Gwen. "Possibly a week. At least until I'd turned in my resignation."

"What're you talking about?" asked Owling.

"Resignation!" gasped Battlemont.

"I just can't toss poor André here to the wolves," said Gwen. "The rest of our men, yes. Once they get inside they'll chew your guts out, anyway."

"What *are* you talking about?" asked Finnister.

"The rest of the men in this agency can take care of themselves...and you, too," said Gwen. "Wolves among wolves. But André here is helpless. All he has is his position...money. He's an accident. Put him someplace where money and position are less important, it'll kill him."

"Regrettable," said Finnister. "Shall we be going, General Owling?"

"I was going to ruin both of you," said Gwen. "But I'll tell you what. You leave André alone and I'll just give *one* of you the business."

"Gwen, what are you saying?" whispered Battlemont.

"Yesss!" hissed Finnister. "Explain yourself!"

"I just want to know the pecking order here," said Gwen. "Which one of you ranks the other?"

"What does that have to do with it?" asked Finnister.

"Just a minute," said Owling. "That intelligence report." He glared at Gwen. "I'm told you've prepared an adecal on the test model we made before coming to you."

"Big Bertha," said Gwen. "And it's not just an adecal. I have everything needed for a full national campaign. Look!"

A solido of the breast-baring test model replaced the transparent suit hanging in the center of the room.

"The idea for Big Bertha here originated with General Owling," said Gwen. "My campaign establishes that fact, then goes on to feature an animated model of Big Bertha. She is a living panic. Funniest thing you ever saw. General Owling, you will be the laughing stock of the nation by nightfall of the day I start this campaign."

Owling took a step forward.

Battlemont said: "Gwen! They will destroy you!"

Owling pointed at the projection. "You . . . you wouldn't!"

"But I would," said Gwen. She smiled at him.

Battlemont tugged at Gwen's arm. She shook him off.

"It would ruin me," whispered Owling.

"Presumably, you are capable of going through with this threat," said Finnister. "Regrettable."

Owling whirled on Finnister. "We must stand together!" he said desperately.

241

"You bet," said Gwen. She pushed another stud on the remote control.

A projection of General Finnister in her famous uniform replaced Big Bertha.

"You may as well know the whole story," said Gwen. "I'm all set with another campaign on the designing of this uniform, right from the Sonnet Bonnet on down through the Sinister Finnister cape and those sneaky walking shoes. I start with a dummy model of the general clad in basic foundation garments. Then I go on to show how each element of the present WOMS uniform was designed for the...ah...Finnister ....ah...figure."

"I'll sue!" barked Finnister.

"Go ahead. Go ahead." Gwen waved a sinuous arm.

*She acts drunk!* thought Battlemont. *But she never drinks.*

"I'm all set to go black market with these campaigns," said Gwen. "You can't stop me. I'll prove every contention I make about that uniform. I'll expose you. I'll show why your enlistment drives flopped."

Red suffused the Finnister face. "All right!" she snapped. "If you're going to ruin us, I guess there's nothing we can do about it. But mark this, Miss Everest. We'll have the men of this agency in the service. You'll have that on your conscience! And the men we draft will serve under friends of ours. I hope you know what that means!"

"You don't have any friends," said Gwen, but her voice lacked conviction. *It's backfiring,* she thought. *Oh, hell. I didn't think they'd defy me.*

"There may even be something we can do about you!" said Finnister. "A presidential order putting you in the service for reasons of national emergency. Or an

242

emergency clause on some bill. And when we get our hands on you, Miss Everest . . ."

"André!" wailed Gwen. It was all getting out of hand. *I didn't want to hurt anybody,* she thought. *I just . . .* She realized that she didn't know what she *had* wanted.

Battlemont was electrified. In 22 years, Gwen Everest had never appealed to anyone for help. And now, for the first time, her appeal was to him! He stepped between Gwen and Finnister. "André is right here," he said. He felt inspired. His Gwen had appealed to him! "You assassin!" he said, shaking a finger under the Finnister nose.

"Now, see here!" snapped Owling. "I won't stand for any more of—"

"And you!" barked Battlemont, whirling. "We have recordings of every conference here, from the first, and including this one! They show what happened! Don't you know what is wrong with this poor girl? You! You've driven her out of her mind!"

Gwen joined in the chorus: "What?"

"Be still, Gwen," said Battlemont. "I will handle this."

Gwen couldn't take her attention off him. Battlemont was magnificent. "Yes, André."

"I will prove it," said Battlemont. "With Interdorma psychiatrists. With all the experts money can buy. You think you have seen something in those campaigns our Gwen set up? Hah! I will show you something." He stabbed a finger at Owling. "Can the military drive you insane?"

"Oh, now see here," said Owling. "This has gone—"

"Yes! It *can* drive you insane!" said Battlemont. "And we will show, step by step, how you drove our poor Gwen out of her mind with fear for her friends.

243

Fear for me!" He slapped himself on the chest, glared at Finnister. "And you know what we will do next? We will say to the public: This could happen to you! Who is next? You? Or you? Or you? Then what happens to your money from Congress? What happens to your enlistment quotas?"

"Now see here," said Owling. "We didn't..."

"Didn't you?" snarled Battlemont. "You think this poor girl is in her right mind?"

"Well, but we didn't..."

"Wait until you see our campaign," said Battlemont. He took Gwen's hand, patted it. "There, there, Gwenny. André will fix."

"Yes, André," she said. They were the only words she could find. She felt stupefied. *He's in love with me*, she thought. Never before had she known anyone to be in love with her. Not even her parents, who had always been repelled by the intellect they had spawned. Gwen felt warmth seeping through her. A cog slipped into motion in her mind. It creaked somewhat from long idleness. She thought: *He's in love with me!* She wanted to hug him.

"We seem to be at a stalemate," muttered Owling.

Finnister said: "But we can't just—"

"Shut up!" ordered Owling. "He'll do it! Can't you see that?"

"But if we draft—"

"He'll do it for sure, then! Buy some other agency to run the campaign."

"But we could turn around and draft—"

"You can't draft everybody who disagrees with you, woman! Not in this country! You'd start a revolution!"

"I..." Finnister said helplessly.

"And it's not just us he'd ruin," said Owling. "The whole service. He'd strike right at the money. I know

244

his type. He wasn't bluffing. It'd be catastrophic!"

Owling shook his head, seeing a parade of crumbling military projects pass before his mind's eye, all falling into an abyss labeled "NSF."

"You are an intelligent man, General Owling," said Battlemont.

"That Psych Branch!" snarled Owling. "Them and their bright ideas!"

"I told you they were fuzzyheads," said Gwen.

"You be still, Gwen," said Battlemont.

"Yes, André."

"Well, what're we going to do?" demanded Owling.

"I tell you what," said Battlemont. "You leave us alone, we leave you alone."

"But what about my enlistments?" wailed Finnister.

"You think our Gwen, sick or well, can't solve your problems?" asked Battlemont. "For your enlistments you use the program as outlined."

"I won't!"

"You will," said Owling.

"General Owling, I refuse to have ..."

"What happens if I have to dump this problem on the General Staff?" asked Owling. "Where will the head-chopping start? In the Psych Branch? Certainly. Who'll be next? The people who could've solved it in the field, that's who!"

Finnister said: "But—"

"For that matter," said Owling, "Miss Everest's idea sounded pretty sensible ... with some modifications, of course."

"No modifications," said Battlemont.

*He's a veritable Napoleon!* thought Gwen.

"Only in minor, unimportant details," soothed Owling. "For engineering reasons."

"Perhaps," agreed Battlemont. "Provided we pass

245

on the modifications before they are made."

"I'm sure we can work it out," said Owling.

Finnister gave up, turned her back on them.

"One little detail," murmured Battlemont. "When you make out the double-fee check to the agency, make a substantial addition—bonus for Miss Everest."

"Naturally," said Owling.

"Naturally," said Battlemont.

When the space brass had departed, Battlemont faced Gwen, stamped his foot. "You have been very bad, Gwen!"

"But, André—"

"Resignation!" barked Battlemont.

"But—"

"Oh, I understand, Gwen. It's my fault. I worked you much too hard. But that is past."

"André, you don't—"

"Yes, I do! I understand. You were going to sink the ship and go down with it. My poor, dear Gwen. A death wish! If you'd only paid attention to your Interdorma telelog."

"I didn't want to hurt anyone here, André. Only those two—"

"Yes, yes. I know. You're all mixed up."

"That's true." She felt like crying. She hadn't cried...since...she couldn't remember when. "You know," she said, "I can't remember ever crying."

"That's it!" said Battlemont. "I cry all the time. You need a stabilizing influence. You need someone to teach you how to cry."

"Would you teach me, André?"

"Would I..." He wiped the tears from his eyes. "You are going on a vaction. Immediately! I am going with you."

"Yes, André."

"And when we return—"

"I don't want to come back to the agency, André. I...can't."

"So that's it!" said Battlemont. "The advertising business! It bugs you!"

She shrugged. "I'm...I just can't face another campaign. I...just...can't."

"You will write a book," announced Battlemont.

"What?"

"Best therapy known," said Battlemont. "Did it myself once. You will write about the advertising business. You will expose all the dirty tricks: the hypno-jingles, the subvisual flicker images, the advertisers who finance textbooks to get their sell into them, the womb rooms where the *you-seekers* are programmed. Everything."

"I could do it," she said.

"You will tell all," said Battlemont.

"Will I!"

"And you will do it under a pseudonym," said Battlemont. "Safer."

"When do we start the vacation, André?"

"Tomorrow." He experienced a moment of his old panic. "You don't mind that I'm...ugly as a pig?"

"You're just beautiful," she said. She smoothed the hair across his bald spot. "You don't mind that I'm smarter than you?"

"Ah, hah!" Battlemont drew himself to attention. "You may be smarter in the head, my darling, but you are *not* smarter in the heart!"

# A GALAXY OF SCIENCE FICTION
# MASTERPIECES AVAILABLE FROM BERKLEY

## EXCITING SCIENCE FICTION
## FROM BERKLEY

### BY FRANK HERBERT